TEMPERED HEARTS

Pamela S. Thibodeaux

"I will give you a new heart & put a new Spirit within you, I will take the heart of stone out of your flesh and give you a heart of flesh." ~Ezek. 36

TEMPERED HEARTS
Book One of the Tempered Series
By: Pamela S. Thibodeaux
Copyright © 2000

Publisher/Distributor:
Temperance Publishing; an imprint of
Pamela S Thibodeaux Enterprises, LLC
PO Box 324
Iowa, LA 70647

ISBN#: 978-0-9896728-2-5

Cover Design: Delia Latham of Delia's Designs

Previous Publications:
Sept. 2005; ComStar Media, LLC.
Salem, Oregon, U.S.A.
ISBN: 1-933866-03-9

Dec. 2000
Writers Exchange E-Publishing Company
Atherton Qld 4883 Australia

All rights have reverted to Author

Note:
This is a work of fiction. Names, characters, places, and incidents either are the product of the author's imaginations or are used fictitiously, and any resemblance to actual persons, living or dead, businesses, establishments, events, or locales is entirely coincidental.

Praise for Pamela S Thibodeaux

"Through Pamela's blessed ability to find God everywhere, even in secular song lyrics, she has written devotions guaranteed to touch the heart and remind the reader of our True Love, the Rose of Sharon." ~ Endorsement for **Love is a Rose** by Linday Yezak, Author, Editor Triple Edge Critique Service

*"**Lori's Redemption** is fast paced, lots of action, gripping storyline.... I loved it. It's gone straight back into my TBR pile."* ~ Clare Revell author of "Monday's Child" series.

"Thibodeaux leads the reader through from the first page to the last without once relinquishing control. She hooks them, holds them, and keeps them enthralled until the last line." ~ Review of **The Visionary** by Delia Latham

*"**In His Sight** caught my attention from the beginning and it made me wonder if I had given all to God as he gave all to me. Thank you, Pamela for a story that I would readily recommend to anyone who needs that extra encouragement!"* ~ Reviewed by Wendy for Happily Ever After Reviews.

*"**Winter Madness** is a wonderful romance and an excellent example of Spiritual growth."* ~Reviewed by Dee Daily for The Romance Studio

*"**A Hero for Jessica** is a good, sweet read charged with attraction but an emphasis on true love. I recommend it to women of all ages."* ~ Reviewed by Violet for LASR

*"**Cathy's Angel** is a short tale that is entertaining as well as inspiring. Well done!"* ~ Reviewed by Marlene for Fallen Angel Reviews

Dedication and Acknowledgements

First and foremost, thanks belong to God without whose gift and direction this story would not have come to life for me or for you. Special thanks to my friends and family for their encouragement, and especially to my husband and children for their infinite patience while I worked for hours, days, weeks and even months on end. And, last but not least, for Mark.

A special note of appreciation to Sandy Cummins, CEO of Writer's Exchange E-Publishing Co. for catching the vision and releasing _Tempered Hearts_ as an e-book in Dec. 2000. Thank you Sandy! May God continually bless you in all that you do.

And a very special **_"Thank You"_** goes to Lauron Sonnier (McCulloch) Stewart, President of Sonnier Marketing for the original artwork for _Tempered Hearts_ and _Tempered Dreams_. You helped make my vision a reality...for this I'll forever be grateful. God Bless you Lauron!

Chapter One

Craig Harris pushed his half-empty plate away and signaled the waitress for a cup of coffee. He scrubbed a hand over his face, rubbed his tired, gritty eyes and looked out the window, hoping to avoid idle chit-chat with the woman as she sidled up to him, coffee pot in hand, seductive sway to her hips, and a hint of suggestion in her smile.

"Wonder when I'll have the opportunity to leave you looking so haggard," she remarked.

His gaze cut to her in a quick, scathing look that stopped further conversation. A flash of movement and color caught the corner of his eye. Craig glanced out the window to see a red Corvette toting a horse trailer drive into the service station across the street.

Impossible, he thought, with a shake of his head. He rubbed his eyes again, positive he was hallucinating. Sure enough, it was there, plain as day. Seen it all now, he thought, and watched a petite blonde disembark from the vehicle, speak to the attendant, then unload her horse. Craig admired the care she lavished on the huge animal. Admiration turned to awe then anger when she loaded the horse back in the trailer and headed in the direction of the diner where he sat. He lay in wait. She was seated comfortably at the counter when he approached her.

"Gonna leave that horse out there long while you sit in here where it's nice and cool?" he asked. As a rancher, Craig detested the misuse of any animal, especially horses.

Tamera Collins turned and looked into the angriest— and prettiest—steel-gray eyes she'd ever seen. "Are you talking to me?"

"No," he snarled. "I'm talking to Harry. Who else would I be talking to? You're the only idiot I've seen put her horse in a trailer in one hundred-degree heat!"

Tamera knew the stranger had no way of knowing her horse trailer was equipped with oscillating fans to keep its occupant cool and it was on the tip of her tongue to tell him, but the sheer audacity of him attacking her stayed her words. She stiffened and desperately held on to her rising temper. "Look, mister, I don't know who you are or where you get off being so rude, but I'll have you know my horse is well taken care of."

With a low growl, he grabbed her by the arm, nearly unseating her. "It's hotter than blazes outside, and even hotter in that trailer! I want to know how long you're going to leave him in there before you get moving?"

Tamera's already strained temper shot up another degree. She jerked free of his grasp. "Don't manhandle me, mister. My daddy never manhandled me. You can bet some half-cocked stranger's not going to either!"

A collective gasp sounded in the cafe, followed by absolute silence as the customers waited to see what happened next. Not one of them would have crossed him in any manner, and everyone wondered what he'd do to the mere slip of a girl who dared to.

Caught between surprise and shock, Craig bit back a curse. *Little spitfire. Got nerve too.* "Looks like your daddy never spanked you, either, sweetheart," he drawled. "Now answer me and make it quick. I'm not used to waiting when I ask a question, and I'm extremely low on patience right now."

Tamera saw red—bright, hot, furious, red. Low on patience? More like low on manners! How dare he manhandle her, insult her father, then calmly demand an answer to an unwarranted attack on her ability to take care of her horse!

Before he could blink, she grabbed her glass of water off the counter and tossed it in his face. "Cool off, Mister. Show some courtesy from now on and next time you just might get your answer."

She stormed into the bathroom, locked the door and burst into tears, the confrontation an overload to her taut emotions. "Arrogant jerk cowboy!"

Craig stared in stunned disbelief, eyes narrowing as he realized she'd succeeded in humiliating him in front of an entire room of his peers. He glared around as customers ducked heads, sipped drinks, or hid snickers and smiles behind their hands. With a muttered curse, he started toward the bathroom.

"No more, Craig," Harry interrupted with quiet authority, fully aware Craig would tear the door down to get to her. God only knew what would happen then. "Leave her alone."

Turning on his heel, Craig stormed out of the cafe. The customers burst into wild laughter the moment he was out the door. Craig Harris owned one of the largest and most successful ranches in the state. *And he never let anyone forget it.*

Craig tore out of the drive, the jeep's tires spun, throwing dust and gravel everywhere. Harry waited until he was gone before he went to the ladies' room.

"Come on out, honey, he's gone," he encouraged the occupant.

Tamera clamped a lid on her whirling emotions, washed her face then opened the door. A flush of embarrassment stained her pale cheeks. "I'm sorry," she whispered.

Harry chuckled, leading her back to her seat as the patrons burst into spontaneous applause. "It's okay, sweetheart. Craig Harris can be a real jerk sometimes. Most of the time actually. He's a fine man, but he does demand respect."

She gasped in petrified shock. "You don't mean the Craig Harris who owns the Rockin' H Ranch do you?"

"Yep, one and the same."

Embarrassment washed over her in angry waves. Tamera hung her head. Of all the strange twists of fate, this certainly topped her list of 'life's little ironies'.

"My daddy always warned me to watch my temper," she said in a humiliated whisper. "Now I know why."

"Don't worry, honey, he'll get over it." Harry assured.

I doubt it, Tamera thought, knowing she'd find out soon enough.

* * * * *

Craig pulled up to the ranch in the same manner he left the cafe. Dust and gravel turned the damp area on the front of his shirt into a dirty mess. Physically exhausted and emotionally strung out, the last thing he looked forward to was explaining his appearance. Which is exactly what I'll have to do, he realized, spotting his grandfather in his wheelchair, on the porch, talking to the ranch foreman. Slamming out of the jeep, he stomped up on the porch.

"What happened to you?"

Craig faced his grandfather squarely, eyes narrowed, jaw muscle twitching. "Some hot-tempered little witch threw water on me."

"A girl?" he asked, not bothering to hide his surprise or amusement. "A girl threw water on you? He chuckled. "Did you hear that, Shorty?" he glanced at the foreman.

Craig eyed Shorty, daring him to comment then returned the glare to his grandfather. "I fail to see the humor in the situation."

His grandfather only laughed. "It's a switch that's for sure. They usually just throw themselves at you."

"Well, that's the price I pay for being known as 'most eligible bachelor'," Craig hissed. "A title I never asked for in the first place."

"Look around you, boy," his grandfather said, gesturing to encompass their surroundings. "You've earned the title, be proud."

"Yeah, well look where pride has gotten me. A face full of water and laughingstock of the town."

The old man grinned. "I said be proud, not arrogant. I've always told you that someone would give you a dressing-down someday. Only wish I'd been there to see it. Where did this happen?"

Craig's eyes narrowed at his grandfather's obvious amusement. Was it anyone else, he'd have thrown him or her off the ranch at the first guffaw. "Harry's."

"Find her, Shorty. I've got to meet this little girl."

The ranch foreman nodded but chose to keep his mouth shut. He struggled not to laugh but couldn't stop the grin tugging at his lips. He held out his hand and waited for Craig to toss him the keys to the jeep, then headed into town.

"Guess my humiliation and your joy will be complete by bringing her here," Craig muttered, slamming into the house only to turn around at his grandfather's command.

"Wait just a minute, Craig," he said, then continued when Craig faced him once more. "I've no desire to humiliate you, son; it's obvious you've done that very well all by yourself. As usual."

"I don't understand you sometimes. Why do you want to bring her here? She's nothing but trouble," Craig insisted.

"Who is she?" his grandfather asked.

"Have no idea. Couldn't care less."

Craig Sr. shook his head and sighed. "You've let that temper get away from you again, with a stranger no less, and forgotten who you are. We Harrises don't go around intimidating strangers. Especially women. What brought this on besides the fact that you've been up for over twenty-four hours?"

"The irresponsible little twit had the nerve to put her horse in a trailer and then park herself on a stool at Harry's. The heat index is pushing the temperature up to a hundred degrees," he insisted at his grandfather's raised eyebrows.

His grandfather shook his head again with another resigned sigh.

"Take a shower Craig. Shorty will be back with her soon, and I expect you present when they get here."

"Ready to apologize no doubt," Craig grumbled. He knew it was a useless waste of energy to face off with his grandfather. Gramps was right, though. After spending the night walking a pregnant, colicky mare, then delivering a premature colt, he'd been up too many hours to consider the consequences.

"You'll do what's expected of you; what's expected of a Harris." His grandfather affirmed.

His voice was as cold as steel and as hard as the glint of anger in the gray eyes that were a part of his legacy to Craig. Without another word, Craig turned on his heel, stomped through the house and stormed up the stairs to do as he was bid.

* * * * *

Tamera swallowed her humiliation and fears long enough to eat her lunch while getting directions to the Rockin' H. She'd barely finished when a man walked into the café.

"No need to follow those directions, missy, just follow him," Harry said, before nodding hello at the little man.

"Shorty," he greeted with a smile and handshake.

Tamera watched the greeting with interest. Not much taller than she, he was the embodiment of a cowboy; bowed legs, skin tanned the color of leather and obviously just as tough, dark eyes that twinkled like stars in a velvet sky. His huge smile was charming despite the discoloration of teeth from age, coffee, and tobacco. He smelled of leather and sweat, strong but not offensive.

"Heard there was some trouble here, Harry," he drawled in a tone Tamera was beginning to associate with the term *'Texas twang'*.

"No trouble, Shorty, just a misunderstanding between Craig and Miss Collins."

Shorty looked at her and grinned. "You? You threw water on him? Why you're no bigger than a fly!"

Tamera blushed at the surprise and disbelief in his voice. "Yes, I'm afraid so," she admitted, her voice softened by embarrassment.

Shorty threw back his head and laughed. "Well, I'll be dipped in horse sh -- hot sauce," he stuttered, amending his usual expression as those who obviously knew it well, laughed. "Knew someone would take him down some day. Boy's had it comin' for quite some time now. Never dreamed it'd be a little bitty thing like you. Mr. Harris asked me to escort you to the ranch. He'd like to get to know you," he informed her, while reaching for her lunch ticket.

Harry shook his head. "This one's on the house. The little lady deserves it," he added, with a wink at Shorty.

Tamera felt a wave of aggravation that everyone seemed to get such a kick out of the humiliation of another human being, whether he deserved it or not. She hesitated, afraid of the consequences now that the time had come to face up to her actions. "I don't want or need any more trouble."

"No trouble miss, I promise," Shorty said.

Tamera looked to Harry for confirmation, hoping she could trust him to steer her right.

Harry nodded. "They're good people. Craig's just a little high-handed at times. As a rancher, he's respected, admired, even envied. Because of his reputation as a rancher his arrogance is usually tolerated; or overlooked."

Tamera sighed. *Might as well face the music*, she resolved, *and see if there's any chance I still have a job.*

Considering what happened, not to mention the fact that she was two weeks late in showing up, Tamera seriously doubted it. With a tiny nod of acquiescence, she followed Shorty to the ranch, the beauty of the drive obscured by the doubts and fears plaguing her. Arriving, Shorty escorted her from her car up to the porch where she found Craig, freshly showered, though still looking haggard and angry, standing beside an older man in a wheelchair.

"Craig Harris, ma'am." He extended a hand toward her. "I hope there are no hard feelings over your run-in with my grandson."

"You're Craig Harris? I thought Harry said he was Craig Harris," she remarked, with a nod in Craig's direction.

The old man laughed. "He is. Craig Harris the Third to be exact."

"Well, sir, I'm afraid I lost my temper also," she apologized, taking the proffered hand. The twinkle in his gray eyes, a lighter shade than his offspring's, eased her embarrassment some.

Again he laughed. "Good for you, honey. Someone needed to bring him down a peg. What's your name?" he asked, enclosing her hand in both of his.

A flush warmed her cheeks. She gently disengaged her hand from his grasp. "Tamera Collins."

A frown creased his brow. "That name sounds familiar. Why's that, I wonder?"

Her flush deepened. "You sent me a letter of acceptance for the summer job," she said, and heard Craig's sharp intake of breath.

"What job?" he demanded.

She dared a look at him. "The veterinarian."

Craig snorted. "You're too young to be a veterinarian."

"That's right," Mr. Harris interjected, giving Craig a warning look. "I remember now. Exceptionally qualified if your résumé was correct."

"It is."

"Job's filled," Craig interrupted.

Tamera dared another glance. One look told her all she needed to know. It would be a long time before he got over their encounter. "I'm sorry to hear that."

She blinked back tears of frustration and exhaustion and turned back to his grandfather. "Mr. Harris, if the job is already filled, I'd appreciate if you could suggest a place for me and my horse to stay over the next few weeks. Harry explained about the charity rodeo you put on each year and I'd like to enter it."

"Craig, your mare's hemorrhaging!" The alarm sounded from the barn before Mr. Harris could answer or Craig could object.

Action exploded around her. Tamera hesitated but a moment before joining in. Jumping off the porch, she grabbed her keys, fumbled with them, threw open the trunk of her car and pulled out her veterinarian bag. Fueled by adrenaline, she pushed her way through the mob of frantic cowboys. Shoving them aside, she knelt beside the mare and began her examination.

Panic seized the animal. She struggled to stand. Tamera knew she would have one heck of a fight on her hands if the mare succeeded. Her sharp whistle brought quiet to the chaos around her.

"Let's not panic, gentlemen," she cautioned with quiet authority. "Craig, get her head." She didn't wait to see if he would obey, just issued orders. "Shorty, is it?" At his nod, she continued. "Get this foal out of the way. You," she nodded at a young man in the crowd. "I need warm water, lots of warm water. And towels."

Without question, they jumped to do her bidding as she continued with her examination. Silence hung in the air: *Thick. Tense. Anxious.* The only sounds penetrating it were the labored breathing of the mare and the senseless, soothing words of the woman beside her.

"She's not hemorrhaging," Tamera muttered, reaching for her bag. "She's in labor."

"What?" Craig exclaimed, shock and surprise evident in his tone. "But that foal's only a few hours old. That's impossible. Veterinarian my ass," he snorted. "You don't know what you're talking about. Get the hell away from my mare!" he ordered through clenched teeth.

Tamera moved, but not to do his bidding. "It happens, Craig," she said and continued her preparations to deliver the foal despite his order to the contrary. "Twins. Sometimes one develops more rapidly. The other either catches up or doesn't make it through delivery. How old is that colt?"

He shrugged. "Three, maybe four hours."

She sighed, fighting back bitter tears. *Now was not the time to lose control.* "Chances are this one will be stillborn or deformed. Either way, it has to be born. You'll lose your mare otherwise," she told him with grave certainty.

Given the alternative, Craig nodded.

It was all she needed. Tamera gave the mare a shot to help with the contractions and prepared for the delivery. Snapping on gloves that covered her from fingertip to armpit, she was ready when the next spasm hit the mare. Reaching in the birth canal, she grabbed the unborn foal and gently pulled, stopping when the contraction ceased, but maintaining her grip. She allowed his direction when Craig barked orders for someone to get the calf puller should it prove necessary in aiding the delivery, then questioned him as to the overall health of the mare, length of term, and condition of this pregnancy. He answered readily, holding and stroking the mare's head, neither of them fully aware they were working in tandem and enjoying it. In less than an hour, the tiny foal made its entrance into the world.

Washing it, Tamera examined the newborn filly. "Breathe," she whispered. "Come on, baby, breathe," she urged, clearing the filly's airway passages and stimulating her heart. The filly uttered a small nicker.

"That's it, baby," Tamera soothed. "Come on now, keep breathing."

Her examination complete, Tamera pulled the filly into her arms, stroking the tiny head and slender neck. "She seems to be normal. She's weak and tiny, but other than that..."

She choked on a sob, but couldn't stop the tears from streaming down her cheeks when she realized she held a living, breathing miracle in her arms.

"Thank you God," she whispered, knowing she'd prayed more in the last hour than she had in weeks.

"What now?" Craig's voice penetrated her thoughts. The mare struggled to get up. He held her still, waiting for Tamera's consent.

Surprised at the tenderness in his tone, Tamera nodded, raising triumphant sapphire eyes to his. "Let her up. It's the best thing for her. Walk her to keep the blood flowing for a while. Make sure she passes the afterbirth, all of it. But watch her for signs of excessive bleeding or extreme weakness. I'll need a bigger stall; clean, dry, and disinfected, with plenty of fresh hay. And heat lamps. The next few hours, maybe even days will be the most critical for her, for all of them really. They'll need constant supervision. She may not be able to nurse them, and even if she does, he'll probably get more than his share. This little one, though, we'll probably have to bottle-feed. Or you will, if I'm not here to help."

Unspoken question hung in the air; Craig heard it, now perfectly aware of her competence. He wondered if she knew how beautiful she looked covered in things most women would find disgusting. Cheeks flushed from excitement and exertion, eyes sparkling with triumph, she sat, holding that filly as though it were her own baby. He let the mare up and rolled to his feet, and offered Tamera a hand.

"You're late." He accused, unable to stop the grin tugging at his mouth.

At a little over six feet tall, Tamera had to tilt her head to look into his eyes. Only temper could have prevented her from being intimidated by the obvious strength in his wide shoulders and broad chest earlier. Admiration shone in the dark gray gaze, though she doubted he'd voice it aloud. She smiled back.

"Looks like I got here just in time."

Innocence combined with pure, female triumph in that one smile made Craig's gut twist with desire. In a few short hours she'd infuriated, humiliated, and amazed him and he wondered how on earth he'd get through the entire summer with her around.

Chapter Two

For the second time that day, cheers and applause surrounded her. After supervising the move of the mare and her foals to a new stall, Tamera gave precise instructions for their immediate care and followed Craig to the porch where he filled his grandfather in on the details.

"Told you she was exceptionally qualified," Craig's grandfather told him. "Looks like God is still in the miracle business too."

He smiled knowingly, and then addressed Tamera. "I took the liberty of having your luggage brought upstairs to your room. Shorty couldn't unload your horse though, he seems a bit temperamental."

She sighed. "Unfortunately, yes. He won't let anyone near. I'll unload him if you just tell me where to put him."

For the first time, Craig noticed how tired she looked and felt a tug of remorse. "I'll tend him for you," he offered. "Maria will show you to your room."

She shook her head. "That's okay, he won't let you."

"Nonsense," he argued, stepping off the porch and heading toward the trailer. "Never met a horse I couldn't handle."

Tamera rolled her eyes. "Arrogant jerk," she muttered under her breath, then blushed when the Senior Craig Harris chuckled. "Wait," she called, as Craig reached for the door. "Please, just let me get him," she insisted, grabbing his hand. Craig grinned at her obvious concern, a smug, lazy smile that made her stomach knot with tension.

"You afraid for me, little one?" he inquired in a soft, husky tone.

Tamera looked into his teasing eyes and ground her teeth in frustration. He was as conceited as he was arrogant! "I couldn't care less if you got your skull kicked in. Probably do you some good," she bit out, pushing him away from the trailer. "My only concern is that he'll hurt himself while doing you the favor."

With that last condemning statement, she flung open the door and entered, only to be met with opposition as the stallion balked, rolling his eyes and stomping his foot. Tamera knew it was because of the blood and afterbirth on her clothing. Taking a few minutes to soothe her horse's mercurial temperament, she backed him out of the trailer.

"Now," she told Craig, noting the awed look on his face as he eyed the big stallion. "If you'll be so kind as to show me where I can put him, I'd like to take a shower sometime this evening."

Craig chose to ignore the sarcasm in her voice, and whistled. "Wow, what an animal. What is he, Thoroughbred, mixed?"

"Arabian," she answered, wondering if he ever saw anything but a Quarter horse. "Full blooded, unblemished, Arabian, from the finest, purest bloodlines. His ancestors have carried nothing but royalty on their backs for a hundred years," she informed him, letting a note of pride enter her voice.

"Well," he snorted, "excuse me."

She grinned. "You're excused. Now, a stall as far away from that mare and her babies as we can get."

Closing the trailer door behind them, Craig noted its nameplate. "Temper Two? Who's Temper One?" He chuckled at the glare she bestowed on him.

"It's a long story. One I'm sure will bore you to death."

"Oh, I doubt that," he argued, drawing his own conclusions. "Can't wait to hear it. Maybe you'll enlighten us at dinner."

She grunted. "Maybe not."

After putting her horse away, Craig led Tamera into the house via the utility room and called for the housekeeper. "Maria, this is..."

"I know who she is," she interrupted. "I'll take her upstairs. After you get out of those clothes," she told Tamera. "You go," she eyed Craig. "Give us some privacy."

Craig's eyes lightened and sparkled with humor, accompanied by a boyish grin that had Tamera doing a double take.

"But I need another shower too," he argued, despite the lack of dirt or sweat on him.

Maria slapped at him. "I said get."

"Aw, shucks Maria. Can't have no fun with you around," he teased, as she shooed him outside.

"Go on now, before I turn you over my knee like I did when you were five."

Tamera felt a pang of emptiness at the obvious closeness between them. "You mean he was five once?" she teased in a deliberate effort not to cry.

She asked the question with such wide-eyed innocence and thinly veiled sarcasm that Maria couldn't help but laugh. "An ornery little cuss even then," she confessed.

"An understatement I'm sure," Tamera muttered.

Maria laughed again. "You'll do just fine here, missy," she predicted. "I do believe Master Craig has met his match."

Again, Tamera regarded her with wide, innocent eyes. "You call him Master?"

Maria laughed once more. "Only behind his back, honey, and don't you ever let on."

Indicating that her lips were sealed, Tamera crossed her heart and promised scout's honor. Taking off her bloodstained clothes, she wrapped a huge bath sheet around her and followed the aging but lively housekeeper upstairs.

Tamera gaped in awe at the room she was given. Decorated in various shades of pink and white, it was light, airy, and undeniably feminine. She didn't know enough about antiques to appraise their value, but knew enough to appreciate the beauty of the huge, four-poster bed and the matching vanity dresser with its one drawer large enough to hold almost all of her belongings. The antique armoire was used to house linens since there was a spacious closet and a private bathroom. She listened in earnest as

Maria showed her where to put her things and informed her that dinner was at six o'clock sharp.

Taking advantage of the luxurious facilities, Tamera stood a long time in the shower washing away the grit and grime from traveling, as well as her other activities, then settled in the tub for a hot bath. She saturated her thick locks with conditioner, wrapped a moist, hot towel around her head and relaxed in scented, frothy water. Her vision blurred as exhaustion numbed her senses and she sank lower in the tub. She awoke with a start an hour later, shivering. She rose, drained the water from the tub and rinsed the conditioner out of her hair. Patting herself dry with a thick, soft towel, she reached for the robe that hung on the door.

Wrapped in the warm terry cloth, she sat at the vanity and combed the tangles out of her mass of blonde hair. She retrieved the blow dryer from her overnight bag, and ran her fingers through the thick tresses while applying heat. When the chore was nearly complete, she sprayed her hair with leave-in conditioner and brushed it. Tamera closed her eyes and mentally counted the strokes as a memory emerged in her mind...*he in his favorite chair, she sitting at her father's feet while he brushed and counted one hundred strokes. She heard his voice in her mind as she completed the task.*

An everyday routine she once thought of as soothing, a time of bonding, she now considered a chore. Tamera blinked back tears, swallowed the lump in her throat, put down the brush, and seriously considered getting it all cut off.

Noticing the time, she unpacked her belongings and pulled on fresh clothes, relishing the feel of clean silk against her bare flesh. She finished her toiletry by cleansing her short but well-manicured nails and then cleaning and replacing her diamond-stud earrings. She slid her feet into sandals and glanced in the full-length mirror, pleased at what she saw.

Wonder what Mr. Craig Harris *the Third* will think now? Tamera mused. For once, she was glad her mother always insisted that she dress and act like a lady when not working, especially at dinner. Tears smarted her eyes as she remembered her mother's voice, lightly admonishing... "You can wear jeans and cutoffs all day long out there working and playing with the horses, but at dinner you'll be a lady. You'll dress and act like one too."

Tears dripped down her cheeks. Tamera pressed a trembling fist to her lips and deliberately fought for control over her emotions. *How could you do this, God? Why? I trusted You! They trusted You! How could You let this happen? How could You hurt us this way?*

Though she didn't voice the questions aloud, Tamera's heart cried out in confusion, pain and anger, momentarily forgetting the joy of holding that filly, that miracle, in her arms. Tamera took a deep, cleansing breath, walked into the bathroom and washed her face, determined not to cry anymore. She wouldn't trust or believe anymore either. Or pray. It hurt too much when you lost.

Faith is the substance of things hoped for...

The scripture floated through her mind. Tamera clamped a lid on it. Well, I won't hope anymore, either. I want nothing from You, she determined.

A knock sounded at the door. Tamera opened it, surprised to find Craig standing there.

Craig looked down at her, noticing the red-rimmed eyes and felt a tug at his conscience. "Is something wrong?"

She shook her head.

"Would you like a drink before dinner?"

Tamera smiled, not quite able to picture him the charming host, and then shoved the thought aside as ungracious, unchristian, and out of character. Nodding, she followed him down the stairs.

Craig led her into the den, then poured her a glass of wine and himself a shot of brandy. He'd spent the better part of the afternoon arguing with his grandfather over her. "She's trouble," he warned.

"She's exceptionally qualified," Gramps had insisted. "She saved your mare."

"Right, and too beautiful for words." Craig snorted. "Did you by any chance get a picture with her application?"

"No, I hired her on merit alone. A picture wouldn't have made any difference. Besides, knowing your weakness for beautiful women, do you think I'd deliberately put that kind of temptation in your face?"

Craig frowned, bit back the angry retort that came to mind, chose kinder words instead. "With the way you and Maria hound me about settling down, getting married and having babies, nothing would surprise me."

Gramps had the grace to chuckle.

"She's going to be trouble. I can feel it," Craig reiterated. "The talk has already started."

"Well, put a stop to it. Protect her if you have to," Gramps insisted.

"I've got a ranch to run. How am I supposed to play bodyguard to some hot-tempered female who happens to be a veterinarian, exceptionally qualified or not?"

Gramps' eyes had narrowed into steely slits.

"You'll do what you have to. Remember who you are, young man."

He remembered, and now he was playing host as his grandfather had bid. She smiled sweetly when he handed her the glass.

Sinking into a chair, Craig watched through lowered lids as she walked around the room. The peach sundress clung in all the right places, showing an incredible amount of tanned legs and tiny feet encased in strappy sandals. Her hair cascaded over her shoulders and down her back in silken waves. *Trouble*, he thought, *with a capital T.*

Tamera could feel his eyes on her as she ran her finger along the intricate carvings on the mantle above the fireplace. "You have a beautiful home, Mr. Harris," she observed, not sure how to address him. He didn't appear to be much older than she, but he was her employer, indirectly at least.

"Mr. Harris? Oh, please, you make me feel as old as my grandfather," he remarked, curious at her sudden show of meekness.

A slight smile tugged at the corners of her mouth. "I've heard it said that you demand respect. As my employer you're entitled to it."

"You didn't bother to consider that when you called me Craig earlier and gave me orders. Or when you threw water in my face."

Her smile brightened, making her eyes sparkle even as color rushed to her cheeks.

"The only thing I considered earlier was the condition of the mare that needed me."

"And before that?"

"The actions of the jerk manhandling me."

His laugh was rich and quick. "Guess I deserve that."

"You do. And did," she admitted.

"Just don't forget who the boss is here," he warned a steely edge to his otherwise soft voice.

She acknowledged the warning with a tiny nod. "I'm sure I'll be reminded quite often."

At Maria's call to dinner, Craig escorted Tamera to her seat then took his own. Gramps was already at the table. They talked quietly while Maria served the food. When she finished and the table laden with the choicest beef, potatoes and vegetables, Maria joined them. A moment of silence preceded the blessing.

Tamera's eyes widened in surprise as the Sr. Mr. Harris began *the Lord's Prayer*. She bowed her head and clasped her hands in her lap to hide their trembling, but fought against reciting the words in her mind. She hadn't heard that prayer before supper since the last time her father said it. Biting her lip, she fought against the tears, determined not to think about what had happened.

"Amen." The chorus broke into her thoughts.

Tamera bit back the refrain with angry determination.

Conversation around her remained light and revolved mostly around Craig's mare and the miracle births. Tamera ate in silence until someone said her name.

"Is something wrong with the food?" the Sr. Harris asked his voice laced with concern.

Tamera realized she'd pushed her food around without eating so much as a bite and put the fork down in defeat. "No. I'm sorry, I guess I'm more tired than hungry."

"Would you like to go upstairs?" he offered.

"No, I'll be fine." She took a sip of her wine and hoped the conversation would steer elsewhere.

"Tell us about yourself," he urged, not wanting her to feel left out of the conversation. "How did someone so young become such an expert on horses? You said your résumé was correct, and I believe you, but how? You're barely a child yourself to be so knowledgeable."

His kind words and gentle smile brought peace to her tumultuous thoughts. Tamera smiled. "I've always had a passion for horses, much to the dismay of my mother." Her smile deepened. "From the time I was very little, my daddy swore I was part horse. He said I squealed with delight every time I saw a pony. As I got older, I wanted to be around them all the time. I went through the usual pony stages, a Shetland then a Welsh, etcetera.

"When I was about ten or eleven, I started hanging around an Arabian ranch not far from our house. That's when I decided I wanted one. I eventually bought Temper from them. Anyway, they got tired of seeing me hang around and do nothing, so they offered me a job brushing the horses. Boy was I thrilled! I'd outgrown my pony so I gave her away and started saving every dime I could. By the time I was thirteen, I knew I wanted to be a veterinarian and work with horses. Again, much to the dismay of my mother."

She sipped her wine, the warm memories helping to ease the dull ache in her heart. "The only drawback as far as I was concerned was completing high school, then eight years of college, before I could do what I wanted. That would make me an old woman in my mind."

Tamera recalled the conversation with her father about that with a tiny laugh. "Then, I saw an advertisement to be a veterinarian assistant. Well, I thought that was my start. I went to private school so it was easy to arrange tutoring and summer classes. I graduated when I was sixteen. By then I'd received my certificate and moved up in my job from just brushing the horses to being a full-fledged groom.

"Mr. Somers, the man I worked for, loved my enthusiasm and respected my ambition. I started college right away, taking a full load while keeping my job. Even though the certificate wasn't really worth the paper it was written on, that plus the experience I had helped me whiz through the first four years. The next four were a little more difficult, but I managed to graduate in the top five percent of my class. Daddy insisted that I take a few months and decide if I wanted to work for someone or open my own practice, since Mr. Somers didn't need a veterinarian on staff at his ranch. That's when I saw your advertisement in *Horse* magazine. So, here I am."

"So that makes you what, twenty-five, twenty-six?"

"Twenty-four."

Craig suppressed a groan. She looked a lot younger than that! The flush on her cheeks and excitement in her eyes had need curling in him like hot flames. "Well, that explains your knowledge and skill. What I want to know is why you're late." He tried not to sound gruff, but couldn't help it. Had she not been there today, he would have lost his prize mare and the filly and, very possibly as a result, the colt.

"We expected you two weeks ago," he continued, ignoring the warning look his grandfather gave him. Sadness clouded her face.

"My parents were killed a month ago," she said, swallowing the hard the lump of tears that clogged her throat. "They were going on vacation; a second honeymoon."

Visibly fighting her emotions, she continued. "You see, where my passion was horses, Daddy's was airplanes. He had his pilot license and leased a twin-engine plane. They were flying off looking forward to adventure, rest and peace. Something went wrong. Everything started out okay. At least it seemed that way, but before they cleared the runway the plane exploded."

Their unanimous gasp echoed in the room.

"You were there?" the Sr. Harris asked, his tone incredulous.

She nodded, unable to stop the tears this time. She brushed them away and struggled against the emotions threatening to overwhelm, fought for enough control to continue. "It was a nightmare. Sometimes I'm still not sure I've awakened. I see that plane explode every time I close my eyes," she mumbled, collapsing under the weight of grief burdening her heart.

He'd been called many things: *cold, hard, callous*, adjectives usually preceding a direct slur on his legitimacy. At that moment, Craig felt every bit the sum total of all the ugly names ever applied to his person. He shoved away from the table, unable to bear her crying.

Tamera looked up, her eyes begging for forgiveness. "I'm sorry. I didn't mean to upset anyone."

Mr. Harris patted her hand as Craig stomped from the room. "Its okay, sweetheart, my grandson is too used to being in control over everything. It's about time he got a little taste of humility."

"I don't think he appreciates me being the one to give it to him. Especially after this afternoon," she wailed.

Maria wiped her eyes and pulled Tamera into her arms. "Don't you worry, honey, he'll get over it. You're safer here with us than somewhere out there alone."

Unable to resist the comfort offered in Maria's ample arms, Tamera clung to her, sobbing until she thought there were no tears left. She didn't normally get so emotional in front of strangers, but no one had held her like this since the death of her parents. When the emotions were spent, leaving nothing but aching emptiness where her heart once was, she pulled away.

She reached for her wine with a trembling hand, took a sip. "I'm sorry, I thought I was all cried out. Anyway, when it was all over I was kind of lost, you know? I found your letter while going through some other papers. I didn't even think that the job might be filled. I just packed up, left, and drove straight through."

"When was that?" Mr. Harris asked his tone gentle.

She shrugged. "A little over twenty-four hours ago. It took longer pulling Temper. Not wanting him to get too stiff in the trailer, I had to stop more often than normal."

Mr. Harris nodded in understanding. "Well, the job's not filled. Craig was just angry when he said it was. It's yours. You're welcome to stay on as long as you like. As long as you want or need to, or until you decide what to do about your future. Is there someone back home to take care of your house?"

Tamera sighed with relief and nodded. "Thank you. I contacted Daddy's attorney. He promised to look after the place. Said he'd hire a caretaker to go a few times a month to clean, and make it look cared for."

She paused. "Mr. Harris, I'm exhausted. Is there a pasture I can put Temper in for the night?"

"Of course. But please, call me Gramps. Everyone does," he added then called Craig in and explained what she wanted.

"You put him out at night? Why?"

Her smile, albeit a wobbly one, was full of pride. "I prefer him to graze at night. I spend a great deal of time, effort and money making sure that his coat is in mint condition, I don't need the sun bleaching or drying it out."

Craig shrugged and led the way to the barn. He watched as she soothed and babied the huge stallion. When she backed him out of the stall, Craig reached a hand to pet him.

Tamera's words of caution were unnecessary when Temper whipped his head around and snapped his teeth, daring Craig to touch him.

Tamera forced the horse's head around, slapped him on the mouth and tightened her grip on the halter. "Stop it," she admonished her tone firm, hold firmer. "He's not hurting anything."

Craig kept his surprise in check as the big horse laid his head on her shoulder and stood passively while he petted and checked him over. The horse's coat was baby soft, his frame huge and muscular, supported by long, thin legs that looked as though they shouldn't be able to hold his weight. At eighteen hands, or almost six feet tall, the stallion towered over his tiny mistress. He was gentle, though, or at least towards her. Craig knew better.

Arabians were known for being temperamental. Temper's flat ears and hoof, lightly resting and ready to kick, assured him that the horse would tolerate his touch merely out of loyalty to Tamera. Regardless, he hadn't seen a more perfect specimen of horseflesh in a long time, his quarter-horse mentality admitted.

Craig finished his inspection then led them to an unoccupied pasture next to the barn. He watched in silence as she turned the horse loose and lovingly encouraged him as he kicked up his heels and ran around the perimeters of the pasture.

"Tamera?" His voice was soft as she turned to go. He reached for her, hesitated, and then brushed his fingertips across her cheek. "I'm sorry."

Though a bit surprised at the tenderness in his voice and actions, Tamera didn't question his sincerity since anyone with such blatant emotions would have no reason to force an apology. There was no doubt in her mind that it cost him a chunk of pride though. Considering everything, she'd seen and heard he was a proud man, of firm opinion, unused to regret or apology. Regardless, she acknowledged his words with a tiny smile and nod.

"Thank you," she whispered, then returned to her room.

Chapter Three

Once in her room, Tamera prepared for bed. Memories assailed her, making sleep difficult. She tossed and turned, seeking the rest she so desperately needed. Sleep, when it came, wasn't peaceful, but haunted.

She ran toward the airplane, begging them not to go. They didn't hear and continued to climb up the steps. They smiled and waved, unmindful of how distraught she was. She ran faster. Suddenly he was there, holding her back, keeping her from warning her parents!

She struggled with him, but he was stronger. He held her easily, undaunted by her struggles, and laughed, calling her names. He reeked of alcohol. She could smell it, taste the fear it evoked. She struggled harder, screamed for her father. Her screams died in her throat as the plane exploded and he forced her down, tearing her dress.

Tamera awoke with a muffled cry. She lunged from the bed, groped around in the dark trying to find the light, unable to gauge where she was, and then sobbed with relief when the doorknob slammed into her hip. Flinging the door open, she raced out of the room. By the time she reached the bottom of the stairs, her breathing had calmed.

She glanced over her shoulder in silent acknowledgement that it would be useless to go back to bed. Not stopping to consider her state of dress, she went out into the night and toward the barn. Guided by instinct, she found her way to the stall which housed the mare and her foals. She talked in a quiet voice to soothe the mare and entered, wondering who was supposed to be staying with the horses and where they were, then blinked in surprise when a flashlight shone in her face.

"What are you doing here? Kinda early huh? The sun's not going to be up for another hour or so."

Tamera remembered him as one in the crowd when she delivered the filly. Suddenly aware she was in her nightgown, Tamera shook her head. "I...I just came to check on them," she stammered, staying hidden from his sight by the bulk of the mare. "And you?"

"I'm supposed to be keeping watch. Just went to get some coffee." He held the thermos toward her with a smile.

"No thanks." She searched her mind for something to say to get rid of him. "I'll take over for a while. You get some sleep."

His eyes narrowed, smile turned into a leer. "We can keep each other company," he offered in a guttural tone that slithered over her like snakeskin. Tamera shivered in disgust.

"That's okay. Mr. Harris is due in shortly," she assured, hoping she didn't sound as shaky as she felt. "You go on and get some rest. I'm sure he'll have plenty for you to do later today. Thank you for pulling your shift."

He snorted, obviously stung by her rejection. "Bossy little chit, aren't you?"

"Not really, just relaying orders."

With a muttered oath, he tossed the thermos in a corner by the door and stomped off.

Tamera sighed with relief that he hadn't pushed the issue or guessed she was lying, and even more relieved he hadn't figured out she was clad only in a silk nightgown. The filly stirred. Tamera knelt and examined her, forgetting the incident in her concern. "There, there, little one," she soothed. "You're going to be just fine."

* * * * *

Craig awoke feeling cotton-mouthed and groggy. From the moment Tamera left him at the barn last night, he'd been consumed by thoughts of her. The desire ignited in him by her excitement at dinner was in no way lessened by the tears she'd shed. Mixed with an alarming sense of protection, the feelings grew in proportions he'd never experienced. He wanted to see her, to touch and hold her, to take away the sadness that lurked deep in her sapphire eyes.

He'd tried to banish the thoughts with a drink, telling himself that what he felt was totally irrational considering he'd known her for less than twenty-four hours. He tried to convince himself he was just grateful because she saved his mare, and that he was impressed with her accomplishments at such a young age. It didn't dawn on him that she was just a few years younger than he. Unable to convince himself, he spent the rest of the evening between the barn and the house, checking on his mare and her foals. After what seemed like the hundredth trip, he vowed to get some rest.

Incapable of getting Tamera off his mind, he'd traded the brandy for sipping whiskey and sat for a while staring at the empty fireplace. Liquor wasn't his usual vice, but he needed something to numb the senses. Every time he closed his eyes he could see her, feel her presence. The memory of the pain in her face, tears on her cheeks, and sobs shaking her slender frame, tormented his heart. Each trip to the barn reminded him of how beautiful she'd looked in her moment of triumph.

The need she aroused in him had him prowling around like a caged tiger and cursing his baser instincts. He found himself in her room wanting desperately to take her in his arms and just as desperately to leave. Craig fought the urge to touch her, to take her in his arms and cradle her against his chest, as she tossed and turned, whimpering in her quest for sleep. Careful to be quiet, Craig berated himself for entering her room in the first place. "What on earth are you thinking? The woman is an employee and a guest in your grandfather's home!"

Going downstairs, he rejected the idea of another drink. Nothing soothed the soul like a long, hard, ride. He'd returned sometime in the midnight hours and dragged himself up to his room only to dream of her.

He stood a long time in the shower and willed his mind and body to behave as she invaded his thoughts again. Acting like an untried teenager, he thought with disgust as lust awoke painfully at her memory.

He'd avoided serious relationships ever since his engagement with the two-timing Stephanie Parker had broken off nearly a year ago. Disgusted and disappointed, he wondered when and if he would ever find a woman to love him and not just his ranch or his wealth.

Again, Tamera's image rose unbidden in his mind.

He snorted aloud at the thought. "Yeah, right, you barely know her and didn't even like her from the moment you met," he argued with himself. She has the temper of a she-cat, a mouth that won't quit, and a body... he cut that thought off with a curse. *Don't even think about it*, he mentally warned himself. It'd be a long, hot summer if he started that kind of thinking now.

Craig completed his shower, dressed and had started down the stairs when Gramps called to him from below. "See if Tamera is awake yet. If so, tell her breakfast will be ready shortly. If not, let her sleep. Lord knows she could use some rest."

"Me too," he muttered, and turned to do as his grandfather bade. He knocked on her door and waited. Not getting an answer, he opened it and called her name in a tone meant to stir, not waken. Though it looked like a small war had taken place in it, the bed was empty and she wasn't in the bathroom.

"She's not in here," he called to Gramps, as he left the room and walked down the stairs. "You haven't seen her?"

"No, not this morning. I can't believe she'd be up yet. The poor child was exhausted."

Craig glanced out the window noting that Temper was still in the pasture. For someone who insisted she didn't need the sun ruining his coat, she hadn't bothered to bring him in yet. Dawning struck with the force of lightning.

"The mare!" he exclaimed, and headed out the door. "I'll beat the little brat if something went wrong and she didn't wake me!"

"Now wait just a minute, Craig," his grandfather called, wheeling himself out on the porch and down the ramp just as Craig reached the last step. "Calm down."

But Craig was too far-gone, driven by fear and anger. He reached the barn door, calling for Tamera.

"Shh!" Shorty waved a hand at him and cautioned Craig to be quiet, then led the way to the stall.

The mare stood quietly in one corner with the colt at her feet. Tamera lay in the other corner cuddling the filly as though it were a baby.

Craig grinned at Shorty, overwhelmed with relief and aching from the longing the innocent picture elicited in him. "I'll get her," he whispered. "Tell Gramps everything's okay, and ask Maria to straighten up the covers on her bed, will you Shorty?"

Shorty nodded. "Poor little thing," he whispered. Gramps had already filled him in on her tragedy.

The mare nickered in recognition as Craig entered the stall. He petted and talked to reassure her then reached down to stroke the colt who simply stretched out in the soft hay. As he turned toward them, the filly nickered. Tamera moaned, turned onto her back and pulled the filly firmly against her. Her gown slipped, exposing a creamy, sun kissed shoulder to his hungry gaze. A mouthwatering sight. Though modest in cut and color, the gown only served to inflame his imagination as to the body beneath it.

Desire, sharp and painful, coursed through him followed by a surge of anger at the thought of her lying there so exposed, so vulnerable, and the fact that he was responsible for her. He vowed to find out who should have been keeping watch over the animals and why he wasn't present. He knelt beside them, touched Tamera's cheek, and frowned at the dark smudges which marred the delicate skin under her eyes like bruises on her creamy flesh. He whispered her name.

Tamera awoke in a mild state of panic and confusion. Glancing around, she realized where she was and who was beside her. A blush warmed her cheeks as she struggled to sit up. She released the filly and fumbled with the front of her gown.

"I couldn't sleep." she explained, glancing into the steel gray eyes. His gaze, soft and warm like liquid metal, made her blush harder as he brushed strands of hay out of her hair with a gentleness that seemed out of character.

Craig knew he was treading on dangerous ground, that people were expecting them, but couldn't seem to get past the moment at hand. "I guess a kiss is out of the question," he queried, his voice tender, gaze unwavering.

Emotions, raw and unfamiliar, shivered through her. Tamera attempted to scoot away from him, emitted a shaky little laugh and tried to quench the feelings escalating to frightening proportions. "A kiss? Why would you want a kiss? I didn't think you even liked me."

Craig wound his hand in her thick hair, stopping her movements. "Like has nothing to do with desire," he moaned and crushed her to him as his mouth covered hers in a thorough kiss. "Absolutely nothing," he assured as she clung to his shirt and trembled in his arms.

Her cheeks flamed. She pushed against his chest, avoiding his gaze. "Craig, please, I want to get dressed and I need to bring Temper in before it gets too hot."

He held her a moment, surprised at his own response to that kiss. He rose and pulled her to her feet. She stumbled. His arms wound around her in an automatic attempt to steady. *Big mistake.* Her soft body brushed against his chest. He could feel her heart pound, smell her intoxicating scent.

He released her abruptly and took a step back.

Too many changes occurring too swiftly assaulted her senses. Seething with embarrassment Tamera tripped in her haste to put some distance between them.

The stench of manure reached Craig's nostrils when she landed neatly in it. *If that don't cool the ardor,* he thought with a chuckle, and regarded her with laughing gray eyes. "Now what are you going to do?"

"I'm going to kill you, Craig Harris," she threatened, and forcefully refrained from throwing a handful at him. "Ugh!" She wrinkled her nose. "Now what? I can't go into the house like this, Maria will kill me."

He chortled. "Or douse you with the water hose. Of course, that would be a sight to behold." He grinned, feeling no remorse. Covered in blood or manure she was stunning.

The thought exasperated him. *It's going to be a long summer.*

Craig grabbed the blanket used by the men keeping vigil through the night and held it up to her.

"What?" she asked, unsure of what he was proposing.

"Just take off the gown and wrap in this."

"Excuse me?" She narrowed her eyes and seriously reconsidered tossing manure at him. "You come in here, kiss me, then pull me up, causing me to lose my balance and fall in a pile of...." She bit back the word that came to mind. "Of *manure*, and now you expect me to undress in front of you?"

"Well, what else do you propose?" he asked. "I won't watch," he promised, closing his eyes. After a long, drawn out pause, he heard the sounds of her undressing and forced himself not to watch as she peeled the gown off and tossed it, that look of disgust on her pretty face.

Tamera snatched the blanket out of his hands and wrapped it securely around her shoulders.

"Jerk," she muttered, teeth clenched as tightly as her fists clinging to the blanket.

He swung her up in his arms. She stiffened. "What on earth do you think you're doing now?"

"You seem to be having trouble staying on your feet," he teased.

"Put me down," she insisted, wondering how on earth a twentieth century man could act like a nineteenth century jerk.

He arched a dark, elaborate brow, and eyed her with deliberate solemnity. "Do you honestly think you can make it out of this barn, into the house and up the stairs without breaking your neck or losing that blanket?"

Tamera shuddered at the images his words conjured. She ground her teeth, buried her hot face into his shoulder and remained tense and silent as he carried her out of the barn.

He stopped just inside the entrance. "What about the gown?"

A dainty shudder shook her. "Burn it."

He carried her up to her room and deposited her on the bed.

Tamera trembled as his fingers brushed over the exposed skin of her shoulders and across the top edge of the blanket. Her flesh burned where his touch lingered. She heard his sharp intake of breath, trembled with an answering shiver and kept her gaze lowered for fear of the need glowing in his eyes, afraid of the hunger that reached into her soul in ways she didn't understand.

Gently, very gently and slowly, his finger traveled from the top of the blanket to lift her chin. When it became obvious he waited for her to look at him, she raised her wary gaze to his.

"Why are you here?" he whispered, his voice so thick, breathing so sharp and painful, he could barely get the words past his raw throat.

Tamera's mind did a quick, frantic search for the answer to what shouldn't have been an unanswerable question. His finger on her lips let her know she need not respond.

Getting a firm grip on his emotions, Craig shook his head. What's happening here? He clenched his fists in a determined effort not to drag her up into his aching arms. He took a step back, hesitated, and shook his head again.

"Breakfast is in ten minutes," he informed her, then forced himself to turn around and walk out of the room. He leaned against the banister for support, willed some semblance of control over his raging senses.

He went out to the barn, retrieved her soiled gown, ordered the stall cleaned, and then asked to see the men who were scheduled to keep watch during the night. They appeared before him one by one. He questioned each until he found the one Tamera had relieved. Craig kept his temper in check until he got the story from the ranch hand as to what happened and why he found her in his stead.

Breakfast was a quiet affair. Tamera avoided his eyes and Craig fought to keep from staring at her; knowing that the anger as well as the longing he felt would be evident in his gaze.

"We need to talk," he insisted, as she rose from the table. Careful to be gentle, he took her by the arm and led her out the door and away from the house, not wanting Gramps to witness what was bound to be a confrontation.

"Who do you think you are, dismissing a ranch hand I ordered to take a turn at staying with the mare?"

She shivered at the unmistakable fury in his voice. "I didn't mean to undermine you, Craig. I woke up confused and disoriented from a nightmare. The next thing I knew, I was in the barn, and the horses were alone. Your man came back from getting coffee. I hadn't realized until he showed up that I was hardly dressed to be outside. I managed to stay out of his sight and to assure him I would stay with the mare and her foals. I didn't intend to fall asleep. I'm just glad it was you and no one else who found me."

"It was Shorty who found you," he ground out between clenched teeth. "And he made sure no one else saw you, either. You're lucky and I'm grateful he's not some randy young buck, otherwise, I'd have to fire him. I very nearly fired the hand that you dismissed without giving him the benefit of the doubt."

"I'm sorry." Embarrassment burned her cheeks, throbbed in her voice.

Craig raked his fingers through his hair, unnerved by the way she avoided his gaze and thrown off-guard by the fear he sensed in her. "Forget it," he muttered. "Just be careful, Tamera. I run a ranch here. Most of the men I can trust. Many are just temporary help. Not one of them has ever been tempted by a female hand. I don't hire female hands for that reason."

He rubbed at the tension in the base of his skull and swore. "I told Gramps it was a mistake to bring you here."

His blatant chauvinism grated on her already raw nerves. "Bull! You don't hire female hands because you think they can't handle themselves around a bunch of chauvinistic jerk cowboys who aren't mature enough to control their animal instincts!"

She hated the catch in her voice, glared at him for it. "I said I was sorry. What more do you want from me? An apology for having a nightmare? My resignation? Forget it, buster, you didn't hire me, your grandfather did!"

She turned away in an angry whirl and stomped off toward the barn, afraid now he would convince his grandfather to send her away.

Craig let her go, knowing he'd strangle her for her belligerence if he didn't.

Tamera took care of Temper before tending to the mare and foals. She wondered what had happened to the gown but was too embarrassed to ask. Though intimately aware when Craig arrived and that he watched her every move, she soon lost all thought of him as she set about examining the animals.

The colt was strong and healthy. He stood up by himself and urgently nudged his mother's bulging udder. The mare stomped her foot and pulled away from his searching muzzle. Tamera watched with concern as she refused to allow him to nurse. She talked gently and tried to examine the mare but was constantly interrupted by the hungry colt. She laughed and tried to shoo him away, relieved when Craig put his arms around the animal and held him out of the way.

Tamera's gentle voice, husky with concern, had him aching all over again, but Craig was determined to know the prognosis of his horses. He squatted in the hay, held the colt firmly in his grasp, and watched as she ran her hand down the length of the mare's stomach, while keeping up her soothing chatter. Reaching a teat, she squeezed some of the warm liquid into her palm. His pulse jerked into an unsteady gallop when she sniffed her palm then touched her tongue to the liquid. Her expression explained everything before she spoke.

"Ugh." She shuddered, wiped her hand on her jeans. "No wonder she won't nurse him. Her milk's no good."

Tamera gave the mare a shot to dry her milk then turned her attention to the colt. She examined him from head to hoof, and back again. He was in perfect health. She giggled when he nuzzled at her shirtfront and rubbed her face against his muzzle. "Sorry little fella, there's nothing for you there, either."

Craig felt another surge of heat and mentally chided himself for reacting like a teenager to her every gesture. He continued to watch in silence as she prepared a bottle and fed the colt.

Satisfied with the colt's response, Tamera moved on to examine the filly while Craig prepared another bottle of milk. She urged the filly to her feet. "Come on, little one. You have to try. Stand up now," she coaxed. "That's a good girl," she soothed, as the filly stood on wobbly legs.

Tamera wrapped an arm around the foal to help steady her during the examination, relieved to find that she, too, was in good health. She was tiny and weak and needed to be worked with in order to build strength, but other than that, she seemed to be normal.

Face flushed and eyes sparkling with triumph, she reached for the bottle when Craig held it toward her.

Tamera felt his gaze linger on her while she fed the filly, but couldn't look at him. Though confident about her knowledge and skill with the horses, she found herself painfully shy and naive when it came to him, especially the way he watched her, his gray eyes glistening with undisguised hunger. So she concentrated on the filly in her arms until the flush of excitement turned into heated embarrassment and she found herself aching in ways she never knew existed.

Thus began her duties at the Rockin' H ranch.

Chapter Four

The days slid one into another and Tamera began to adjust to her position at the ranch. The crux of her duties consisted of working with the new foals and yearlings, more of a pleasure than a job. She also had to worm cattle, horses, or even dogs, and give routine shots, but her duties revolved mostly around the horses. As one week passed into two, she began to relax and enjoy the ranch. She visited with Gramps, at times spent hours with him. His gentle strength and solid faith were a balm to her shattered soul

He told her of his younger days, the days before rheumatoid arthritis took over his body but not his spirit. He talked of how the death of Craig's parents when he was fifteen left him to shoulder most of the responsibility of the ranch.

The stories of how Craig managed and succeeded filled her with a new sense of respect for him and in those particular moments, she missed him the most. She could identify with the stress of losing both parents. The difference was, where Craig had his grandfather, she had nobody. Whatever else she felt, she missed him. Not the confused feelings he aroused in her, but definitely his magnetic presence.

As usual for this time of the year, Craig was gone more than he was home. Tamera made certain Shorty and Jimmy, the boy assigned to assist her, had a full report on the progress of the mare, Silver, and her foals.

As the days continued to pass, she found herself laughing and smiling, living again. She still missed her parents, sometimes cried deep into the night with grief and anger—anger aimed mostly at God—but healing had begun. The nightmares became less frequent, less vivid and in the quiet moments before dawn, Tamera prayed a little, questioned a lot and searched for the peace she once knew. At Gramps' urging, she joined him in prayer and Bible study, hoping to find some answers.

Life continued and Tamera slipped into a routine. One of her strongest assets was the ability to create routine in her life, and stick to it. She arose around four-thirty, slipped downstairs to bring Temper, Silver, and the foals into the barn, and returned to her room to workout and shower before breakfast.

She was used to having the run of the house early in the morning, and usually beat the men out of bed, but they always managed to be up and about, and Craig gone, before she went down to breakfast. Therefore, she wasn't expecting the soft knock on her bedroom door early one morning barely into her third week.

* * * * *

Craig hesitated three times before stopping at Tamera's door. He knew that she was an early riser because the horses were always in the barn by the time he saddled up. In the days since that first morning, he'd avoided her, but she continued to haunt his thoughts. He stayed away from the ranch house, even spent several nights on the range checking fences to the far-reaching corners of his property, but nothing worked.

He spent hours with the yearly regulars who attended the rodeo event they hosted, got reacquainted with them, settled them down, and made sure his ranch stayed in some semblance of order. He loved the rodeo, what it represented, and the fact they used the proceeds from it to help the less fortunate. What he didn't like was the extra work involved in roping off several provisional locations for tents and horse trailers, as well as constructing temporary arenas. But, even with the extra work, he couldn't get Tamera off his mind. Especially since she seemed to be the only topic of conversation with everyone he talked to!

He'd asked Shorty to keep an eye out for her. "For goodness sake, Shorty, don't let her know I asked this of you, either. She'll have a hissy-fit."

Seeing as he'd seen Craig raised, Shorty felt it his duty to chide him for his chauvinistic attitude. "And right she should, boy, that girl can take care of herself. If you'd hang around long enough and quit avoiding what you feel for her, you'd see that."

He shook his head, spit tobacco juice, missed Craig's boot by mere inches. Craig snorted. "I don't have time to *hang around*, and the only thing I feel for her is constant irritation."

That was a lie though, and he knew it. Shorty knew it too. He shook his head, spit again.

Craig mounted his horse. "Disgusting habit you have there, Shorty."

"Yeah, well, we all have a few of those."

He'd whirled away before Shorty could start listing his.

Every evening he got home long after everyone was in bed, and fought the urge to go to her. He was like a man obsessed, out of control, and it bothered him. What bothered him the most was the confusion that warred with his baser emotions. Desire was uppermost in his thoughts, but mixed with a range of feelings he'd never dreamt of feeling...tenderness, respect and white-hot jealousy. He'd never been so confused in his life and didn't understand his feelings one bit!

He heard stories of her many abilities and how talented a rider she was. He knew of the time she spent with Gramps and the affection he showed her. He heard the men talk, and knew every one of them wished he had the guts to ask her out. All of them, including Jimmy, the seventeen year old boy he'd hired for the summer and stupidly assigned to assist her.

His whole life was in turmoil because of one tiny, hot-tempered, extremely beautiful, blue-eyed brat and it infuriated him!

This morning was no different. He took a deep breath and hesitated yet again. His own hesitancy infuriated him. Careful not to take his frustration out on the door, he knocked. Getting no answer, he opened the door, and then wished to heaven he hadn't.

She sat on the floor, scantily clad in leotard and tights. Her head rested on the between widespread legs as she evidently stretched or cooled down from a workout of some kind. She rose in slow, controlled movements, closed her legs and drew them up to her chest, took a deep breath, hugged, released, then arched her back and rolled her head. Her eyes were closed and she seemed to concentrate only on the muscles she'd worked. Headphones explained why she hadn't responded to his knock. Opening her eyes, she caught a glimpse of him leaning against the doorframe. A startled gasp escaped. She jerked the headphones off and scrambled to her feet.

"Craig! I didn't hear you knock."

"Evidently," he drawled. Color rushed to her cheeks.

Tamera looked away, reached for a towel, and buried her face in the soft cloth in an attempt to regain her composure. Her heart thumped madly in her chest.

"What do you want?" she asked, darting a glance at him.

Though he seemed to rest against the doorframe, tension coiled the entire length of him. She could feel it, see it in his face. He looked flushed, angry. His eyes glowed with an inner fire. Hardness furrowed his expression and a muscle in his jaw twitched.

"You do this every day?"

The accusation in his tone puzzled her. Tamera nodded, and looked down to unbuckle the portable tape player attached to a belt around her waist.

He turned on his heel, ground out the words, "No wonder you have the body of a goddess," and stomped away.

Tamera rushed to the door. "Wait! Did you want something?"

He turned. His eyes flared. Craig visibly bit back his retort when she gasped, took a step back, and regarded him with wide, innocent eyes.

He took a deep breath, clenched and unclenched his hands then tucked them into his pockets. "I wanted to talk to you about Silver and her foals."

"I'll be down as quick as I can," she assured and closed the door. She hurried into the bathroom, locking that door behind her and ran a tubful of warm water. The desire in his gaze left her weak and trembling. She leaned against the sink, willed control to her racing pulse and wondered how long he'd watched her.

Long enough to note I have the body of a goddess, she mused. A wry smile curved her lips. Considering his expression and attitude, she couldn't help but wonder if he'd meant it as a compliment or an insult.

She hurried to finish her bath, dress and arrange her hair into a thick French braid. She bounded down the stairs and took a deep breath, steeling herself against any more sarcastic remarks. None were forthcoming. Craig was already in the barn waiting, pacing. He turned at the sound of her footsteps, nearly muffled in the soft hay. She inhaled a deep breath and smiled. "I love this barn."

The tension in his expression eased. Craig grinned. "We could turn one of the stalls into a room."

She giggled, kept pace with him as he headed toward Silver's stall. "I don't like it that much. What I do like though, is the wide open space in the center. There is plenty of room to work the horses even if it's raining."

"That was the whole point of building it this way. We're in the business to make money. Not many people want green-broke, unbroken or untrained horses these days."

She nodded. "True."

He paused at the stall's entrance. "I noticed you were letting them out at night, too."

She nodded. "It's better for them."

"Well, let's see what you've done with them."

"Do you want a quick run down or what?" she asked.

Craig shook his head. In the time it took for her to meet him, he'd decided he would not go out on the range today. He'd stay home, spend time with her, get to know her a little better and just maybe figure out his feelings. "I'm not in a big hurry today, so give me a full report."

Tamera opened the stall door and called to the colt. "C'mon boy, let's give Craig a show."

She snapped a lead rope onto his halter and spoke while they walked to the center of the barn. "As you can see, he's developing nicely. Good muscle tone, well defined. He learns quickly, too."

She led him through his paces, slowed him to a walk and called him to a halt then showed Craig his hooves and teeth, remarking on his growth and progress, and then laughed when the colt nudged her shirtfront.

"I know, little fella, it's time to eat." She handed Craig the rope then prepared a bottle. "He's already begun grazing some, but he's not too pleased with the feed or hay. You know they sometimes nurse up to six or even nine months. It may take a little longer with these two. We'll just have to wait and see."

"What about the mare? How soon can I breed her?"

Tamera's cheeks flamed. She finished feeding the colt and led him back to the stall to get the filly but dared not look Craig in the eye. "How often do you usually breed her?"

"Every chance I get," he answered, then stammered. "I mean...."

He cleared his throat. "Uh, you know what I mean. I'm a rancher. I breed my stock as often as possible."

She nodded in understanding but avoided his gaze, and examined the mare while gathering thoughts that were scrambled by unusual embarrassment. "Well, she seems to be doing okay, but my recommendation is that she get a break."

"How long a break?"

"A year," she suggested, and glanced up in time to see that his reaction was just as she imagined it'd be.

"A year!"

"Yes Craig, a year. She'll probably come in-heat within a couple of months, then not for another six months after that. I think she should be left alone until after these next two times. Having twins was hard enough, not to mention the premature births and her milk being bad. She needs a break. After that, I'd recommend you breed her every other time she comes in. She'll last longer and give you better colts if you take it easy on her. Even women don't do well having a child every year and an animal is no different. She needs love, attention, and time to heal. Take good care of her, and she'll deliver well every time."

He frowned but refrained from comment. Tamera arched an eyebrow at him. "Don't ask a question if the answer is going to tick you off."

She smiled to take the sting out of the words. His answering grin made her pulse scramble. Tamera snapped the lead rope on the filly's halter and took her out to the center of the barn for a workout. "Now, Baby, here, is a little weaker than her brother, but doing well."

She walked alongside her and put the filly through her paces but at a much slower rate. "C'mon, can't let that old boy show us up now, can we?"

She quickened her steps and got the filly up to a light trot, then let out the lead rope, talking all the while. "That's right now, come on, typical arrogant male won't show us up. Let's show Mr. Harris what we can do."

Craig laughed. "That's great, Tamera. All I need is a liberated mare. You trying to change the way I run this ranch?"

Tamera realized he'd overheard her senseless chatter to the filly and flushed. "No, just the way you raise your horses."

She shortened the filly's lead rope, slowed their pace to a walk, and urged the filly to take just a few more steps.

"Come on, girl, you've got to keep it up. Just a little farther now. It'll be all right. I promise. It'll make you stronger. Come on," she urged, walking backward until she backed into the hard, firm wall of Craig Harris.

Craig grabbed her by the waist when she crashed into him. She struggled to stay on balance but only managed to rub against him, eliciting an immediate and intimate response. His arms snaked around her waist and pulled her closer. She heard his sharp intake of breath as electricity surged through them, galvanizing in its wake.

"I could get used to this," he purred into her ear, his voice husky.

"No, you can't." She trembled in his grasp; strained against his grip.

"Why not?"

Caught off guard by the longing in his voice, Tamera relaxed a bit. "Because, I have to feed this filly and work Temper and..."

She trailed off, not knowing what else to say, unable to think straight from the scent of his aftershave, the weight of his embrace, and the feel of his hard body pressed against hers. With a reluctant sigh, she rested against his firm chest. Her legs trembled nearly as violently as the filly's. Her breath caught as he rubbed his jaw absently against her head.

"Nice, huh?" he queried, and in a smooth gesture ran his hand down the length of her arm and over hers to grasp the filly's halter.

Tamera nodded, unable to speak, not knowing what to say even if she could. She felt flushed, her limbs heavy, breathing sharp, almost painful. She turned wide, pleading, eyes to gaze up at him.

Craig saw confusion and fear warring with a deeper emotion in those beautiful gems. He knew he shouldn't hold her like this, but the feel of her in his arms, her body in such intimate contact with his, obliterated all common sense. He breathed her name, turned her in his arms, and lowered his lips to hers for a gentle, tender kiss.

She tensed. Her clenched fists bored into his chest. Craig relaxed his grasp and pressed her face against his chest in a hug. Without a word, he caressed her from shoulder to waist, and held her a moment longer. "Relax," he whispered, relieved when the tension eased out of her.

Clucking his tongue, Craig kept one arm around Tamera and led the filly back into the stall. He released them and watched, silent, aware, as she fixed a bottle and fed the animal.

"You're doing a fine job with them," he said, breaking the silence that sprang up between them.

"Thank you," she beamed, then turned when they heard a high, feminine voice from the barn entrance.

"Don't worry Shorty, I'll find him," she said, stepping through the entrance despite Shorty's protests.

Craig noted Shorty's apologetic grimace and bit back a groan as Stephanie Parker sidled up to him and placed a kiss on his cheek.

"There you are," she cooed. "I just got back from Dallas. Heard about your mare and her twins, thought I'd run out and check on them."

"Right," he growled, jerking away when she tried to wipe the lipstick off his cheek. "If you've heard about them, I'm sure you've heard about our veterinarian, too. Somehow, Stephanie, I wonder just who you've run out to check on."

"That's not fair."

Craig ignored the pouting mouth; it just didn't affect him as it once had. "Well, you've come just in time, whatever your reason. This is Tamera Collins, the veterinarian we've hired for the summer."

The wary look she gave him told Craig Tamera sensed there was more going on than what met the eye. She didn't move, simply nodded hello at the stately brunette who edged closer to him.

"She looks too young to be a veterinarian," Stephanie remarked snidely, and batted long, heavily mascaraed eyelashes at him. Craig turned her away, rolled his eyes then winked at Tamera.

"Don't worry, Stephanie, she's a lot older than she looks and extremely qualified," he assured, his tone placating as he led Stephanie out of the barn.

"Now," he said, once they were away from Tamera. "What do you really want? You didn't come all this way just to insult my new veterinarian, did you? 'Cause I know you didn't come to see the horses."

She smiled up at him in a way that would have once made Craig's insides melt and trailed her fingers down his chest.

"I've been doing some thinking while I was in Dallas. Do you think we could work things out, Craig?" she asked, and lowered her gaze in an attempt to appear demure.

Craig looked down at her fingers and snorted, not even trying to hide his annoyance. "Oh really? *You've* been doing some thinking?"

She nodded, lifting wide, innocent eyes to his. Craig wasn't fooled for a moment.

"And just who helped you do that, Stephanie?" he asked, not bothering to hide his disgust any longer; no doubt in his mind that she hadn't been in Dallas alone. It wasn't the first time she had stepped out on him, but it was well past the last, which was exactly why he'd broken off their engagement nine months ago.

Her eyes flashed fire. She reared back in an attempt to slap his face. Craig grabbed her hand before her palm connected with his cheek and fought the urge to break her arm. "I wouldn't, if I were you. I just might forget I'm a gentleman and slap you back."

She hissed an unladylike insult, followed by an equally unladylike curse.

He shoved her toward her car. "That's right, but know this, I'll not be played for a fool by you or anyone else, ever again."

Craig didn't bother to wait for her response, but turned on his heel and walked back into the barn as Stephanie gunned the engine of her car and whirled away in a gale of dust and gravel. He returned to the stall where Tamera brushed Silver in short, furious strokes. Her eyes shot lightning sparks at him.

"Who was *that*?"

He leaned against the stall with a grunt. "My *ex-fiancée.*"

"Figures."

"What?" he asked, exasperated. *Women!*

She threw the brush in a corner and stomped her foot, a low growl sounded in her throat. "I don't need you to defend me to anyone, especially the likes of her! And if you hadn't whisked her out of here, I'd have given her a piece of my mind!"

He fought not to laugh, grinned instead, and walked toward her. "I'm sure you would've."

The laugh escaped, rich and full. He grabbed her hands and pressed her clenched fists to his lips. "Sheathe your pretty claws, Tamera; she's not worth getting them dirty over."

"Don't think you can come in here and pacify me with a kiss, mister, I'm not that gullible."

"Of course you're not," he agreed with a soft chuckle, and did just that.

Chapter Five

Things began to change for Craig and Tamera. He was still gone more than home, but after the morning he checked with her on the progress of his mare and foals, he made a point to see and talk with her whenever he could. He was pleased with her work and told her so. A mutual respect formed between them hampered only by the desire that caused confusion by its depth and strength.

Things seemed to be going smoothly until he came home early one day to find her mail on the hall table next to his. There was nothing unusual about that, except for the Victoria's Secret Catalog. Without even opening the magazine, his imagination went wild, picturing her in flimsy lingerie. Desire erupted in him with volcanic force and he cursed himself for thinking and acting like a teenager.

He dropped the magazine in disgust and stomped outside to find her, only to be told she was working Temper in one of the arenas. It wasn't hard to know which one, all he had to do was look for the crowd.

He joined the throng of onlookers just as Temper reared up. Tamera jerked back on the reins, muttered something. She got him under control, jumped out of the saddle, pulled firmly on the reins and brought his head down to eye level.

"What *is* your problem?" she asked the big animal. Temper pawed the ground and snorted. She threw her arms up in disgust. *"What?"*

With a shrill, angry neigh, he fought against the hold she had on him. Breaking free, he reared. His huge hooves pawed the air in a threatening gesture.

"Stupid brat is going to get killed by her own horse," Craig mumbled and started over the fence. Shorty halted him. Temper stopped just short of hitting Tamera coming down.

"Oh, yeah?" Craig heard her exclaim as she swung at the horse. Her clenched fist connected with his big jaw in a resounding *thwack*.

"You do that again and I'll beat you within an inch of your miserable life! What's wrong with you?" she raged at the horse as if he could actually answer. "We've been through these patterns a million times!"

Craig groaned. The girl was crazy! He said as much.

Shorty laughed. "She's a woman Craig. She's had to handle that stud since he was a colt. She knows what she's doing."

For a small woman, she packed a powerful punch. Temper went down to his knees. He nickered softly. His head swayed back and forth, and he nudged her in what appeared to be an apology.

"Okay," she relented with a sigh. "I forgive you. Give me a kiss." She leaned down to him and he nuzzled her cheek in a caressing gesture. Tamera took a step backward, and allowed Temper to get to his feet. He arose and rested his head on her shoulder as she wrapped her arms around his neck and hugged him, murmuring soft, soothing words.

She remounted, galloped him to the far end of the arena and then worked him around the barrels and poles, in one of the smoothest, fastest, exhibitions Craig had ever seen.

The crowd of onlookers burst into cheers and applause as Temper slid to a halt along the fence. Tamera flushed with pleasure when Jimmy assured her their time was faster than the day before. Dismounting, she declined Jimmy's offer of help and loosened the saddle then walked Temper to cool him off. The crowd dispersed, muttering about how slim their chances of winning were if she entered the rodeo.

Craig leaned on the fence. "Pretty smooth riding there, hot shot, after you got him calmed down. Is he always so edgy?"

Tamera shook her head. "No, only when..."

She bit her tongue, blushing profusely at what she'd almost said. "Only sometimes."

Craig realized what she meant and grinned. As Shorty had said, she was a woman and she'd had to deal with that horse since he was a colt. Temper had to know that she was boss at all times.

"Well," he drawled with a chuckle. "If you handle your men the same way you handle that horse, I pity the poor guy that ends up with you."

Tamera shrugged, grinned. Her eyes laughed and mocked him.

"Probably have to. Men are all animals, anyway. Don't you worry though, I'll know how to handle my man when the time comes," she assured him, a smug, confident ring to her voice.

"I'll just bet you will."

So it continued. Craig came and went as his feelings allowed. When the desire to see Tamera and to be near her outweighed the need to be away from her, he stayed home. When he ached from restraint, he rode the range, still trying to figure out exactly what his feelings for her were. He wanted her—that much he knew; with a hunger that reached deep inside in ways he'd never experienced.

Hell couldn't be worse than unanswered desire, he decided. It's not that he couldn't control the desires of his flesh; that had never been a problem. The problem was he'd never had to work so hard at it. Need was a hunger, a greedy appetite that gnawed at his heart and mind and he wanted her more with each passing day and every breath he took; though the desire he initially felt was quickly giving way to deeper emotions.

To top it all off, every man he met seemed to be having the same problem when it came to her. The situation came to a tumultuous head on the one-month anniversary of her arrival.

Craig was out making the usual rounds when his horse, Rocky, stepped in a hole. The big stallion stumbled and fell, bringing Craig down with him. Stunned, he lay dazed for a moment. Moving cautiously, he got to his feet as Rocky struggled to stand. Nothing seemed to be broken by Craig's examination, but Rocky refused to put weight on his left forefoot.

Craig loosened the cinch of his saddle and walked the remaining three miles to the house, leading his horse, cursing his stupidity and frustrated by his preoccupation. If he'd had his mind on riding instead of on Tamera he may have avoided the accident altogether! To make matters worse, when he got home she wasn't there.

* * * * *

Tamera arrived back at the ranch shortly before dark. She'd left that morning after tending to her duties and spent the day shopping, picking up supplies, and exploring the countryside.

Bandera was beautiful; surrounded by lush green fields, rivers and lakes that sported some of the *'best fishing in Texas'*, ranches that grew some of the *'best cowboys in the country'* as well as National Parks and several dude ranches where you could rest and relax or play cowboy. The city itself, though modern and busy, retained its small-town demeanor. The atmosphere made Tamera feel right at home. The people she met were friendly, treating her as one of their own instead of an outsider, especially at Harry's Diner where she went for lunch.

"How ya doin', missy?" Harry inquired.

"Fine."

"Got ole Craig tamed yet?" he teased.

She smiled and shook her head. "I'm a veterinarian not a miracle worker."

The patrons laughed and talked with her, giving her hints and suggestions on how she should tame him.

"I think I can hold my own," she remarked. Realizing how quickly the conversation turned from teasing toward insult, she regretted her part in instigating the whole conversation. "Besides, I don't think he needs taming, a little understanding and compassion maybe, but not taming. And besides that, I don't want to tame him; I just want to work for him."

She heaved a grateful sigh when her lunch arrived. Harry patted her hand and gave her an encouraging wink.

"My bet's on you, sweetheart. You just might be what the Rockin' H needs."

Filled with discovery and adventure Tamera enjoyed every single minute of her day and with a bit of reluctance, headed back to the ranch, but promised herself another day of exploration in the near future. Shorty and Jimmy met her at the car as she drove up.

"The boss was just fixing to go looking for you," Shorty informed her.

Something in his voice sent a shiver of apprehension down her spine. Tamera instructed Jimmy as to which packages to take to the tack and feed rooms then took the others herself. She ran upstairs, put them in her room and then went to find Gramps. Relieved there was no problem there, she filled him in on her day.

She glowed with excitement as she talked about her adventures, making her more beautiful, which only further infuriated Craig when he found her in the den with Gramps.

"Where on earth have you been?" he demanded. "I've been calling all over the country!"

She tensed, arched an eyebrow at him. "Out. Why?"

"You could have left word on how to reach you, or occasionally checked in. I have a horse nearly crippled by a fall, and you're out gallivanting all over God's creation!"

Her eyes flared. She growled as her temper rose to meet his. "Well, excuse me. I didn't know I was expected to report my every move. I work here, I wasn't aware that I'm a prisoner. Now what horse and what happened?"

"Leave the girl alone, Craig," his grandfather warned as Craig took an ominous step toward her. His gray eyes flashed furiously. "She has the right to a day off. Tell her what happened so she can check on Rocky."

Anger, desire, jealousy, and frustration were more than Craig could take. "I run a ranch here, and a ranch runs twenty-four seven. There's no such thing as a day off. And as for you..."

He turned on his grandfather. "It's a shame all it takes is a pretty face to turn you into a traitor."

Tamera ground her teeth. She stepped toward him and her eyes dared him to say more as fury overrode her common sense. "Don't you dare talk to him like that!"

Craig's eyes narrowed and jaw muscle twitched as he forcefully refrained from putting his hands on her. "He's my grandfather; I'll talk to him any way I please!"

"Not around me you won't."

"Tamera, you're pushing it," he warned. "You better back off before something happens that I'll regret."

Tamera glared at him for a moment, turned on her heel. "God forbid you should ever say or do something you'd regret."

Craig grabbed her arm, twirling her around to face him. "The last thing I need right now is your smart mouth."

Her reaction was instinctive, fueled by fury, as her palm connected with his cheek. "I told you once before not to manhandle me. I won't tell you again."

Wheeling his chair closer, Gramps tried again to diffuse the situation. Craig ignored his soft command, pulled Tamera firmly against his chest and forcefully restrained from beating her.

His hands bit into the soft flesh of her arms, his eyes narrowed into dangerous slits of steel. His jaw muscle throbbed furiously. Tamera's chin lifted another notch. They glared at each other, neither willing to back down; both waiting for the other to continue or end the fight.

"Enough." Gramps insisted when she continued to hold her ground despite the tear that rolled down her cheek.

Craig ground his teeth and pushed her away, releasing her from his punishing grip. Pride warred with the pain and anger in her eyes but Tamera made no attempt to rub her arms or brush the tear away. Head held high, fists clenched, she turned and stalked up the stairs. The door slammed behind her with a resounding thud.

"Oh God," Craig groaned, trembling with the force of emotions running rampant through his blood. He leaned against the mantle and buried his face in his arm.

"You want to tell me what's bothering you?" Gramps coaxed.

Craig raked his fingers through his hair. "I wish I knew. Everything about her bothers me, in more ways than than one, ways I don't even understand."

"You falling in love with her?"

"I want her. That much I know. That's about *all* I know," he added in a frustrated under breath.

For the first time in a long time Craig saw anger so raw, so fierce he could barely contain it, harden his grandfather's features. "You mean you'd like to bed her, but with no thoughts of marriage. Right?"

"Not really," Craig mumbled. "She's brought those infantile, impossible dreams to life again."

He turned and faced his grandfather's anger. "Gramps, you and I both know that marriage and this family don't fare well together."

"Bull," Gramps snorted. "Don't give me that *'sins of the father'* crap. I raised you better than that. The sins of the father only follow the son when allowed. Besides, your grandmother and I had a beautiful marriage."

Craig shrugged. "I guess."

"You guess?" He wheeled his chair closer to Craig. "What do you mean, you guess?"

Craig squatted down in front of him, his eyes huge and pleading.

"I don't know Gramps. She's so beautiful. She's strong, smart and talented. And beautiful." The word sounded more like a curse than a compliment.

"She's young and good with animals. And beautiful. She's passionate and open and honest. She's a terrific rider and she's so outrageously... beautiful."

He growled. "She makes me feel things I've never felt. Hell, most of the time, I feel like a stupid teenager on his first date whenever I'm around her; running on hormones and nothing else. It's confusing and infuriating. I've never felt so out of control in my life and I don't like it one bit!"

Gramps chuckled. "Sounds like love to me."

Craig pondered the words his grandfather spoke a moment then rose to pace the room. "I thought I was in love with Stephanie and Pam before that. How do I know if it's real love? And how do I know if she feels the same?"

"You'll know when you stop fighting your feelings. Stop analyzing them and listen to your heart. Did you ever feel about Stephanie or Pam the way you feel about Tamera?"

"No. I knew them better than they knew themselves. I could see right through them. They *loved* me because it was advantageous. I had all the right assets," Craig muttered, remembering his naiveté and foolishness with disgust.

"She's nothing like either of them, and I think you know it."

"How do you know for sure?"

"All you have to do is look at her, talk to her, and watch her around the animals and other people. She's as genuine as they come," Gramps assured.

"She is something else," Craig admitted ruefully. "I'm sorry, Gramps. I should never have talked to you the way I did. Nothing gives me that right. I love you. Sometimes I think I take it for granted that you know it. I'm sorry."

Gramps saw past the proud, strong, arrogant man, to the boy he loved so much. "Listen to me, Craig," he said, his voice soft, urgent. "If there's one thing I've learned being in this chair so long, it's that only when hearts are tempered, minds are open and wills are softened, that man can discern the will of God for his life. You've been too busy fighting everything you feel to see what He's showing you."

"You think she's the will of God for my life?"

"It's not for me to say. I know she's here for a reason. I know this much too, she's certainly been a blessing in my life. She's brought joy and laughter into this old heart. And I believe being here has done her some good also. She's been through a lot lately. She's been joining me for prayer and Bible study, and believe me, she's hurting. Her faith is being tested, painfully so, and you're only adding to that pain. It's not like you to be so insensitive. That worries me," Gramps admitted.

"She's a very precious child, pure in spirit and in heart. Open up to her, Craig. Quit fighting yourself and give her your heart. Even if she ends up not staying past the summer or your relationship doesn't develop into more than friendship, you'll be richer for knowing her. Gaining her friendship, if not her heart, is a blessing you'd do well not to ignore. And I think you know that too," he added, his tone soft.

"I guess," Craig agreed with a sigh, hating the fact that he didn't know anymore. He could only guess.

"You know what you have to do, don't you, son?"

"Yes sir. The one thing I do know about this whole mess is that I've made an ass of myself. *Again.* I'll apologize," he promised as they heard the front door shut. Craig walked to the window and watched Tamera walk to the barn.

"I guess now's as good a time as any," he mumbled, following in her wake. Craig knew without a doubt that she was going to check on Rocky. He walked quietly, and listened to the sweetness of her soft, soothing, voice. He didn't realize she was crying until Rocky pulled away with a nicker when she touched the tender area of his ankle.

"I'm sorry, boy," she wiped her eyes on her shirt. "I'm sorry I wasn't here. You'll be all right, I promise. It's just a little sprain."

Remorse washed over Craig in angry waves. He whispered her name, his voice thick with regret.

Tamera stiffened at the sound of his voice.

"What?"

Anger and humiliation colored her tone and Craig imagined she wished he would just go away and leave her alone. "I'm sorry."

"Me too, Craig, I'm sorry I was gone when you needed me. I'm sorry I was late getting back today. I'm sorry I was late getting to the ranch in the first place. I'm sorry my presence offends you, and I'm sorry for whatever I've done to make you hate me so much."

She began to cry in earnest. "And if I had anywhere to go but home, I'd leave this blasted ranch tonight!"

"No!" He reached for her. "Please, don't cry."

She pushed him away. Her eyes bored into his. "Why not? Do my red eyes, snotty nose, and blubbering offend you too?"

For the first time, Craig realized how much he'd hurt her. And for the first time he didn't think about what he should say; only said what was in his heart. "No. You don't offend me."

"Then will you please tell me what I've done to upset you so much?"

He sighed, raked his fingers through his hair. "Nothing...everything...honestly, I don't even know."

"Well, if you don't know, who does? You're so unpredictable!" she accused.

"I mean, half the time you're almost nice; you're charming and sweet and wanting to kiss me and the other half, I feel as though you can't stand the sight of me! And I don't know what I've done to make you mad at me," she wailed.

"Nothing," he groaned, pulling her firmly in his arms. "You've done nothing. I'm sorry I hurt you. It kills me to see you cry, and I feel like a jackass for making you."

Craig stroked her hair in a soothing gesture and tried to find the words to explain to her what he was just beginning to understand and admit to himself. "It's me. I've been acting like a fool. I don't hate you. In fact, I like you. Too much, so much it scares me, and I don't understand what's happening between us. But something is definitely happening. That's what I don't like: the not knowing, and not being in control of my thoughts and feelings. I'm so sorry. Will you forgive me?"

She nodded.

"Thank you," he breathed and wrapped his arms tighter around her.

Tamera trembled in the aftermath of emotions. Draping her arms around his waist, she gave in to the overwhelming need to cry, dampening his shirt with her hot tears, tears of pain and anger, of humiliation and rejection and too many nights of loneliness.

When her trembling stopped and her sobs subsided into soft, hiccupping sounds, Craig cupped her face in his hands and brushed his thumbs over her hot cheeks and apologized again.

"Oh, man," he whispered. "Even with red eyes and a snotty nose, you're more beautiful than any woman I've ever laid eyes on."

He brushed his lips over hers then handed her his bandanna. Tamera took a deep breath and buried her flushed face in the soft cloth.

"Right and you've got land for sale in California," she muttered, finding comfort in his musky, male scent combined with the fresh smell of the outdoors and the subtle aftershave lotion he wore. It wasn't as much comfort, however, as she found in his arms when he wound them around her and pulled her against him once more.

Chapter Six

Tamera awoke the next morning a little heavy-headed from the tears she'd shed. Though not much was said between them after Craig's apology, she felt as though they'd reached some kind of understanding or solved an unknown problem between them. She rose at her usual time, hurried downstairs to bring the horses in and check on Rocky, then hastened back up for her workout and shower. She was surprised to find Craig hanging around outside her bedroom door when she finished.

Craig waited for her to finish her morning ritual, not willing to subject himself to interrupt her workout again. He was just too vulnerable to handle seeing her in such a state of undress this morning. He cringed at the thought. *Vulnerability.* Another emotion he didn't understand and hated. He turned as she walked out of her room, and greeted her with a halfhearted smile. Without stopping to analyze the reasons behind what he was doing, he spoke. "How would you like to ride the range with me today?"

Tamera hesitated, uncertainty flickered in her eyes. "Why?"

Craig shrugged. "I don't know. Get you away from all these people, away from here. Spend some time alone. Get to know each other a little more. Start over. A new beginning."

He hesitated and shrugged again, feeling like an idiot, and positive he sounded like one. "Just an idea."

Something about his demeanor reminded Tamera of a little boy solemnly trying to make up for his misbehavior. She smiled. "I'd love to. Just let me feed the foals and brush Temper. Rocky won't be able to carry you for a few days. His foot is sprained pretty badly, but nothing permanent. He just needs a few days of rest and alternating ice and heat packs to recover."

Craig nodded. "I'll ride Red. Let Jimmy feed and work the foals. Instruct him on Rocky's care. Get Temper saddled while I pack us a lunch."

"Should I bring a bed roll?"

"Do you want to stay out all night?"

Desire darkened his steel-gray eyes to a gunmetal color. A surge of electricity coursed through her. Tamera trembled. "No. I don't think so."

His curt nod assured Tamera he was very aware of why she hesitated.

"I'll meet you in the barn in ten minutes."

"Craig, is something wrong?"

He raked his fingers through his hair. "Rough night."

"I'm sorry," she whispered, resisting the urge to stroke the throbbing muscle in his jaw. She bounded down the stairs and hurried to do his bidding.

Craig followed at a more sedate pace and hoped this wasn't a mistake. So far, he'd been able to protect her by simple threat, which put a halt to the less-appropriate talk about her. Taking her away for the day, alone, was bound to start it up again. He shrugged mentally. Devil take the talk, he thought, he'd handle whatever he had to handle. They, *he*, needed this day.

He packed enough lunch for the both of them, loaded his saddlebags and went to saddle his horse. He led Red out of the barn where he met Tamera who'd brushed and saddled Temper and was fooling with his bridle. "What are you doing?"

"Changing his bit."

He noticed the curb bit in her hand. "I don't like those bits at all."

She sighed. "Neither do I, but like spurs, they serve a purpose. The good thing is I rarely have to put it to use. Just putting it in his mouth assures him I won't tolerate any misbehavior. I had to use it so much when he was growing up that I seldom have to force him to behave any more. I just don't feel like fighting him today. This assures me I won't have to."

Craig swallowed his argument. She was right. *As usual.* "You just about ready?"

She nodded, put the bridle on Temper and mounted up.

Craig handed her a canteen of water, and they headed out. He wanted her all to himself today, so he took her in the opposite direction of the rodeo guests and arenas.

As they rode, he began to relax and enjoy her company. She was an avid listener, her questions intelligent, as they talked about the ranch and he explained the boundaries of his property.

One of the largest ranches in Texas, it covered nearly fifty thousand acres of prime land. He raised cattle, horses, sheep, and goats, not to mention the pigs and chickens in the barnyard. He grew his own feed and hay as well as providing for some of the smaller ranches. Livestock, though, was his main source of revenue.

"It's beautiful," she breathed when they stopped to take a break. "No wonder you spend hours each day out here. It's so beautiful. So peaceful. Close to nature."

Her voice softened, "close to God." She pulled the bandanna from around her throat, moistened it and wiped her face.

"Whew, it's hot," she remarked, then braided her hair and tucked it up under her hat. "I usually carry a ponytail holder with me, but I forgot."

"You want to head back?" he asked. She shook her head, eyes shining.

"Not unless you do. I love it out here. Thank you for bringing me."

Looking at it through her eyes, Craig felt a new sense of wonder and awe at the graciousness of God. Pride filled his soul, and his heart whispered *Thank You.* He tugged the brim of her hat down over her eyes and smiled. "Let's go, then. I know the perfect spot for lunch. We'll stop there for a while. The horses need a break too."

They rode in a northeasterly direction, and Craig checked fences and moved cattle until they crossed Bear Creek, one of the many tributaries of the Medina River.

They dismounted and let the horses drink a little before leading them to a grassy knoll just past the water's edge where huge shade trees offered relief from the heat. Craig unsaddled Red, propped the saddle against the tree and spread his saddle blankets on the ground. He handed her the extra rope he usually carried, then looped his through the bridle, allowing enough slack so the horse could graze in the lush grass along the bank of the creek.

Tamera followed his lead and did the same with her saddle and blankets. She removed the bit from Temper's mouth and looped the reins around his neck, tying them to the bridle so he could not slip it off, then tied him up, but allowed him enough rope to graze.

Together they walked to the creek to wash their hands and face in the stream. Craig watched as she re-wet her bandanna in the cool water, then wiped her face and throat and the skin exposed from the open collar of her shirt. She shook her long hair loose from its braid and ran her fingers through it until it cascaded across her shoulders and down her back in a silken mass.

Craig went back to the blankets and watched through lowered lids as she walked over to check on Temper then slipped behind some bushes for a moment of privacy. Desire, sharp and painful, curled in him as she shyly slipped back to the edge of the creek and washed her hands again in the cool, running water. When she settled beside him, he unpacked their lunch in a desperate attempt to have his hands on something besides her.

Sandwiches made with thick slices of ham and cheese, a flask filled with iced tea, and homemade cookies lay before them like a feast.

"Mmmm, cookies. I'm impressed. You thought of everything, including desert."

The teasing innocence in her remark cooled the desire he was trying to put a chokehold on. Craig chuckled. "You like cookies?"

She nodded. "Oh yeah, especially Maria's, they remind me of Mama's. My mother baked the most delicious cookies in the world and she always made sure there were plenty in the house whenever Daddy or I came in from work or play."

His heart ached at the sadness that clouded her beautiful sapphire eyes. He watched in silence as she savored each bite of her sandwich, and sipped the tea he'd poured for her in the cap of the flask. A soft laugh escaped him when, after finishing her sandwich and two cookies, she reached for a third one. "Gee whiz, where do you put it all, and how do you stay so slim eating like that?"

Tamera blushed and flopped down on her back. "It's a shame, I know. I just can't seem to help it; that was so good."

She rubbed her stomach, turned over and regarded him with laughing eyes. "I'd probably be as big as a house if I didn't workout every day."

Her sapphire eyes sparkled with mirth, her feet swung back and forth in a gentle arch. Craig fought the urge to touch her, to taste those smiling lips. He reached for a cookie instead, hoping its sweetness would suffice. It failed so bitterly that he found himself laughing at his own folly.

"What's so funny?"

Craig shook his head, finished his cookie then reached for another with a wry grin. "Nothing."

Tamera rolled her eyes and shook her head. Instinct warned her not to ask again. They spent the next hour or so laughing and talking, sharing childhood memories and future dreams.

"And what did your father call you as a child?" he queried after one of her many stories of growing up.

"Bet you can't guess," she challenged.

He shrugged. "Probably something dumb like princess or pumpkin or honey bunch."

She shook her head. "Nope, nope, nope. Three strikes, you're out."

"So tell me," he urged, enjoying her tinkling laugh and shining eyes.

She grinned. "Will anything I say be used against me in any way, shape, or form?"

He chuckled. "Probably. But tell me anyway."

"Temper Tantrum. He used to get so tickled at me. When I didn't get my way, I'd throw a fit. He'd just laugh and say: 'Go ahead, my little Temper Tantrum, throw a big one. It won't work.' It usually didn't, and I usually realized he was right in telling me no. I mean, it was so seldom he told me no anyway. Then as I got older and a little more mature, the nickname was shortened to Temper."

"Bet he never spanked you either," Craig taunted.

Her eyes narrowed, but she smiled. "Not that I can remember."

He tossed his head with a shout of laughter. "I knew it! No wonder you're so insolent."

She smiled a sugary, innocent smile and batted her eyelashes at him. "At least I'm not arrogant and conceited."

Craig had the grace to grin. "Point taken. That's how Temper got his name?"

"Yes. When I got him and he turned out to be so temperamental, it was just natural to name him that. In fact, he's registered under *Temper Tantrum Too*. When Daddy got the license plate for my trailer, they goofed, using the number version instead of the correct word. He wanted to take it back, but I kept it anyway. It fits also."

She sat up, drew her knees to her chest, wrapped her arms around them and rested her chin. Sadness clouded her face. A tear dripped slowly down her cheek. She whisked it away, struggled to stem more.

"Sometimes I miss them so much, especially Daddy. Mama and I were close, but my father was my life. He was my hero. When I was little I used to tell him, that when I grew up I was going to marry someone just like him. I don't think there's another man like him in this world."

Craig brushed the tear off her cheek and fought the urge to take her in his arms. "I'm so sorry you had to go through that."

She sniffed and smiled. "You know, the Bible says that *'all things work together for good,'* but for the life of me I can't figure this out. Why did they have to die? What good can possibly come of it?"

Craig shrugged. "It's hard when God doesn't make sense to us. In those times, we just have to trust. After all, He is God."

"That's what Gramps says, too. His strength and faith have helped me a lot. Thank you for sharing him with me."

A smug, cocky grin tugged at the corners of his mouth. "What can I say? He *is* my grandfather."

Determined not to ruin the day with gloom, Tamera shook off her sadness and laughed. "Such arrogance, only you can turn something like that around to your credit. I didn't know you were so philosophical when it came to God."

He laughed, but refrained from comment.

"Your turn, 'fess up, what was your nickname? 'Little Craig' or 'Tee-boy?' How about 'junior'? No, that couldn't be right. You're not a junior, you're Craig the Third. I know! It's Trey."

He shook his head. "No to all of the above. My parents were not the affectionate type. I've never had a nickname. Gramps has always called me Craig. My father was called Adam, so Craig was fine with me."

"So your full name is, Craig Adam Harris the Third?"

He shook his head. "Adam Craig."

Giving up, he pulled her in his arms and leaned back against his saddle. She tensed against him.

"What are you doing?"

"I just want to hold you," he whispered. "I won't bite, I promise."

She fought the smile tugging at her lips and did her best to look serious.

"You'd better not, I'll bite you back," she threatened in a solemn voice.

But she couldn't hide the laughter in those beautiful eyes. Craig swallowed a groan.

"Oh, please," he said, his voice laced with sarcasm. "Punish me."

She nipped playfully at his shoulder, ignorant of the effect it would have on him.

"Ouch, witch." He chuckled, tossed her onto her back and towered above her. His hand roamed lazily up her body in a subtle caress.

"You asked for it," she remarked, her eyes wide and innocent then pushed against his buckle which bit painfully into her side.

The innocence in her gaze was unfamiliar and unnerving. Craig resisted the urge to kiss her and pulled her against him in their original position.

"I'll get you back," he threatened in a soft, tender tone then held her lightly when she snuggled closer.

"Temper?" he whispered.

"What?"

"I'm glad you came with me." He was, too, exceptionally glad. In a few short hours, he'd realized how accurate Gramps's opinion was. She was precious, pure in spirit and in heart. He'd never met a woman like her before, and mentally kicked himself for being such a jerk.

"I'm glad you invited me. It's a beautiful day."

He brushed the hair off her cheek with a tender smile. "Thank you for giving me another chance."

"Every one deserves another chance," she murmured.

He chuckled. "Even arrogant jerks?"

She nodded, smiled. "Especially those."

They sat quietly while large, puffy, white clouds floated across the soft summer sky. Tamera's eyelids drooped, breathing deepened and she dozed into a light sleep. Craig found it extremely gratifying to know she trusted him enough to fall asleep in his arms, especially after the way he'd treated her. Lulled by the warmth of the afternoon sun, the coolness offered by the shade trees, the kittenish sounds she emitted in her sleep, and the poignant feelings she aroused in him, he closed his eyes, and savored the memories of the morning.

Longing filled him, more than physical; the sharp ache of desire tempered by the sweet innocence of the sleeping beauty in his arms. Soul-deep longing brought on by unanswered prayer and unfulfilled dreams of a wife and children. While he held her, those dreams come alive again and Craig wondered if she might be the one to fulfill them. He wrapped his other arm around her waist, pulled her more firmly against him, and deeply inhaled her intoxicating scent.

The sun hung low in the west Texas sky when he opened his eyes again. Careful not to disturb Tamera, Craig consulted his watch. Three and a half hours had passed since they stopped for lunch. His gaze roamed lazily and located the horses which grazed contentedly along the edge of the creek. He smiled as a soft sigh escaped her and she snuggled closer to him. She stirred on the verge of waking up. Craig took a length of silky blonde hair in his hand and tickled her nose with the ends. A throaty chuckle punctuated by a soft grunt escaped him when she punched him with her elbow and mumbled for him to quit.

"Wake up, Sleeping Beauty. Or is this where Prince Charming is supposed to kiss you?"

Her eyes flew open. "I'm awake."

"I want to kiss you, anyway," he whispered. His lips covered hers in a gentle caress as he pulled her firmly against him.

Tamera's breath lodged in her throat when his lips took sweet possession of her mouth and his hand roamed over her waist to rest just below her breast. She nudged it away with her elbow and clung to his shirt as a sweet lethargy infused her limbs. Instinctively her arms crept around his neck and she buried her fingers in his thick black hair, pressing her body against his passion-hardened one.

A whimper escaped when his mouth left hers, trailed tiny kisses to her ear then nibbled gently on the lobe before continuing its sweet torture across her cheek, down her neck, and over her throat to nip at her chin and return to her lips.

"Oh, man," he muttered in a thick, hoarse voice, then released her from his heated grasp. "What do you do to me?" he moaned, kissing her closed eyes and forehead.

Tamera trembled as the heat of his hard body pressed intimately against her. Fear rose up to choke her, fire rushed to her cheeks. She stiffened in his arms and avoided his gaze. "You started it."

He nodded, accepting the guilt of her accusation. "Someday I'll finish it," he promised in a husky whisper.

"But unless you want to spend the night out here, we'd better get going. It's liable to be dark before we get home and I'd better bring you back safe and sound or Gramps will have my hide."

"Can't have that, now can we?" Tamera forced her voice to be light in a desperate attempt to squelch the desire running rampant between them, and the fear following close on its heels. Craig grabbed one of her hands as she slid her arms from around his neck and kissed the palm.

"I'd risk Gramps' wrath and the wrath of God, to spend the night in your arms."

She closed her fingers instinctively over the area branded by his lips and fought the hysteria, as desire mixed with fear jolted through her system once more.

"Please," she pleaded, and desperately tried to avoid his gaze in a frantic attempt to still the fear that made her pulse race. "Let me up."

Craig watched as emotions changed the color of her eyes from brilliant sapphire to a smoky, midnight blue. He wondered at the flush on her cheeks, the hint of unease in her eyes, and the fear he sensed in her. "What's wrong?"

She shook her head and lowered her gaze.

"Tamera? Look at me. Answer me," he insisted when she didn't budge.

"I'm just not used to being handled so easily."

Craig bit back the questions burning his tongue, pressed his lips to her forehead and released her. Rising to his feet, he pulled her up with him, amazed at how well her tiny five-foot, two-inch frame fit against his six-foot length. He ran his hands down her back, freed her from his embrace and went to collect his horse, leaving her to do the same.

Chapter Seven

They started the trek home at a leisurely pace, laughing and talking, and competing in short races until they discovered each was letting the other win. Passing one of his smaller herds of cattle, Craig picked a calf and 'cut' it from the rest. Tamera watched with pleasure and envy at the skill of the cutting horse.

"He's not half as good as Rocky," Craig assured when she commented on their performance. "He needs more work, but he's coming along nicely. I guess Rocky hurting himself could be a blessing in disguise."

She smiled. "Maybe. That's one thing I never learned. I can break horses and train them. I can race, work barrels and poles, and Temper knows a slew of tricks, but I've never been around cattle to train him for that. I'd love to be able to, though."

"I'm sure you're quite talented in all those areas, but I don't want you breaking any horses. I have seasoned men to do that."

She eyed him with disdain, shook her head and sighed. "That's a chauvinistic remark if I've ever heard one. Coming from you, it shouldn't surprise me. Speaking of breaking, who's going to break the foals when it's time? By the way, when are you going to name them?"

"I mean it, Tamera. These are not horses you've been around since their birth. Most of them have never been inside a corral. They're wild. I don't want you getting hurt."

She closed her eyes and ground her teeth, a low growl sounded in her throat. *I will not be baited into an argument,* she determined. *But one day he's going to have to trust me.*

A low growl sounded in her throat but she kept her expression polite and remarked, "Yes, boss."

Craig eyed her warily. The innocent expression belied her stubborn nature. He stopped Red alongside Temper, reached over, and covered her hand with his; sure she would react violently to his next statement.

"If I even *hear* you defy me and attempt to break a horse, I'll beat you and fire you on the spot," he threatened, a thread of steel in his otherwise soft voice.

Tamera rolled her eyes and pulled away. "I said okay."

He grinned at her angry expression tempted to kiss that pretty, pouting mouth and offered a truce. "Maybe I'll help you teach Temper to cut. But to answer your question, the colt is already named. I thought I'd let the new owner name the filly."

"What did you name him?" she asked, unable to mask her disappointment.

"Silverado, after his dam Silver and his sire Desperado."

Tamera grunted. "Oh, please! He even names his horses chauvinistic, arrogant, cowboy names."

Craig chuckled. "So what would you name the filly?"

"You mean if she were mine?"

"Yeah."

"Silver Angel."

He mimicked her gesture and rolled his eyes. "Oh, please! She names her horses fanciful, fairy-tale names."

"I could call her Silver Miracle or Silver Surprise."

He grinned, his mind made up in a split second. "Name her anything you want. She's yours."

It took a moment for his words to register. She grinned. "She's mine?"

Craig loved the way her eyes sparkled. "Yeah, I figured I'd give her to you. Kind of like a bonus. She probably won't be much use to me for a long time, if ever, being so small, and you've probably ruined her for anyone else, coddling her so much."

Tamera threw back her head, laughed, and turned Temper around in a fancy whirl. "I could kiss you, if you weren't such an arrogant jerk!"

Craig laughed as she proceeded to entertain him with her horse's skills. It amazed him that Temper was so well behaved and gentle with his young mistress as she encouraged him to side step, prance, mimic a Tennessee Walker, count, and walk on his rear legs. She ran him in a tight, perfect figure eight and ended the performance with a bow, then leaned forward in her saddle as he turned his long, slender neck and nuzzled her for a kiss.

Craig applauded then quieted as a movement in the grass and distinct rattle got his attention. Red began to balk and rear. He called a warning to Tamera while trying to keep control of his horse.

The warning came too late. Temper reared, snorting in fright. Unprepared for the sudden change, Tamera tumbled from his back, using her left arm to break the fall, which broke with an audible snap. She screamed in terror and pain as the fangs of the rattlesnake sank into her right arm just above the wrist.

She jerked hard and rolled away as the snake recoiled to strike again, only to be deterred by Temper's angry hooves. She watched in horror as it coiled around his legs when he neighed and reared then fainted, not seeing him stomp repeatedly until it lay in shreds at his feet.

"Oh, God!" Craig exclaimed, and leapt from his saddle. The moment he hit the ground Red reared again and ran off, taking the snakebite kit with him. Craig reached Tamera as she fainted. He whipped off his belt, made a tourniquet and wrapped it around her upper arm, praying all the while for the strength to do what had to be done. He used his pocketknife to cut tiny slits across the angry, red fang marks in her arm. He took a deep breath, raised it to his mouth, then sucked and spit to draw the poison from her blood, repeating the process until he felt too nauseated to continue. He loosened the belt and let her arm bleed freely.

As gently as possible in his haste, he searched her body for evidence of another bite. Satisfied to find none, he repeated the process as before, tightening the belt then drawing the poison from her with his mouth. He loosened the belt once more, and massaged her arm in a downward motion, urging it to bleed. Cold beads of sweat covered his body as he searched his mind frantically as to what to do next. He ripped his shirt off and wrapped it around her broken arm in a makeshift sling.

What now? he wondered, overwhelmed by a sudden sense of helplessness. Even if Red did make it back to the barn, it would be hours before anyone found them. His eyes searched the horizon, and spotted Temper in the distance. Craig whistled in an effort to call the horse. He might not be able to mount Temper, but maybe he could figure out a way to strap Tamera to the saddle and lead them home. Temper reared, and neighed shrilly, but wouldn't come near enough to be caught.

Not knowing what else to do, Craig picked Tamera up and started walking in the general direction of the ranch house. He walked as long and as far as he could until shock and fatigue took over his body and his steps faltered. He stumbled and fell to his knees, jolting her in the process.

She whimpered.

Craig cradled her to his chest, afraid he'd hurt her or compound her injuries. "I'm sorry," he whispered. "Oh, God, help me."

Shivers of shock shook his mind and body. Craig watched in defeat as the sun sank from the west Texas sky and darkness descended on them. There was no way he could carry her in the dark. He'd risk getting turned around and it would be harder for anyone to find them. There was nothing he could do now but wait and pray. He thought about starting a fire, but quickly discarded the idea. In the middle of more than a hundred acres of grazing land he couldn't risk it getting out of control.

Craig had no idea how long they sat there before she started to moan and writhe in his arms. One moment she mumbled that she was hot, and the next she shivered so hard her teeth chattered from chills of shock and fever. He held her close in an effort to share his body heat with her.

"And they shall tread on serpents..." he quoted over and over in the form of a prayer, wishing he knew the rest of the Scripture then sighed with relief as she quieted once more. Illuminated only by the full moon, he gazed into the sapphire gems when she opened her eyes. A soft prayer of gratitude died on his lips and a shiver of fear pierced his soul when she gazed right through him.

"Daddy?" she queried in a tiny, little girl voice.

"I'm here, sweetheart." Craig whispered, hoping to soothe her delirious mind.

She whimpered. "Mama? Where's Mama?"

"We're here, sweetheart. She's right here with me."

A tear dripped down her cheek. She shook her head. "I can't see her. Call me Temper, Daddy. It's been so long since you called me that."

Craig had no idea what else to do except try and keep her calm so he whispered, "I'm here, Temper, I love you, Sweetheart."

"I love you too, Daddy. I miss you. Is it beautiful, Daddy? Is heaven as beautiful as you always said it would be with Jesus?"

"Yes, baby, it's beautiful."

"And Mama's there too? And Tony?"

Craig's mind went blank. Who the hell was Tony? She'd never mentioned a brother, or any other family for that matter.

"Daddy? They're there, too, aren't they?"

She sounded frightened, as though heaven wouldn't be complete without them.

"Yes Temper, we're all here, darling," he assured her softly.

"Can I go, Daddy? It's so lonely without you all. I want to come meet you in heaven," she whined, her eyes huge and pleading.

Craig's heart stopped. Gut-wrenching fear gnawed at his soul and ripped him to shreds. She was begging to die. *God, no!* his mind screamed.

"No!" he rasped, hugging her close.

"Why not?" she cried.

He searched his mind frantically, for words to reassure her. "Because, sweetheart, it's not time. You have to hang on, Temper. Hang on, baby. Promise you'll hang on and I promise we'll be right here watching over you."

She didn't answer. Craig sighed in relief when her breath slowed and evened as she slipped back into a place of rest in her mind. Anguish hurled through him at the realization of how near she hovered between life and death and how close he was to losing her. Tears clogged his throat. He swallowed hard, tried to pray.

"Oh God...God, please help me," he begged, then raged at the heavens, angry at his own helplessness. "Damn it! You can't take her when I've just found her!"

"Craig." He heard the Voice deep in the night, deep in his soul, as a dark cloud covered the moon.

"What?" he whispered into the stillness. "What do You want from me? I'll do anything, God. I'll give You anything You ask. Please, just don't let her die."

"There's nothing you can offer, for it is all mine. What I want is you—all of you Craig: your heart, your soul and your mind. You've been playing at it all along, but you've never really surrendered or trusted. I will not force you. It's a decision you must make, the decision to trust me with your most precious treasures."

Kind and gentle, the Voice urged, but didn't force, his willful surrender.

"Okay," Craig whispered. "Okay."

He sensed the light. Even with his eyes closed, he could see as it penetrated the darkness. As though a single moonbeam penetrated the clouds, lightened the night, surrounded them, and filled him to the darkest recesses of his mind. A deep peace filled his soul. A cool breeze ruffled the still air. Tamera stirred in his arms.

"Craig?"

He hugged her tight but kept his eyes closed for fear of the darkness taking over again. "I've got you, sweetheart."

"Don't leave me."

"Never," he promised as she dozed once more. For a moment, she felt cooler, but it wasn't long before the fever rose again, ravishing her with chills and she trembled violently in his arms.

Craig flinched in surprise when he heard a soft, tender snort. He opened his eyes as Temper gently nuzzled Tamera's cheek.

"Temper," he whispered, his voice hoarse even to his own ears.

"You've got to help me, boy. She's hurt real bad. We've got to get her home." He kept his voice soft and reached for the bridle. The moment he touched it, Temper reared up, screaming in agitation. Craig cursed the horse ran in a tight circle around them and continued to rear and neigh, the sound an eerie echo in the still night air. Suddenly he heard the roar of an engine and frantic voices call their names.

He cradled Tamera close with one arm, waved the other. "Here! Over here! Thank you, God!"

"Craig! My God, what happened?"

He stared blankly up at Shorty and whispered, "She's hurt bad, Shorty, real bad."

"Let me have her," Shorty urged.

He jerked away. "No, I've got her."

"Okay, Craig, easy now," Shorty said, seeing the signs of shock in him. "Let's get y'all home."

He nodded as two other men joined him and helped get Craig to his feet and in the jeep while Craig cradled Tamera in his arms, refusing to let her go. They kept him talking, gleaned bits and pieces of what happened, and banished the shock from his mind while filling him in on the details of what occurred since Red had arrived, riderless, at the barn.

"We weren't too worried at first. Figured you got thrown and Tamera would bring you on Temper, come and get help, or y'all would walk. Then Temper got there. He was plumb crazy, Craig, running around like a wild horse, neighing and bucking. Jimmy finally got close enough to see the blood on his legs. We knew then that something bad had happened. We loaded up in the jeep and on horseback, and split up. Suddenly, Temper appeared out of nowhere, bucking and raisin' hell. Man, I've never heard a sound like that horse made. It was eerie, like he was really desperate— or loco. When he took off, we followed, hoping and praying he'd lead us to y'all."

Craig's eyes searched for the horse that loved his mistress so much he would go to such lengths to get help for her. He whistled and called to him, urging Temper to follow them home, and promised the horse she would be okay. They arrived at the ranch house and the hands helped Craig out of the jeep.

"Hey," Shorty exclaimed as Temper butted him out of the way.

Craig turned so the big horse could see his mistress. "She's gonna be all right, boy. I promise."

Temper nickered softly then nudged them both in a tender gesture of affection.

Shorty held the door open as Craig carried Tamera into the house and laid her on the couch.

Gramps spoke from his wheelchair by the window. "Doc Hensley is on his way."

Craig sighed with relief. "Thanks, Gramps."

"Come here, Craig. Are you all right?"

Craig knelt in front of him with a nod, and welcomed his grandfather's embrace. As they waited for the doctor to arrive, Craig told him what happened, of the light in the darkness, the Voice in the night.

"It was so real," he concluded.

"What makes you think it wasn't?" his grandfather asked. "The Bible says, *'And I will pour out my Spirit in the last days. Your daughters will prophesy, your old men will dream dreams and your young men will see visions.'* Don't dissect what happened with your mind. Believe it with your heart."

Craig nodded and sighed. "I've depended on your faith for so long. I guess it's time to stand on my own."

He grinned ruefully. "I just have a hard time picturing myself on my knees, groveling before an unseen entity. I mean I believe He's real. I see evidence of His existence and blessings, and there's no doubt what I experienced, but..."

He shrugged. "I know all the rules, and I try to follow them, mostly, but it doesn't seem to be enough. What's next?"

Gramps chuckled. "You think *'humbling yourself under the mighty hand of God'* means on your knees and groveling?"

He shook his head and smiled. "That's not it at all, Craig. Believe me, it's very simply an act of your will to ask for and accept His will in your life, to seek His face, His wisdom and His direction. It doesn't have to be complicated, Craig. Religion and Doctrine have made it so, but that's not how it's supposed to be. It is a very simple, heartfelt decision, and the desire and determination to get to know Him on a more personal, more intimate level through prayer and Bible reading. Trust what you've experienced, use it as a beginning.

"The Bible says, *'Ask and it will be given you; seek, and you will find; knock, and it will be opened to you.'* It's really that simple, Craig. You just have to believe in God, in His willingness to speak to you, and in your ability to hear from Him." Their conversation was interrupted by the clatter of hoof-beats near the porch.

"Craig," Shorty called from the door. "It's Temper. He's gone crazy again."

"Go see him," Gramps urged. "You've been holding Tamera. Maybe you can calm him down and get him in a pasture. Otherwise we'll have to bring him in. He'll tear down the door to get to her, to protect her."

"I don't want to leave her," Craig whispered.

"Go, Craig. I'll stay right beside her. The doctor will be here soon."

Craig went out. "Come here, boy," he urged the big horse. "She's okay. I promise. Come on, now."

He approached Temper with open arms, allowing the horse to smell Tamera's scent on him. Temper neighed and shook his head but allowed Craig to lead him into his pasture. Craig filled his water trough and removed his bridle and saddle. He handed the tack over to Jimmy to be cleaned, then went back inside to wait for the doctor with Gramps.

Chapter Eight

Dr. Scott Hensley strode into the den only to be met at the door.

"What took you so darn long?" Craig demanded.

"I got here as quick as I could. I was making rounds when I got the call. Since no one said there was an emergency, I finished up before heading out." Growing up on a neighboring ranch, he was used to Craig's arrogance.

"Now, what happened?" he asked, expecting to find Gramps on the couch. What he didn't expect was to find a young woman of heart-breaking beauty there.

"Gee, Craig, how did the most beautiful woman in Texas end up on your couch?" he asked, taking in the petite form, finely chiseled features, and thick mass of blonde hair he'd bet his last dollar was as natural as the day she was born.

"She's the most beautiful woman in Texas because she's from Mississippi. She's here because we hired her for the summer, and she's on the couch because she was thrown from her horse, broke her arm, and bitten by a rattler. Any other stupid questions?"

Scott grinned at Craig's tone, the only man in Bandera County allowed the privilege, and only because they had grown up the best of friends.

"No, that about covers them. I heard she was pretty, but, well, let's just say that was an understatement." He chuckled at Craig's heated glare and watched in concern as she began to mumble and writhe on the couch.

Craig knelt beside her, brushed the hair off her face and whispered, "Temper?"

When she opened her eyes, they weren't wide with fear or pain, but alive with anger: *cold, formidable anger.* Craig felt it like a shaft of ice in his heart.

"I hate you," she growled, striking out.

Craig tried to duck, but not before her hand caught him soundly on the jaw. She whimpered and pulled it protectively against her while she continued to glower at him.

"I thought you loved me. How could you love me and hurt me that way? You have no idea what love is!"

Before he could utter a word in his defense, she slipped out of consciousness. He looked at Scott, dumbfounded. Tamera began to weep; soft sobs shook her frame. Craig gathered her in his arms.

"He hurt me, Daddy," she whimpered. "He hurt me so bad."

"Who hurt you?" Craig asked.

"Tony. He hurt me so bad, Daddy," she whined then glared. "You said he was in heaven with you. How could God let him in heaven after what he did?"

"It's okay, sweetheart, no one will ever hurt you again," he promised, and rocked her gently as she quieted once more.

"She's been like this off and on since the accident," he told Scott, his voice husky with emotion.

Tears of shock, fatigue, and concern moistened Craig's eyes, making them glisten like dew drops on sheet metal.

"Tell me everything." Scott knelt beside them, checked her pulse and pupils and listened attentively, while Craig filled him in on the facts of what happened and what he had done.

"You did well," he assured, and gazed at Craig with the respect that was mutual between them.

As boys, they'd played together and gone to school together. Fate declared them neighbors; scandal insisted they were brothers. The fact they looked enough alike to be twins only added fuel to the rumors flying about their parentage.

They favored each other in their identical build: six-foot height, broad shoulders, slim hips and long, muscular legs. Similar facial features added to the suspicions that they were related. The most significant difference in their looks was the eyes. Where Craig was blessed with the gray eyes of his father and grandfather, Scott's were a deep, doe-eyed brown. Both possessed an air of confidence that came across as purely sensual. But in looks only were they alike.

God had ended the similarities there. In attitude they were completely different.

Craig was proud and arrogant. His degree in Agriculture, as well as courses in Business Administration and Marketing & Finance had been obtained despite the long working hours and the mental strain of managing the ranch. Education enabled him to bring the ranch from near ruin (as his father had left it) to one of the most profitable in Texas. He couldn't stand incompetence and demanded perfection in nearly everything, especially when it came to his ranch. He wielded his knowledge as power, and demanded the respect that he felt he'd earned and deserved.

On the other hand, Scott was a shy, humble man, with a burning desire to help others. He used his medical degree for just that and often offered his services to the poor at no charge. He was the only doctor who still made house calls, or, in many instances, ranch calls, and he spent many summers with missionaries. The only time Scott expressed the depth of passion that was evident in Craig's demeanor was when a patient was at risk. Then, outside of Craig's, his wrath met no match.

Despite, or perhaps due to the scandalous rumor that they shared the same father, the boys had vowed to remain friends no matter what. So it was to his friend Craig entrusted Tamera's life.

"Has she been unconscious the whole time? Did she hit her head?" Scott took mental notes as Craig answered his questions and examined her for other broken bones or a head injury.

"Okay, there's not much we can do about the bite, it's been too long. We need to keep the arm elevated and ice on it for a while. I don't see any signs of a head injury or internal bleeding. We ought to get her to the hospital, though there's not much they can do for her now, except watch her around the clock."

"I can watch her," Craig insisted.

Scott knew that stubborn look and the futility of arguing with it. "Okay. The first thing we need to do is set that arm, then wake her up and get that fever down. She may have a slight concussion. I can't give her anything for pain because of the venom. You're going to have to hold her," he told Craig.

"I'll get what I need." He hurried outside, then back, and laid out his supplies. "Ready?"

Craig lifted her slight form, cradled her in his lap and nodded.

"Okay, here we go," Scott, muttered. The moment he removed Craig's shirt from around her shoulder, she whimpered.

"Take it easy, Scott, you're hurting her!"

Scott glared into the accusing gray gaze. "Do you want her to be able to use this arm?"

He continued at Craig's nod. "Then hold her, or get out!"

"Craig, why don't you go take a shower, son," Gramps interrupted, hoping to defuse the situation. He knew all too well that if these two wills clashed, the outcome would no doubt be a bloody one and time was of the essence.

"Shorty will hold her," he reassured, when Craig started to refuse.

"Go on, son, you're too upset to help," he urged when his grandson lifted a worried gray gaze that mirrored his own.

Craig relented with a frown and allowed Shorty to take his place. He and Scott rose together, toe-to-toe, and eye-to-eye.

"Forget the malpractice suit if something happens to her," he warned, glaring at Scott. "I'll just kick your sorry carcass clear across Texas."

"I wouldn't expect less of you," Scott said through teeth clenched as tightly as the fists by his sides, his anger tempered by the hint of desperation in Craig's voice.

"You've got to help her, Scott," he pleaded, suddenly overwhelmed. "Please."

"I'll do my best," he promised, surprised at the depth of emotions in his friend's eyes. Kneeling beside her once more, Scott knew he made a promise he'd need help to keep.

Divine help.

"God help me," he whispered. Simple words, but powerful. He'd learned long ago how powerful. Saying a soft prayer for guidance, he set her arm. Finishing that task, he brushed the silky hair back from her face, spoke her name, and gave her a gentle shake.

"Wake up, sweetheart," he urged. When she failed to do so, he retrieved a vial of potent-smelling liquid designed to bring about a response.

"This should do it. It may make her sick, so be prepared," he warned Shorty, pulling a small trashcan next to the couch. He waved the vial under her nose. Tamera groaned and her head to get away from the awful smell.

"Stop."

"Come on, sweetheart, wake up," Scott urged. "Open your eyes. Talk to me."

"Please, Craig." She moaned and, as the smell got to her, turned onto her side, and retched into the trashcan. "Please stop."

"That's it, sweetheart, get it all out of your system," Scott soothed. "What's your name?"

"Tamera, you idiot. What's my name...?" she muttered in a soft, scathing tone.

"How do you feel, Tamera?"

"Sore and sick." She vomited again then glared at him with the most beautiful sapphire eyes he'd ever seen. "You're not Craig."

Scott chuckled. "How do you know?"

"Because Craig doesn't have a mustache," she mumbled groggily, and closed her eyes again. "Or brown eyes."

Satisfied with her response, Scott let her doze off again. He picked her up, carried her up to her room, and helped Maria bathe and dress her in a pair of silky pajamas. He propped pillows under both of her arms and made her as comfortable as he could, then left Maria to sit with her. He'd barely made it down the stairs when Craig stormed out of the den.

"How is she?"

"I'm sure she'll be okay. Keep both arms elevated and ice on that bite for a couple of hours. Switch to cool compresses. Tap water will be fine. Watch to make sure that the fever and the swelling go down. Wake her up every couple of hours; just make her tell you her name or something simple. I'm sure she's okay, but if she does have a concussion, we don't want her to sleep for too long of a stretch or she could slip into a coma. Try to get some liquids in her, water or juice. Other than that, we've done all we can. I'll come out in the morning and check on her. Oh, and watch that right hook," he warned with a laugh.

Craig rubbed his jaw and grinned, showing a glimpse of his old self. "I'll be more prepared next time. Thanks, Scott, I owe you one."

Scott grinned. "You'll get my bill. How about a drink?"

"Gramps will get you one," Craig said and bounded up the stairs.

Scott walked into the den chuckling. "He's got it bad, huh?"

Gramps laughed. "I'm afraid so. It took an act of Congress to keep him down here while you put her to bed."

"I'm a doctor!"

Gramps smiled and handed Scott a drink. "Yes, but you're also a man."

* * * * *

Tamera swam up from darkness to the light of consciousness. Her first feelings weren't of pain or discomfort, but agitation. After hours of torture where she was allowed to doze briefly then awakened within what seemed like minutes, and forced to drink until she thought she'd drown, she was given a reprieve. Now that she had finally gotten a chance to rest, she was uncomfortable. A heavy weight around her waist pinned her down, and some awful noise sounded in her ear. She turned her head toward the sound, and opened her eyes ready to do battle for a little bit of peace and quiet.

A smile curved her lips when she noticed Craig asleep beside her. The weight around her waist was his arm tucked between the pillows propping up her arm and curved around her in a protective manner. The awful noise was actually the sound of his gentle snoring. She gazed at his handsome face a moment, noticing how boyish he looked in his sleep. Gone was the arrogant rancher. Her heart swelled with tenderness. Despite her effort not to disturb him, she couldn't suppress the soft moan of pain that escaped when she tried to get a little more comfortable. His eyes flew open.

"Talk to me," he urged.

She smiled and arched an eyebrow at him. "What are you doing in my bed?"

A teasing light replaced the worry in his gaze. He grinned. "Your bed? I own this ranch, remember? And everything on it, including this bed."

She rolled her eyes and fought the tug of a smile. "Arrogant jerk."

"Thank God you're back," he said with a chuckle, then brushed his lips over her forehead. "Fever's down too. Do you remember much?"

She frowned for a moment. Her eyes widened in fear and she struggled to get up. "Temper!"

Craig tightened his grip on her. "Easy, Temper's fine."

"Tell me everything."

Craig told her what had happened and how Temper had brought help, then tried to get into the house after he had carried her in; omitting only the details of her delirious outbursts. "In fact, unless you need something, I'll go see if he'll let me feed and brush him."

"Take me with you."

Those wide, pleading eyes would be his undoing. "Oh no, you're staying right where you are until Scott checks you over later this morning."

"Who's Scott?"

"Scott Hensley, the doctor."

"He was here last night?"

Craig nodded. "He set your arm. Don't you remember?"

She shook her head. "Not really."

"You will," he promised, and brushed his lips across hers in a tender caress. "Can I get you anything?"

Her eyes rolled sleepily. She shook her head.

"Rest, sweetheart. I'll be right back," he whispered.

"Craig?"

"More questions?" he teased. "I thought I told you to rest."

She frowned at him and asked anyway. "How did I get up here? Like this?"

"Scott carried you up and helped Maria put you to bed."

"You let a man help her?" she asked in a mortified whisper, a hot blush staining her cheeks.

"He's a doctor, Temper," he soothed, forgetting the fact that he hadn't liked the idea last night either. "Any more questions?"

She shook her head.

"Okay, I'll be right back," he promised, as she dozed off once more.

When Tamera woke up again, Craig was asleep in a chair beside the bed; his long legs stretched out and propped up next to her. His eyes opened the moment she moved.

"How do you feel?"

"Like I'm drowning in the *Great Sea of Pillows* and starving to death," she remarked, moving in an effort to get up.

"Where do you think you're going?"

She glared at him. "I need to get up."

"Hang on; I'll get Maria to help you."

"Oh, please, I think I can go to the bathroom by myself." She pushed the pillows away, swung her legs over the side of the bed and stood, then swayed weakly. Craig caught her as she slumped toward the floor and laid her gently back down.

"Now do you believe me?"

She nodded, disarmed by her weakness.

Maria came in carrying a huge tray of breakfast. Craig left them alone until she called him back into the room.

When he came back, he wasn't alone. Tamera's eyes widened in surprise when the two men walked in together.

"How come no one ever told me you had a brother?"

They laughed in unison.

"I don't. This is Scott Hensley."

Her eyes narrowed, a flush heated her cheeks. "*He's* the doctor you told me about?"

Craig's eyes danced merrily as he leaned down and kissed her on the forehead. "It's okay, I'd trust Scott with my life. He's the best doctor around."

Scott's charming bedside manner rushed to the surface. "Don't worry, sweetheart, I see beautiful women every day in my profession, though none quite as lovely as you."

If he hoped to appease her, he failed. Tamera glared at him, and then turned her gaze on Maria, her eyes wide and pleading. "Please don't leave me alone in the room with two arrogant jerks."

"I'm really not as bad as Craig," Scott assured Tamera after Maria succeeded in getting Craig out of the room so they could have some privacy.

"He just brings out the worst in me," he confessed with a grin, then wisely put a thermometer in her mouth before she could say anything.

Those flashing sapphire eyes, however, spoke volumes.

Chapter Nine

"How's our patient today?" Scott asked cheerfully, as he entered Tamera's room. Three days had passed since the accident, and her progress was remarkable. The first day was the worst. Her temperature had fluctuated as her body fought against the feverish effects of toxins injected into her bloodstream by the rattler's bite. Yesterday, she was much better with a low-grade temperature that broke during the night. So far, it hadn't returned, and the swelling in both arms had subsided quite a bit. This afternoon, however, she seemed agitated.

"Depends," she remarked without a single glance up from her magazine.

Scott sent Craig a questioning look to which he merely shrugged. "On what?"

Tamer glared at Craig then up at him. "On how soon I can get out of this bed and you can get him out of here. He's growing roots in my chair and getting on my nerves."

Craig grunted. "Nice to know I'm appreciated."

Scott chuckled. "Out, buddy, so I can examine my patient."

Craig rose and strode toward the door. "I'll send Maria in."

"Don't bother, Craig. Maria has more important things to do than run up here at your every beck and call," Tamera grumbled.

Her eyes shot sparks at him.

"What is your problem?" Craig drawled. Ungrateful brat, he thought. For three days, he'd neglected everything in his concern over her, so much so that everyone, especially Gramps and Shorty, went around with smug, knowing grins on their faces. He'd held her when she cried, stopped her from hurting herself when she fought, and left her side long enough to get his men started, tend to her horse, or take a shower. He ate in her room, and slept in snatches when she rested. The muscle in his jaw began to twitch as he fought not to lose his cool.

Tamera bit back her reply with an audible hiss and took a deep breath. Her expression was carefully blank despite the turbulence in those expressive sapphire eyes. "Nothing, I'm just tired of being in this bed. You said you trusted Scott, and I trust him too. I don't think Maria has to be bothered again."

Something told the men it went much deeper, but neither wanted her upset. Craig shrugged and left the room.

"You want to tell me what's wrong, sweetheart?" Scott asked when he attempted to take her pulse and she stiffened at his touch. Tamera closed her eyes and fought back tears of frustration and fatigue. She did not want to appear ungrateful.

"He's driving me crazy, Scott," she whispered with a weary sigh, confiding in him. In the past three days, she'd grown to like and trust Scott Hensley. In him, she saw the tenderness she'd glimpsed only a few times in Craig. It still amazed her how much they looked alike, but she'd come to appreciate the differences in their personalities.

Scott was the humility to Craig's pride, the buffer to his ego. Though he had the same tendency toward arrogance, he didn't wield it the way Craig did. In Scott, she saw the man that Craig was underneath all of his worldly pride. Scott was the physical manifestation of the gentleman Craig hid beneath his rough and tough exterior. As she recognized that fact, Tamera realized she was coming to care a great deal for that gentleman.

"That first day when I was so weak, someone, usually Craig, was here, wiping my forehead with a cool rag. Yesterday I was much better, resting more, and still, he was here, insisting that Maria help anytime, every time, I needed to get up. Today I'm even better, and he's worse. He's oblivious to the fact that I'm feeling much better."

She let out a disgusted snort. "I can't even go to the bathroom without him calling Maria in to help me. I don't want to sound ungrateful, but enough is enough. The longer I lie here, the weaker I'll get."

Scott suppressed a grin, tried to soothe. "That sounds just like Craig, always in control. I'm sure he's just worried. You were one sick puppy, there. From what I can gather, he hasn't left your side unless it was absolutely necessary. Even Maria has remarked on how attentive and tender he's been toward you."

"Probably afraid I'll croak; then he'll have another problem on his hands," Tamera muttered then sighed, feeling at once childish and petulant. "I'm sorry, that was rude, ungrateful, and uncalled for."

Scott chuckled. "And probably true."

He laughed at her guilty flush and self-conscious giggle which confirmed she really felt that way despite her apology.

"Let's not be ugly," Tamera chided, glad he understood her frustration. "But the fever's been gone since last night and the swelling has gone down. That means I'm healing, doesn't it?"

He nodded. "It means you're getting better, but healing will take time. Have you told him how you feel?"

She shook her head. "I tried but he's adamant. It's like butting my head up against a brick wall."

Scott chuckled. "How about we get your temperature and pulse and measure the swelling around that bite, then I'll let you walk to the chair by the window."

Tamera heard the emphasis he put on the word let and rolled her eyes at him. "Bless you, you arrogant jerk," she muttered before he shoved the thermometer in her mouth with a roguish grin.

Scott finished his examination then helped her into the chair and handed her a blanket. "Okay, there you go. Now, don't try and do too much. You're a smart woman, Tamera; don't push yourself too soon. You could still get real sick if there's even a trace of poison in your system."

She smiled up at him, her eyes shining with gratitude. "Thank you. It feels so good to be out of that bed."

Scott left her and sought Craig downstairs. "We need to talk."

He led the way into the den then turned on Craig in an angry whirl. "Don't you think you're being a little overprotective?"

"What do you mean?" Craig asked, clearly puzzled.

"Look Buddy, I know you went through a lot out there, alone that night, but you're not coming across as protective as much as arrogant and bossy." Craig eyes narrowed into shimmering slits of steel.

"You don't know what I went through. I held her in my arms while she begged to die. She looked right through me, talked to her dead father, and begged to go meet him in heaven. You saw how delirious she was. You don't know her. She's stubborn and willful. She'll expect too much out of herself and then I'll lose her. No, I don't think I'm being overprotective!"

Scott knew there was no winning when Craig was of such a mind-set, so he tried another tactic. "Okay, Craig, maybe so; she might be stubborn and willful, but she's not stupid. You said yourself that she's a brilliant veterinarian. Do you think she would push herself any more than an injured animal?"

"I guess not," Craig said with a sigh. "But I'm scared, Scott," he admitted, his tone rueful. "I've never been as scared in my whole life as I was that night. What am I supposed to do?" he questioned, clearly at a loss as how to behave.

Scott shrugged and considered his words carefully. "Some say delirious people are out of their minds when they talk. That's not quite true. They talk from the deepest part of their heart and soul. Old memories surface. Old wounds open. She's been hurt; my guess is, badly. That much is evident by her outbursts. Just be gentle. Be patient."

He shrugged again. "Just be yourself. And trust her to know her limitations."

Craig rolled his eyes and grunted. "Easy for you to say. I don't even know myself anymore. She's got me twisted up in knots. One minute I could kiss her, the next, strangle her. The hot-tempered little twit probably doesn't think she has any limitations."

Scott laughed. "Sounds like love to me."

"Thank you, Dr. Hensley," Craig muttered, his voice thick with sarcasm.

"Oh, come on, Craig. Why do you think women gather around you like pretty moths to a flame?"

He snorted. "Because of my money."

"No," Scott argued with a smile. "Because of your charm. I've heard it said you're a very tender and generous man when you want to be."

His eyebrow arched meaningfully. When Craig refrained from comment, he continued. "C'mon Buddy, we both know you're a fake."

He chuckled when Craig leveled a glare at him. "I know you, remember? The real you. And when you're on an intimate level with a person, especially a woman, they get a glimpse of the real you: the gentleman beneath the rancher. Beneath all this liberation humbug, most women still want to be treated like ladies. They want to know they're loved and cherished. They want equality in the office and sensitivity outside of it."

Craig shook his head with a shrug. "I still don't know about Tamera. How am I supposed to know how to treat her, or even act around her, when I've never met a woman like her in my life? She's smart, talented, and beautiful, but she comes across as innocent. Almost virginal."

"What makes you think she's not?" Scott challenged, and was rewarded with one of Craig's rare, blank, caught-off-guard stares.

Craig grunted. "Yeah, right, no one who looks like her, with a body like that reaches her age still a virgin. Those eyes alone would tempt a saint."

Scott grinned. "Which you're not."

Craig's answering grin was self-mocking but he refrained from comment. Scott laughed.

"Just because she's beautiful gives you no reason to lump her in the same category as other women. Regardless of what you think, virtue isn't as scarce as you believe," he cautioned, to which Craig merely snorted.

Scott hesitated and eyed his friend thoughtfully. "It's more than just Tamera, isn't it?"

Craig hesitated a moment then confided everything that had transpired the night of Tamera's accident.

"Sometimes I'm so sure, Scott, about her, about myself, and about God. And yet, at other times, I feel as though it was all a hallucination and I'm losing my mind. You, yourself, know I would never tolerate out of a man what I've put up with from her."

Scott sent up a silent, "Thank You." He'd prayed for his friend for a long time. He also knew Craig was dealing with feelings he'd never dealt with before. If he weren't careful, though, he'd push Tamera away. He smiled secretly as an idea came to him.

"Okay, buddy, I get the picture. But you're coming on too strong. If you don't take it easy, you're going to push her right into someone else's arms. Maybe even mine," Scott warned, ignoring the fact that he didn't date patients. Craig knew that too, so Scott tossed in the bait.

"Tell you what, since you met her first, I'll give you until the cast comes off. If you don't pull it together, you may just have a little competition on your hands," he challenged.

Craig accepted the challenge with an answering grin. "I thought you didn't date patients."

Scott shrugged. "After that cast comes off, she won't be a patient."

"You don't stand a chance," Craig said with the confidence born of love.

"We'll see," Scott remarked, knowing he would never make a move on her. Craig was his best friend. They'd vowed long ago that nothing, not even a woman, would come between them. But, Scott knew Craig better than most people did. He knew the boy beneath the man, and he knew that once Craig let go of all of his pent-up frustration at the world and anger over past experiences with women—once he let that charming little boy show—Tamera didn't stand a chance. Especially since, unless he missed his guess, she was already half in love with Craig. He grabbed his bag and headed toward the door. "I left her sitting in the chair by the window."

"I do love her," Craig confessed. The admission obviously surprised him more than it did his best friend. "No doubt too much for my own peace of mind."

"Figures," Scott muttered with a defeated sigh, and a shake of his head. "Well, then, my advice is to back off. Take it," he insisted. "Advice is free you know."

"Thanks, Scott," Craig said, and then bounded up the stairs as Scott let himself out. He stopped for a moment outside Tamera's door to collect his thoughts.

"Lord," he prayed silently. "You said to trust You with everything. Whatever it is, please help me," his heart begged. "I need Your wisdom now. Help me to be the man You want—and she needs—me to be."

A sense of peace filled him. Craig took a deep breath and marveled at how easy learning to trust the Lord sometimes was. He stood a moment longer, trying to be conscious of God's presence and to hear His voice. Though he hadn't had much time to read the Bible since the accident, he had prayed, a lot. Scriptures from his youth filled his mind... Love is patient and kind. Love never fails. In all things, with prayer and supplication, let your requests be known to God.

"Thank You," he whispered, then opened Tamera's door.

She sat in the chair, her face raised in welcome of the warm rays of sun penetrating the glass pane. Though she didn't move, he sensed the quick tensing of her tiny frame; saw the slight clench of her fists and the subtle, defiant lift to her chin. He grinned, shook his head, and walked toward her.

"Hey, Sweetheart, how do you feel?" he asked, then knelt beside her.

"Fine."

"Was Scott pleased with your progress?"

She nodded.

"What did he say?"

"That I could go jogging tomorrow," she mumbled, her agitation evident.

He chuckled. "Really?"

"No."

She glared at him, her blue eyes flashing. A flush of anger stained her cheeks. "But he did say I could go to the bathroom by myself."

Craig smothered a grin. "He did?"

"You're driving me crazy, Craig," she whispered. Tears filled her eyes. "I'm not an invalid, and I'm not an irresponsible child."

He cupped her hot cheeks in his hands and confessed, "Scott chewed me out for the same thing. I'm sorry for being such a tyrant. I'm just worried. You don't remember much about that night, or the next day, but you were real sick. One minute you fought my embrace because you were hot, and the next you shivered so bad your teeth chattered. And on top of that," he whispered, his voice filled with emotion, "you opened those beautiful eyes, looked right through me and begged your father to go meet him in heaven."

Her eyes widened in surprise. "I would never consciously ask to die, Craig," she chided in a gentle tone.

"I know. But I don't think you realize how close you came."

"What else did I say?"

He shrugged. "You asked about your mother and Tony. Who is Tony?"

He noticed the quick flash of pain and fear in her eyes, the panicked expression, and the flush of discomfort.

"What did I say?"

"Only that he hurt you really bad. Who was he, Tamera? How did he hurt you? What happened that would make you wonder if he was in heaven, then resent it if he was? Are you just angry because he died and left you too, or is it more than that?"

Tears filled her eyes. She bit her lip, shook her head.

"Okay," he whispered. A nagging sensation suggested he might not want to know, anyway. "You don't have to answer. But the day will come when there'll be no secrets between us," he vowed. "Deal?"

His tenderness beckoned. Tamera quit fighting her response and brushed a stray lock of hair off his forehead with a smile. "Deal."

Craig grabbed her hand, kissed the palm. "Okay. Are you ready to get back in bed?" he asked, then raised his hands in defeat when she glared at him. "Just asking."

"No."

He smiled. "Okay, you sit right here. I'll be back in a minute."

Tamera relaxed once more when he left the room. She closed her eyes, rested her head against the back of the chair, and enjoyed the serenity of being alone. Within minutes, she heard a soft whistle and her name being called. She leaned forward, and looked out of the window.

A huge smile curved her lips and her spirits lifted when she saw Craig beneath her window holding on to Temper's halter. She opened the window and called to the big stallion.

Temper fought Craig's hold with a tug and shake of his head. He reared up and greeted his mistress with a welcoming neigh. Craig let him go and watched as the horse neighed and pranced around for her in a tight circle.

Know just how you feel, boy, he thought. She makes me feel like prancing and showing off too.

Craig chuckled as she called to Temper, blew him kisses and waved while the horse responded with soft, blowing snorts. When they both settled down, he led the horse back to the barn. He fed and groomed him, amazed at how close he and the animal had become since that night. He may never be able to ride the horse, but Temper was beginning to trust him.

His mistress would, too, Craig vowed.

Chapter Ten

Tamera awoke the next morning, surprised and a little disappointed to find Craig was not sitting in the chair by the bed then chided herself for being so fickle. Dozing, she was awakened by a loud noise outside her door. She turned over and watched as Craig opened the door and Gramps wheeled in, followed by Scott.

"'Morning, sweetheart," Craig drawled, walking to her side as Scott opened the drapes and Gramps wheeled himself to the other side of the bed. "How are you feeling?"

"Better. What was all the commotion?"

"Gramps' wheelchair. We carried him up. Hungry?"

She nodded.

"Maria will bring breakfast up in a minute. I have some errands to run so Gramps decided to visit with you for a while after Scott checks you over. Unless you'd rather be alone?"

She eyed him warily, unsure how to take the change in him then glanced over at Gramps and smiled. "Of course I'd love to visit with you."

Gramps chuckled. "I brought up the chess set. Craig will set it up in a minute and we'll play after Scott examines you."

"Sounds great. Have you brought Temper in yet?" she asked Craig, then frowned when he nodded. "I was hoping I could go with you to see about him."

Scott sat on the bed beside her and checked her blood pressure. "I'm afraid that's not possible yet. I know you're feeling better, but you're going to have to take it easy a few more days. Number one, that cast is getting loose and will continue to do so until the swelling in your arm is completely gone. We're going to have to replace it real soon, so we can't take any chances there. Number two; you need to regain your strength slowly. Your system has been through a horrible shock, and we don't want to push it. And, number three; you have to keep that bite very, very clean. So that means staying out of the barn for a few more days.”

“But...” Scott cut off her protests by putting the thermometer in her mouth.

Craig laughed. “I may have to keep one of those handy,” he teased. “It’s very effective in shutting her up.”

Tamera reached up and deliberately withdrew the offending object from her mouth. “You two have been conspiring against me,” she accused, her eyes slashing them both like daggers.

“Wouldn’t dream of it,” Craig assured, and kissed her on the forehead. “I’ve got to go. Can I bring you anything?”

“Something to read.”

“Like what?”

“Anything,” she breathed.

“You got it, darling,” he assured with a grin. “And, if you’re real good, I might let you join us downstairs for supper tonight,” he teased.

“How gallant,” she muttered, her tone dry.

“Oh, here, Gramps,” he remarked, and handed him a small riding crop he pulled from his pocket. “If she gives you too much trouble, use this on her.”

“Get out of here, Craig Harris, before I throw something at you,” she warned as he reached the door.

“Yes Ma’am,” he obliged with a grin. He tipped his hat then gave her a wink. His gaze, warm and tender, swept over her in a way that left her breathless and blushing to the very roots of her blonde hair.

She looked up at Scott with heartfelt gratitude after Craig left. “I don’t know what you said to him or how long it’s going to work, but thank you.”

Scott shrugged, “I just assured him you’ll live,” he answered, glad to see Craig had taken his advice.

* * * * *

Later that afternoon Craig headed back to the ranch. He ran errands, shopped, and had lunch, then took a ride to a neighboring town. He deliberately stayed away in order to give Tamera some space and hoped she missed him as much as he missed her. He arrived with an armload of packages and a dozen roses. Maria met him at the door.

"Shh," she cautioned as he stumbled through it, whistling.

"Where is everybody?"

"Your grandfather is resting upstairs, and Tamera was asleep when I picked up her tray after lunch."

On impulse, Craig picked a single rose from the center of the bouquet and handed it to her. "For you, my lady," he whispered, kissing her on the cheek.

"Why don't you try some of that charm on her, upstairs?" she admonished in a tender voice, her eyes shining with the love she reserved just for him.

He chuckled. "Think it'll work?"

"It certainly wouldn't hurt. Besides, it's time for you to quit fooling around and settle down. This house needs babies in it."

Craig laughed. "Yes, Ma'am."

He walked slowly up the stairs, surprised to find the door to Tamera's room open. He stopped in the doorway and gazed inside. She lay on her side facing the opposite wall. Her shoulders rose and fell with the rhythm of her gentle breathing. He stood immobilized as emotions rocketed through him. Love, desire, hunger, need; emotions so deep and fierce they left him breathless and weak and rooted to the spot. Craig closed his eyes and reveled in the feelings. A tremble shook him clear to the soul.

He took a deep breath, entered the room and walked quietly around the bed. He knelt beside her and removed another rose from the bouquet. Very gently, he ran it across her cheek. She brushed a hand in its wake, and rolled onto her back. Her pajama top fell off her shoulder, exposing the tender skin to his hungry gaze.

Craig suppressed a groan as desire, sharp and painful, coursed through him. He leaned closer and rubbed the rose across her cheek once more, trailed it over her lips and down her throat. She mumbled and opened her eyes. Time stood still as they gazed at each other.

Tamera trembled. His eyes were soft and warm, like liquid metal. Instinctively she knew he was going to kiss her. The thought sent tiny sparks shivering through her body. She felt paralyzed. She couldn't move and she couldn't tear her eyes away from his hypnotic gaze.

Slowly, teasingly, he lowered his lips to hers, stopping a breath away. He swallowed a chuckle when her eyes closed and lips parted slightly, waiting. She didn't wait long. As though of their own accord, his lips closed over hers in a tender caress. Careful of her injuries, he wrapped his arm around her waist and hauled her gently against him as the kiss deepened. Realizing that he was getting very close to kissing her past the point of propriety, Craig ended the kiss and lay her gently back against the pillows.

"God, you're beautiful," he murmured in a thick voice. Her smile was tender.

"Is this for me, or did you buy it just to torture me with?" she asked, picking the rose up from where he had dropped it and burying her nose shyly in the soft petals.

He grinned and handed her the bouquet. "I bought a whole bunch to torture you with," he teased.

"They're beautiful," she breathed, a soft blush covering her cheeks.

"Not as beautiful as the one holding them," he assured tenderly, and was rewarded with another sweet blush. "Want to see what else I bought you?"

She nodded, laying the roses beside her as he handed her a package. Excitement curled in the pit of her stomach as she un-wrapped the box. The *VS* inscribed on it made her blush even more. She closed her eyes, almost afraid to open it. "I can't believe you went into a woman's lingerie shop to buy me a gift," she whispered, surprised and touched at this side of his nature.

He grinned. "The sales lady was very helpful," he teased. "Especially when I told her I was buying something for my veterinarian."

She giggled. "I'll just bet she was." Opening the box, she gasped in surprise, pulling out peach silk pajamas and a matching robe. "Oh, Craig," she breathed, fingering the soft lace trimming the collar and the tiny rose embroidered on the top. "They're beautiful. Almost too pretty to wear," she remarked. "Thank you."

"I was going to get the gown, but I figured you'd be more comfortable in pajamas. I'll get you the gown later," he promised. The tone of his voice and the look in his eyes indicated that he intended to see her in it, too.

"Besides," he continued, "I thought you would feel better wearing them after taking your bath."

Her eyes widened. "You mean a whole bath? A real one in a tub full of water?"

He laughed softly at the look of joy on her face. "Yep, and I even bought scrubbing bubbles," he said, holding up a bottle of peach-scented bubble bath, also from Victoria's Secret.

"They work hard, so you don't have to," he teased, chuckling when she tossed her head and laughed.

Excitement made her eyes sparkle like rare, precious gems. Love rushed through his veins like hot, molten lava; Craig fought the urge to take her in his arms again.

"I had lunch with Scott. He said it would be okay as long as you take it easy and are careful not to get that cast wet, so I bought you this." He held up a man's rubber glove that would cover it.

"You thought of everything!"

"That's not all."

"You mean there's more?" she asked, her eyes shining. "I could get used to this," she teased.

"I could get used to spoiling you, too," he admitted, moving the stuff out of his way. Picking up the last bag, he emptied it on her lap. "I didn't know exactly what you liked to read, so I got a variety."

"I'll say," she stated, sorting through the pile. There was a historical romance novel, a contemporary romance novel, a murder mystery, a horror novel, a *Horse* magazine, a woman's magazine, a combination crossword puzzle and word-find book, and the latest inspirational book.

"I can't wait to get started on all of them," she remarked. "I love to read, anything and everything. I used to relish rainy weekends because they gave me a chance to catch up on my reading. I don't know how to thank you," she whispered, a shy flush covering her cheeks. His eyes darkened, making her tremble.

"I'll think of something," he promised. "Now, how about that bath? How do you like your water?"

"Real warm. Do you think Maria can help me wash my hair?"

He shook his head. "Maria is probably busy with supper by now. I'll help you."

"That's okay. It can wait another day."

"Nonsense," he countered. "It'll make you feel better." He cleaned off the bed then picked up her hairbrush off the vanity table, surprised to see the absence of bottles. His mother's vanity was always cluttered with a variety of lotions, creams and cosmetics. Tamera's was refreshingly empty.

"Ah hah!" he exclaimed picking up a bottle of baby lotion. "I always wondered how a woman could work around horses and animals all day and still smell as fresh as a baby. Now I know your secret."

She grinned. "I figured if it's gentle enough for babies, it's gentle enough for me."

Settling himself beside her on the bed, he turned her so that he could reach the thick braid that hung down her back. Very gently, he undid it and brushed her hair. Unable to resist, he wrapped an arm around her waist and buried his face in the silken mass.

I love you.

Craig bit back the endearment; afraid she would think they were just words to describe his physical reaction to her. When the time was right, he'd tell her and he'd never let her go.

"I'm not sure all this excitement is good for you," he whispered huskily, feeling her tremble, resisting the urge to kiss the pulse visibly throbbing in her throat.

"I'll take my chances," she moaned, resting against his strong frame.

He held her as long as he could stand the sweet ache then released her with a reluctant sigh. Propping a chair against the bathroom sink, he started the water, adjusting the temperature until it ran tepid. Walking back to the bed, he helped her into the chair and admonished her to relax as he gently washed and conditioned her hair.

A sigh rose up from her toes as Tamera relaxed under his tender administrations. "Hmm, feels good," she remarked. "I don't think I've ever gone this long without washing my hair."

"You should have said something before."

She shrugged. "Maria's always so busy. It's been a blessing just to have her brush it out and re-braid it once a day. It's so long and hard to take care of, sometimes I'm tempted to cut it all off."

"It'd be a sin to cut off such beautiful hair," he murmured huskily.

"You sound just like my father. He loved to brush it, every night, one hundred strokes. I guess I wouldn't be happy with it too short, but I'd like to take a couple of inches off."

Craig agreed that it might be easier to take care of if she did. With painstaking tenderness, he combed the tangles out of her hair then twisted it up and secured it on top of her head with a huge barrette. Cautioning her to sit still and rest a moment, he ran a tub of warm water, adding the peach-scented liquid. He then washed the hairbrush per her instructions and set it on the windowsill to dry.

"I love peaches," he commented inhaling deeply, "especially the sweet, fresh, tender ones."

He chuckled knowing that she'd caught the innuendo, when a blush rushed to her cheeks. When the tub was full, he helped put the glove over her cast. "This is the point where I have to leave you alone," he whispered achingly, though his expression said he'd rather not. "Please be careful."

She rested her forehead against his, still unnerved at her weakness. "I will," she promised, anxious to sink into the warm, scented froth. "Thank you. For everything."

Utilizing the strength of a saint, Craig left, closing the door behind him. It took every ounce of self-control he possessed to walk out of that room. Thirty minutes later he knocked on the door. "Everything okay in there?"

"Yes."

"You ready to get out?"

"I can get out by myself!"

He laughed, imagining her hot blush. "I meant that I would ask Maria to come help you, Sweetheart."

"I'm okay," she assured him.

"Okay, I'll be back in twenty minutes to help you downstairs."

When he returned she was sitting in the chair by the window, holding the roses and hairbrush in her lap. Tears clung to her thick lashes.

"What's wrong?"

"I can't even brush my own hair," she sniffled.

Craig knelt in front of her, cupping her hot cheeks in his hands. "It'll get easier, Sweetheart. I promise. How do you normally take care of it?" he asked, taking the brush from her hands.

"I blow-dry it. When it's almost completely dry, I spray it with that conditioner," she nodded toward the vanity, "then brush it. I managed to get it dry and spray it, but now my arm hurts too much to brush." Her voice broke as she swallowed a sob.

"Don't cry," he pleaded, brushing his lips across her cheek as she blinked back tears and bit her lip to keep it from trembling.

"Come here," he said, helping her to sit on the vanity stool. Turning the chair around, he sat behind her. Picking up the brush, his eyes met hers in the mirror. "One hundred strokes right?" At her nod, he brushed, counting mentally; long, slow, sensuous strokes; a pleasantly erotic chore.

"Did you buy a dozen roses?" she queried.

He grinned at the puzzled frown on her pretty face and put down the brush. "Yes, but I had to give one to my favorite lady in the whole world."

"Oh, really?" she asked, arching an eyebrow at him.

"I gave one to Maria," he confessed with a tender smile.

"How sweet," she breathed. "All right, where's my arrogant jerk cowboy?" she asked, eyeing him warily.

"I thought you didn't like him," he remarked, standing.

"I guess he kinda grew on me," Tamera admitted softly, as he put the chair back by the window.

Craig chuckled, walking back to where she sat. "He's available at your beck and call my lady," he informed her, bowing gracefully. Reaching down, he swung her up in his arms.

"What are you doing?" she asked, stiffening.

"I'm carrying you downstairs for supper."

"I can walk," she insisted.

"Bull! You're too weak to manage those stairs just yet. Besides," he conspired in a husky whisper. "I enjoy holding this luscious little body of yours every chance I get."

"Arrogant jerk," she muttered resting her head on his shoulder, then smiled, enjoying every facet of his personality.

Gramps and Maria shared secret smiles and tender gazes as Craig waited on Tamera, fixing her plate and cutting up her meat. After supper, Craig carried her into the den for a while, then out onto the porch to see Temper when he let him out in the pasture for the night. He let her visit with Shorty and the hands that came to inquire about her health. Sensing that she was getting tired, he carried her back upstairs despite her protests to the contrary. When he stepped in to check on her the next morning, she was already up and sitting in the chair.

"Take me with you to see about Temper," she begged, her eyes wide and pleading.

The denial froze on his lips. He sighed heavily. "Okay. I can deny you nothing when you look at me like that. I'll take you, but only if you promise you'll sit still and watch, and not argue over my carrying you to the barn."

"I promise," she remarked as he lifted her into his arms. "This time," she muttered under her breath.

"I heard that," he insisted, tightening his hold on her. Tamera met his glare with wide-eyed innocence.

Chapter Eleven

Tamera hesitated on the way to her room when Jimmy rushed through the back door calling for her. "Miss Tamera!"

"Lower your voice, young man," Maria admonished.

"And take off that hat," Gramps added.

"Yes sir, sorry ma'am," he addressed both, his eyes showing relief when Tamera returned to the kitchen.

"What is it, Jimmy?"

"There's been an accident. Debbie Ryder's horse fell with her. We can't get him up. She's pinned beneath him!" he added as they rushed out the back door.

* * * * *

Craig walked in the house, surprised at the quietness within. "Is everything okay?" he asked Tamera, who was heading up the stairs toward her room. Though she accompanied him each morning to see about Temper, and had been getting around more and more, she still seemed a bit weak from her accident two weeks ago. Scott had deemed her recovery from the snakebite as nothing short of miraculous and assured them she would recover completely, but cautioned her not to overdo it.

"Fine," she muttered over her shoulder.

Craig's ears perked up at the sulky tone of her voice. "What's wrong?"

She turned to face him. Her cast was dirty. Dust and sweat streaked her face.

"Where have you been, and what have you been doing?"

"One of the contestants had a riding accident. She turned a barrel too sharply. They fell. The horse broke his leg, pinning her beneath him. She's pretty shaken up, but seems to be okay. We called an ambulance, anyway. I set the leg as best I could, but he'll need surgery. I then helped to get him up off of her, and waited with them until the ambulance came for her and the animal hospital for him."

Craig ground his teeth. "Does Scott know about this?"

"Shh," she interrupted, his raised voice grating on her constantly raw nerves. He was way too insistent about her taking it easy. "You're going to wake Gramps and Maria."

"I'll definitely wake them when I beat you, you idiotic little twit," he threatened. "You shouldn't be doing so much yet!"

"I didn't have the time, nor did I think it necessary, to ask Scott's permission. I'm a veterinarian. What was I supposed to do?" Turning on her heel, she stomped on. "Idiotic little twit my eye," she muttered, "at least I'm not an arrogant jerk."

It was all the insolence he could tolerate. Taking the stairs two at a time he grabbed her, swinging her up in his arms. Tossing her none-too-gently onto her bed he followed, pinning her down with his body. "If I have to, I'll hog-tie you to this blasted bed until you get clearance from Scott to go back to work. Is that understood?"

"What?" The angry flare in her eyes prompted him to ask.

"You're hurting me."

"No, I'm not," he countered, making sure neither of her arms was in a bind. "Talk to me," he urged.

"You're driving me nuts! How on earth can I earn my paycheck and pay my medical bills if I don't get back to work? You've left strict orders that I don't do anything, even with the colts," she hissed, "and you've threatened anyone who even thinks about helping me saddle my horse! I'll have you know, you arrogant jerk, that I don't need a saddle, or a bridle for that matter. Temper will do whatever I want him to the minute I get on his back! I am not an invalid and I wish you would quit treating me like one!" she raged, each statement punctuated by an angry poke in his chest.

He tried, but couldn't suppress a grin. "Do you know how beautiful you are when you're angry?" His voice was soft, husky.

Tamera fought a response to that seductive tone. He would not manipulate her that way! She rolled her eyes. "Get off of me," she ordered despite her melting resistance. But he knew. She could tell by his glittering gray gaze that he knew everything she felt. The jerk!

He chuckled. "Say please," he whispered, nibbling at the corners of her mouth.

She tensed, fighting the sweet warmth infusing her limbs and pushed against him with what little strength she had. "I will not say please. I said, get off me."

Craig didn't budge. He couldn't. Holding her like this was wreaking havoc on his senses. He pulled her closer and chuckled, thrilled at the flare of passion in her eyes. Very slowly he lowered his head, his lips capturing hers in a thorough kiss. Rolling over, he pulled her with him, rubbed her back in a tender gesture.

"Make a deal with you. You get a release from Scott and I'll leave your recovery up to you."

"What about my work?"

A grin tugged at his mouth. "Don't push it, Temper. Don't worry about your check, and there are no medical bills. Consider the accident work-related."

She rolled her eyes. "You are the most pigheaded, chauvinistic, egotistical, arrogant man I've ever had the misfortune to meet."

"And you're the most stubborn, willful, hot-tempered, beautiful woman I've ever had the good fortune to meet," he countered in a husky whisper.

"I can't win with you, can I?" she queried with a smile, getting used to his subtle, domineering ways. She snuggled closer to his hard body as he wrapped his arms tighter around her.

"I can't lose with you." He urged her closer, succumbing to the need to taste her sweetness and fire again.

"Okay, okay," she relented when he released her lips an eternity later. "I'll get a release from Scott."

"Does that mean I have to stop and let you go?"

His throaty chuckle shivered through her. Knowing he should, but not yet willing for him to do so, Tamera didn't answer. Feeling shy yet somewhat brave she rubbed her cheek against his, then kissed it.

Leather and lace.

Craig's breath escaped with a moan as desire rocketed through him. Her shy, inexperienced passion affected him more than any expert touch he'd ever known. He groaned. "Lord, You've presented me with the physical manifestation of temptation. Help me."

It was Tamera's turn to grin. "Call on someone closer, Craig."

He laughed. "Right. I don't think He'd appreciate me consorting with a witch, and a seductive one at that."

She wrinkled her nose at him. "If I were a witch, of any sort, I'd turn you into a frog. Just like that," she snapped her fingers. "There'd be one less arrogant jerk for the world to put up with."

His high-pitched voice, punctuated with frog-like croaks, reduced her to a helpless mass of giggles as he begged her to kiss him again and turn him back into her prince. She turned her nose up haughtily, ignoring his pleas until she could no longer resist. With the regality of a queen bestowing favors on a lowly knight, she lowered her lips to his cheek.

Craig turned his head, capturing her lips with his. He held her lightly, forcing himself to be gentle, when what he really wanted was to roll her over and ravish her.

I love you.

He checked the words, afraid of her reaction, afraid of putting a strain on the relationship developing between them, afraid of scaring her off. Gut instinct told him that Tony was, or had been, someone special to her. Jealousy insisted he question her; love cautioned him not to; pride stopped him. So he gazed into her shining sapphire eyes with all the tenderness he possessed and said nothing.

"So," she began, breaking the silence that sprang up between them. "What are you doing home so early, anyway?"

Craig glanced at his watch. "I was going to town and wanted to see if you'd like to ride along with me."

She smiled. "Really?"

"Sure."

"I'd love to." She scrambled from the bed and hurried into the bathroom to retrieve a wet washcloth. "Just let me wash up, brush my hair and..."

"You look fine for where we're going," he told her as she wiped her face and neck. "Besides, we're going in the jeep."

"The jeep?" She walked to the vanity table and picked up her brush. "But what about this mop?" she queried, shaking a hand-full of hair at him as he walked up behind her.

"Beautiful," he breathed with a tender stroke. "Like silk. Who ever heard of a silk mop?"

She rolled her eyes, groaned. "Oh, Craig, be serious. It may look like a silk mop now, but if we go in that jeep and I don't do something with it, it'll be a tangled mess."

He shrugged. "Braid it or something."

"Easier said than done." She raised her cast for emphasis. In a single motion he turned her around and sat her down. He raked his fingers through it, and separated her hair then plaited it into a thick braid down her back.

"I can't believe..." she breathed.

He shrugged a teasing grin on his face. "No different than braiding a horse's tail, except you don't kick or bite."

She rose with a very unladylike snort and walked toward the door. "Yeah, well just don't push your luck, mister."

Catching up with her, he swung her up in his arms. Tamera stiffened. "What are you doing now?"

"Carrying you down the stairs. Until you get a release from Scott. Remember?"

"I can walk. I've been walking up and down the stairs for days now, and you know it."

"And your point might be...?"

The innocent smile belied the devilish glint in his eyes. "My point is that you're an arrogant, bossy, jerk."

He laughed and carried her anyway. Reaching the bottom, he let her slide down his body before he released her from his embrace. It didn't hurt his ego one bit to feel her tremble and hear the soft purr of pleasure she couldn't suppress.

* * * * *

Two weeks slid into three. After she obtained her release from Scott, Tamera's strength returned steadily. She was often seen walking, jogging, or running, determined to stay in shape while regaining her strength. After Scott had changed her cast for the third time, and admonished her for its appearance, she decided not to spend as much time with the horses. It was easier to supervise their training and care than to put up with a filthy cast and Scott's displeasure. He reminded her so much of Craig, especially when he was angry. Thankfully there had been no more accidents or injured animals with which she had to contend.

The rodeo took place as scheduled. Forbidden by Craig and Scott from competing, Tamera joined the throng of spectators, cheering for the winners and applauding encouragement to the losers. She watched with an absurd amount of pride when Craig was called to give an exhibition of the cutting event. She could feel his intense concentration as he sat nimbly in the saddle while holding the reins loosely.

Rocky was magnificent, obeying the slightest command of Craig's legs or the reins. He was well bred, superbly trained, and it showed. Craig galloped him out of the arena as the announcer told of the horse sale following the rodeo.

She was watching the cutting competition when Craig appeared at her side. "You were great," she complimented, her smile dazzling.

He grunted. "It's a miracle I could do anything. How am I supposed to concentrate with you sitting up here dressed like that?"

The look in his eyes sent tremors down her spine. "I'm not dressed any differently than ninety percent of the people here," she countered, glancing around and indicating others dressed similarly in cutoffs and T-shirts. "The only women wearing jeans are those competing."

Craig glanced around with a snort. "There's not another pair of legs like yours anywhere on this property," he assured, his gaze traveling up the slender length of her legs and over her body. "Or body, or lips," he whispered hoarsely.

His eyes darkened. Hunger and need reached deep inside her in ways she didn't understand. Desire coursed through her so sharp and hot, it made the sweltering Texas heat seem like an old blue northern. Tamera shivered as a blush rushed to heat her cheeks. He continued to gaze at her with a longing that created chaos in her mind and made her say things she normally wouldn't say. "Been a long time out on the trail, cowboy?"

He nodded. "Too long," he assured her in a velvety-rough voice that shivered over her like a caress. "Hell can't be any worse than celibacy."

"Craig!" she admonished blushing harder, torn between surprise and horror at his words. "Don't talk like that," she warned. "Why don't you go find some fat, sassy cowgirl to help you take care of that little problem? There's plenty around here drooling over you," she insisted, wondering why the thought made her angry.

Craig saw the anger for what it was: jealousy. He locked his heated gaze to hers. "I want you."

Stated simply and honestly, the words had the same effect on her as a kick to the midsection. Her breath stuck in her throat, her heart skipped a beat. She gasped softly as desire washed over her in angry waves, followed by fear.

"No," she whispered, lunging away from him. Jumping off the stands, she headed toward the house.

Craig saw the desire, but consumed by need, missed the fear. He caught up to her with ground-eating strides as she reached the barn. He grabbed her gently by the arm; urging her into its dark, cool recesses.

Suddenly, he was everywhere. His arms wound around her, pulling her firmly against his hard body as his lips covered hers in a hungry gesture. The kiss deepened.

When she began to tremble he picked her up, wrapping her legs around his waist as need shuddered through him with a force he had never experienced. One arm held her firmly in place while his other tugged at her ponytail until her hair fell across her shoulders in a thick, silken, mass. A primitive grunt escaped him as he sank his fingers in it while his mouth feasted greedily on the sweetness of her lips.

Swept up in the storm of passion, all Tamera could do was cling weakly to him and ride it out as her own need rose swiftly and powerfully to match his.

The storm raged on, wild, hot, fierce, consuming.

Craig nearly lost it when she relaxed more fully against him with a soft moan of surrender. He could take her here and now, but instinctively knew that she would regret it. So would he. His feelings for her being what they were, he would later regret the fact that he'd taken her in the barn, no better than an animal. A soft, insistent voice in his mind urged him to release her while he still had the strength and sense to do so. He dragged his lips from hers and buried his face against her neck. Breathing heavily, he fought for control of his raging senses.

"No wonder your daddy called you Temper," he whispered hoarsely. "Your temper was only a hint of the fire in you," he breathed, his lips traveling up her throat to capture hers again, gently this time. "You're so beautiful," he murmured against her mouth.

Brushing the hair off her face, he cupped her cheek and gazed warmly into her soft sapphire eyes. "I want you," he confessed. "But not like this. Not like some lust-filled teenager out of control. You're much too precious for that."

He saw the fear this time as she realized how close he'd come to losing control. Two huge tears rolled slowly down her cheeks. He swore softly, letting her slide from his embrace. He cupped her face in his hands brushing the tears away with his thumbs. "I'm sorry, if I frightened or hurt you," he whispered.

The fear was quickly replaced by anger, an irrepressible rage that exploded in a blinding red haze. She jerked away from him. When her eyes met his they weren't tear-drenched but furious. Instinct alone had him catching her clenched fist before it connected with his jaw. Fear of hurting her had him releasing it at the slightest whimper.

"What on earth..?" he muttered, as her balled fists slammed into his chest pushing him away from her.

"Don't touch me like that!" she raged. "Don't you ever touch me like that again. You have no right! No one has the right to touch me like that!"

"Temper, wait," he reached for her, stunned by her outburst.

"No!" she cried, jerking out of his reach. Turning, she ran into the house sobbing.

He started after her, but stopped when a thought struck him. *"She's been hurt. My guess is, badly,"* Scott's words rang in his ears.

Craig shook his head, denying it. "No," he whispered. "Oh, God, no."

But he knew. God help him, he knew and there was absolutely nothing he could do about it until she trusted him enough to confide in him.

Trusting God and instinct that he was doing the right thing, Craig went back to the rodeo. Supper that evening was strained when Tamera declined eating with the excuse that she wasn't feeling well. When Maria fixed her a tray, he took it up to her.

He knocked on her door. "Tamera," his voice was soft, coaxing. "I brought you a tray."

"Go away, Craig. I'm not hungry."

"You need to eat, Sweetheart."

She reluctantly opened the door.

"Are you okay?"

She nodded, a flush of humiliation rushing to her cheeks.

"I want to apologize again for what happened, Tamera. I'd never intentionally hurt you or frighten you. I hope you know that. I hope you'll forgive me for overstepping my boundaries. I know how you were raised and what your convictions are. I know what the Bible says, but I've always kept that part of my life separate from my faith, what little faith I had. God's been dealing with me about that all afternoon."

Fully aware that her fear stemmed not from his passion but from within herself, Tamera softly assured him it was okay. "There's nothing to forgive, but thank you. I know you would never intentionally hurt me, Craig. I was frightened and I overreacted. I'm sorry."

Despite the words, she stiffened when he reached out and stroked her cheek with a gentle hand, and her gaze never reached his. His prayer that night was for patience, gentleness, wisdom, and a double dose of self- control.

Chapter Twelve

Tamera woke in a cold sweat, her breathing labored, her body rigid with fear, as the nightmare she'd had continued to haunt her thoughts. Lunging from the bed, she paced the floor. She felt wired, her nerves taut, like a bow ready to fire. She hadn't slept in days, not since the rodeo. *And that kiss.* The memory of it shivered through her, the nightmare in its wake. She glanced around the room, from the bed to the window to the door, trying to subdue her thoughts. Her breath quickened as panic enveloped her. She had to get out of here!

Throwing on her robe, she barely made it to the door before her trembling legs collapsed. I can't do it, she thought, fighting down another wave of panic. I can't, not here, not like this!

Tamera knew what she had to do. Methodically she packed her things. It was two-thirty in the morning. She had plenty of time to get away. Biting her trembling lip, she wrote a note and left the ranch.

* * * * *

Craig awoke in a cold sweat, his breathing labored, his body rigid with need from the memory of a kiss and the dreams it evoked. Rolling over, he cursed. Six-thirty! He'd overslept. Stumbling from the bed, he stood a long time in the shower, one of many cold ones he'd endured the past few weeks. Shaking the water from his eyes, he willed his thoughts into some semblance of order, trying to control his raging senses. After dressing, he bounded down the stairs, grabbed a couple of biscuits, and wolfed down a glass of juice.

"Gotta go, overslept," he mumbled, picking up his thermos of coffee and heading out the door.

Gramps frowned at Maria. "Craig overslept; Tamera's not up yet. What in the world is going on?"

Maria smiled. "Maybe they're both having trouble sleeping."

He chuckled. "Good. It's done him a world of good to have his life turned upside down. I've never seen him looking better. Have you?"

Maria frowned. "No. But, now that you mention it, Tamera's been a little quiet the past few days. Kinda withdrawn and peaked."

Gramps' eyes narrowed suspiciously. "You don't think...? Nah," he rejected the thought. He knew his grandson well enough to know Craig would not bed the girl in this house unwed. And he knew Tamera well enough to know she wouldn't allow it. He shrugged. Kids! Everyone could see they were in love. Why didn't they just admit it and start making a life together? It sure was simpler in the old days, he thought with a sigh.

* * * * *

Craig arrived at the house around four-thirty; too late for lunch, too early for supper. He'd been leaving early and coming in late. Tamera's reaction to him the day of the rodeo haunted his mind as vividly as the memory of the kiss tortured his body. Just night before last, he'd paused at the door of her room and heard her cry out. Without hesitation, he went in to check on her. "What's wrong, Sweetheart?"

She shook her head. "Nothing. Just a bad dream."

"Sure?"

She nodded, unable to meet his gaze.

"Talk to me, Temper," he urged.

"I can't," she mumbled, her voice hitching on a sob.

He'd kissed her forehead wanting desperately to tell her of his love. Now he wished he had. And, now that the ranch was once again in some semblance of order and the last rodeo guest was gone, he intended to spend more time with her, and, hopefully, gain her trust.

"Any leftovers? Seen Tamera? Where's Gramps?" he asked Maria, rummaging around in the refrigerator then fixing himself a sandwich.

He heard her sniff as she dabbed at her eyes with her apron. "How many questions do you want me to answer at once?"

Stunned by her sharp tone, his head jerked up, gaze leveled on her. "What's the matter?" he asked, feeling the tension and noticing her red- rimmed eyes. "Where's Gramps? Is something wrong?"

He took a bite of his sandwich as she nodded in the direction of the den. Fear curled in the pit of his stomach. He left the sandwich forgotten on the table and sought out his grandfather. He found him sitting in his wheelchair, his face pale and drawn. "Gramps?"

"She's gone, Craig," he mumbled, tears filling his gray eyes.

"What?" Craig gasped.

"Tamera. She's gone."

"When? Where?"

Gramps answered, oblivious to Craig's distress. "When she didn't come down for breakfast we didn't worry much; figured she was just sleeping late for a change. Then it got late and," his voice broke. He struggled with his emotions for a moment then continued.

"Maria went to check on her. At first we just thought she went into town early or something. It's not unusual for her to skip breakfast or lunch. Then Maria found this." He handed him a note.

Craig's mind whirled. His hand trembled as he read: *Gramps, I love you. Please forgive me.*

"I don't understand," he rasped.

"Something happened, Craig. Maria said she'd been a little withdrawn the last couple of days. Did something happen between you? Another fight? Do you have any ideas?"

A memory rose vividly in his mind, a kiss that had tortured his mind and body for the past four days. A guilty flush heated his cheeks when he remembered her fear.

Gramps hissed a curse his eyes narrowing dangerously. Seeing the guilt on Craig's face, he jumped to conclusions, assuming the worst. "You seduced her!" he accused, for the first time in his life wanting to strangle the grandson he adored.

"No!" Craig lunged away from his angry, accusing gaze. He paced the floor. "No. I swear, Gramps, I didn't. It was just a kiss, a kiss that got a little out of hand. That's all. I swear."

"Why would she leave over a kiss?"

Craig shrugged, the impact of the situation trampling his heart like a stampede. She's gone! "I don't know, Gramps. She seemed afraid, like I would hurt her, or force her, but when I questioned her she assured me it was all right. Night before last she had a nightmare. When I checked on her, she said she was all right. And I've been too busy to...." *care?*

Had he been too busy to care?

Craig shook his head in denial.

He hadn't even noticed she was gone.

Remorse settled like a lead weight in his stomach. "Oh, God," he raked his fingers through his hair. "Why didn't you send for me earlier?"

Gramps shrugged, immediately regretting his hasty conclusion. He had no reason to doubt Craig. "We just found the note a little while ago, and I wasn't sure which direction you rode out this morning. I've been praying that you'd come in early."

"Where do you think she's gone?" Craig whispered his voice hoarse with emotion, thick with fear that she wouldn't come back.

"I can only assume, home."

"I'm going after her. She can't have too much of a head start." He headed out the door but turned at his grandfather's soft command.

"Wait, Craig. I'm sorry I doubted you. Don't let her get away, son. She's the best thing that's happened to this family in a long time."

Craig walked to his grandfather's side and gave him a hug. "It's okay, Gramps, I probably would've thought the same thing if I were you. I'll find her. I promise. And I'll bring her back," he vowed. "Even if I have to drag her, kicking and screaming."

At Maria's insistence, Craig forced down his sandwich, talked with Shorty, took a shower, packed a bag, and loaded it and the basket of food Maria packed into the jeep. By then, two hours had passed. It took another hour to get to town and service the jeep, making it nearly eight o'clock before he hit the highway and headed east. Four hours and one speeding ticket later, he stopped and called home.

Gramps was relieved to hear from Craig. Though a bit frustrated and tired, he was okay. "Listen to me, Craig," he urged. "I've been thinking and praying since you left. I want you to take it easy. The last thing we need to worry about is you getting in a wreck somewhere between here and there."

"I'm not worried about wrecking, more like getting thrown in jail in some hick town for speeding," Craig interrupted.

"Listen, I feel sure she's gone home. You have that address don't you?"

"Written down and memorized."

"Okay. Take it easy. Whatever her reasons, I'm sure we'll hear from her soon. I feel positive she's all right. You get some rest and continue in the morning. Promise, Craig," he urged when Craig protested.

"Okay," Craig relented. He was exhausted. "I'll rest a while." He didn't stop just then but drove for another couple of hours. Then, fighting fatigue to the point of questioning his ability to drive safely, he pulled off the highway. Sleep, when it came, wasn't easy or restful.

* * * * *

Tamera awoke to sunlight streaming through the blinds. When she arrived at five-thirty last evening, she unloaded her horse but didn't unpack her car. Where it took nearly eighteen hours to get to Bandera, the trip home took only fifteen. She'd felt a twinge of remorse when she led Temper on stiff, trembling legs to his pasture. She watched as he walked gingerly around then, recognizing the familiar surroundings, trotted and ran around the perimeters of his home. She fixed his feed and water, and then went into the house. Numb from exhaustion, she couldn't think or function. Tugging off her boots, she curled up on the couch and fell asleep.

Now, in the bright light of morning, it was time to exorcise the demons in her soul. She walked through the house, opening one door after another as homesickness washed over her in waves. Memories crowded her mind as she entered her bedroom to take a quick bath before continuing her quest for peace.

Reaching for the knob on her parents' door, she rested her head against the cool wood. Taking a deep breath, she opened it and went in. She walked around, finding comfort in touching their things. "Oh, Daddy," she whispered. "Help me now." Tears fell unchecked down her cheeks as she made her way through the rest of the house.

Mustering up as much courage as she could, she entered the den; the room where her faith -along with other things- had been stolen. Emotions overwhelmed her: pain, anger, bitterness, hatred.

So much stolen. So much lost.

She didn't know when the first item hit the floor, nor the last. When she regained her senses, she was in a crumpled heap on her knees. The room looked as though a small tornado had swept through it.

In a mild state of shock, she got up. Cleaning the room helped in sorting out her feelings. She'd righted the last piece of furniture, swept up the last piece of glass, and was scrubbing the rug when a knock sounded on the front door. Wiping her hands on her jeans, she went to open it. Her eyes widened in surprise, as she stared up at the man she never thought she'd see again.

* * * * *

Anthony Gerard glared down at the girl, hatred boiling inside him. He'd been angry for so long. But anger was far preferable to the pain in his heart. "Where've you been? We haven't seen or heard from you in months! And you were supposed to have loved him," he snarled, stepping through the doorway.

Tamera sighed. "Mr. Gerard, don't you think it's a little late to pretend you care? You never liked me, so what difference does it make where I've been?"

"That's right!" he growled. "You always thought you were too good for Tony. So high and mighty! So ambitious! You killed him! And you didn't even go to the funeral."

Tamera blinked back tears at his accusations. Squaring her shoulders, she lifted her chin defiantly. "I was there," she told him. "And I buried a lot more than just your son that day. If the only reason you've come here is to blame me for his death, you can leave."

"It is your fault," he insisted. "He wouldn't have missed that curve if he hadn't been here to see you that night! I tried to tell him you were playing games but he wouldn't listen!"

"How dare you! How dare you come into my home and talk to me like that? He wouldn't have missed that curve if he hadn't been drunk!"

"Well, if you knew he was drunk, why did you let him drive away from here?"

Tamera saw red—bright, hot, furious red. "Oh, no, you don't," she snarled. "I didn't let him leave. He left of his own accord. I couldn't have stopped him even if I'd wanted to. Which I didn't; especially after what he did to me."

"What are you talking about, what he did to you? He loved you!"

She snorted. "If what Tony demonstrated that night was love, then he was sorrier than I thought."

"What are you saying?" he demanded in a cold, hard, voice.

Tamera hadn't wanted it to come out like this. She hadn't wanted to tell him anything, to hurt him or cause him any more pain over the loss of his son, but his accusations were more than she could stomach. She closed her eyes, memories of that night replaying with vivid clarity in her mind. When she opened them again, they were dull, devoid of emotion save pain. Still, she tried to temper the blow, to soften the truth.

"He abused me, Mr. Gerard. Your precious son forced himself on me against my will, then walked out of here not knowing or even caring how I was," she informed him in a quiet, cold, emotionless voice.

Anthony fought the onslaught of emotions; anger, pain and an alarming sense of betrayal. Violent rage erupted and boiled over in a curse. "Liar!" he screamed. "You lying, slanderous, little..." he struggled with the feelings that were causing such pain in his heart. In some deep region of his mind, he suspected she was telling the truth. Still, he denied it. He was afraid, so afraid.

"How dare you say something so cruel?"

"I'm not lying!" she insisted, storming back into the den. Grabbing something out of the trashcan, she slung it at him. "That was the dress I was wearing that night, Mr. Gerard. Right here! In this room! On this floor! In my own home! He came here, and he raped me!"

There, she said it! Humiliation and shame washed over her in heated waves.

Emotion colored her cheeks a vivid red. Wrath sparkled to life in those expressive sapphire eyes until they slashed at his composure, daring him to say more. Anthony Gerard stared down at the torn, soiled dress in his hand. Rage twisted his guts. Never in his life had he felt such fury.

Hatred marred his features as he took an ominous step toward her and completely lost control. "You...harlot!" he snarled, grabbing her. "You play with him for months, and then you accuse him of something so vile after he's dead and can't defend himself! How can you live with yourself?"

She lifted angry blue eyes to glare into his. "Because it's the truth," she told him in a soft, bitter, voice. "And I think you know it. You're his father. You, yourself, know how selfish Tony was. What Tony wanted, Tony got, regardless of what it cost. Well, it cost me dearly," she remarked bitterly.

"Now, get out of my house and leave me alone," she ordered, not wanting to discuss it anymore. All she wanted to do was face it, deal with it and be healed of it. To feel worthy again. To feel whole.

"Liar!" he raged, slapping her across the face and shoving her down on the floor.

Tamera whimpered as her cast banged against the coffee table. Holding her arm against her protectively she waited for the next blow as he raised his hand.

"I wouldn't if I were you."

Anthony turned at the warning, oblivious to everything but the burning pain in his chest and the desire to block out everything he'd heard; to fight against the sickening sense of truth churning in his stomach. "She just accused my son, my dead son, of..."

"I heard," Craig interrupted, afraid that if he heard the word again he'd lose control. He'd arrived a few minutes ago. Hearing their raised, angry voices, he hadn't bothered knocking. Her accusation stopped him dead in his tracks. It took every ounce of self-control he possessed to stop himself from attacking the man the minute he put his hands on her. If he touched her again, he would kill him.

"Let her go and get out," he ordered in a calm, deadly voice.

Although his voice was soft and he didn't move, Tamera knew Craig was furious. Every muscle in his body was tensed for battle. His eyes were a dark, dangerous gray, and his jaw muscle throbbed madly.

"Who are you?" Anthony demanded. "What business is it of yours if I beat the girl for lying?"

Craig uncoiled his long frame, moving slowly, like a panther stalking his prey. His gaze assessed the situation: Tamera cowed in fright, an angry hand-print marking her beautiful skin, the torn dress at the man's feet, her words ringing in his ears.

Blood pounded in his veins. Revenge screamed through his soul. He stopped toe-to-toe with his adversary. Clenching his fists in a deliberate effort not to put his hands around the man's throat, he glared down at him. "Just call me Prince Charming," he answered his voice deceptively soft.

"I told you to let her go and get out. I'm not going to repeat myself. And if I ever hear of you coming around here again, I'll personally hunt you down and kill you."

At five-foot nine-inches, Anthony had to look up into the man's blistering gray gaze. It was a very intimidating feeling, being forced to look up into such deadly eyes. He glanced back at Tamera. "You just make sure you keep your lies to yourself," he warned.

Craig's patience snapped. A low growl escaped as he grabbed the man by the shirtfront. "Listen, Mister, if you persist in intimidating the girl, you're asking for a full-blown war," he muttered, shoving him toward the door.

"Get out of here before I hurt you," he insisted, glaring at him as the disgusting little man escaped his wrath.

He turned back to Tamera, wanting desperately to go to her, to wrap her in his love and make her forget the horror she'd been through and cursed himself again for not telling her sooner that he loved her. He whispered her name, opening his arms to her. She looked at him with such horror, such anguish, as though she were being ravished from within, and collapsed.

Craig stood helplessly as she curled up into a tiny ball and wept.

Chapter Thirteen

Craig let her cry as long as he could stand it. *The total of about thirty seconds.* "Temper," he moaned, reaching for her.

"Don't," she croaked, recoiling from his touch. "Please, don't touch me. I'm not fit for you to touch me," she sobbed.

"That's bull," he insisted, forcefully refraining from dragging her up in his arms and cradling her against his chest. "Why don't you tell me everything and let me be the judge of that," he urged, lifting her chin and encouraging her to look at him. The pain and fear in her eyes cut him like a knife.

Tamera saw the warmth and tenderness in his eyes. And the anger. Instinctively she knew it was not directed at her. With a nod she let Craig help her to her feet. Unable to stand still, she paced the floor. In a soft, hesitant voice she began.

"Tony was my boyfriend. I met him in college. He was older, so suave, so sophisticated. I thought the sun rose and set in him. Daddy couldn't stand him." A bitter smile twisted her lips. "It was the only thing we really disagreed over. I guess he saw something I didn't. Anyway," she continued. "I thought I was in love. He seemed sweet enough but he wasn't impressed with my desire to be a vet. I think he thought he would be able to change that if we got married."

Jealousy rose, unbidden and strong, but Craig didn't interrupt.

"When I got the letter from Gramps about the job, Tony was furious. That is, until he found out where it was. See, he was due to leave for Basic Training in San Antonio. We'd be close enough to visit. So he decided to pacify me and let me take the job. Not that I wouldn't have anyway. Then my parents were killed. At first, he was so supportive, but then he got impatient with my grief and me. After all, he was there. My loving and honorable fiancé." She snorted in disgust.

"And since my father was gone, he felt he had even more control over what I did. He wanted me to sell everything including my home and my horse, and move in with his parents. That's when I realized how selfish he was. And how utterly two-faced. He thought the engagement ring I accepted gave him certain rights to my affections. He came over one night, drunk, and tried, for lack of a better word, to persuade me to consummate our relationship. He said he wanted me to give him something to keep him warm during the weeks between Basic Training and our wedding, something to think about so he wouldn't be tempted to look elsewhere. He gave all the usual reasons. Other people did it before they got married, he argued. But I'm not other people. When I refused and asked him to leave, he got angry. Really angry," her voice trembled.

Craig felt his blood boil as her eyes darkened with the pain of remembering. He waited for the story to end.

Tamera turned away, unable to stand the anger and sorrow on his face. "He ripped my dress and pushed me down. I struggled, but he held me easily." Her voice broke. She bit her trembling lip and took a deep breath.

"When I woke up the police were knocking on my door. He was dead. He'd been driving too fast and missed a curve down the road. He was killed instantly. I hadn't even had time to change or shower. The officer questioned me, but I didn't tell him anything. Tony was dead. What good would it do? So, I went to the funeral, but I didn't sit with the family or anyone else. I stayed back from the crowd, afraid to face anyone; afraid they'd be able to tell by looking at me that something had happened; afraid they'd guess the truth and somehow blame me for his death."

"Why on earth would anyone think that?" he interrupted.

"It's a small town, Craig. People talk. They think what they want and say what they want, the truth be damned. And these days, it's not a 'sin' to sleep around, but it is a 'sin' to let someone drive drunk and die."

She shrugged, unable to explain the paradox of living in a small town that thrived on gossip to someone who spent his life with fifty thousand acres separating him from civilization, especially someone who'd made his own way and didn't give a darn what people thought.

"To hell with scandal and small town talk," Craig insisted. He'd experienced his share, risen above it, and didn't care what people thought. "People will always find something to talk about, whether it's true or not."

Tamera sighed, her eyes searching his for understanding. "I know. These are supposed to be enlightened times with women's liberation and equal opportunities. Still, despite the progress we've made over the years, it's sometimes difficult for a woman. Some men don't know how to deal with a woman with ambition and drive. Anyway, I buried my faith with Tony, along with my feelings. I thought if I just put it all away—the anger and the pain, the betrayal and guilt—I could get over it. I left right after and drove straight to Bandera."

"You have no reason to feel guilt," he ground out. "It's a good thing the son-of-a-bitch is dead, otherwise I'd have to kill him." Something about her story puzzled him. "What do you mean after you woke up?"

"When he, uh," she stammered, blushed. "I fainted."

Craig raked his fingers through his hair. "Oh, God, Tamera. I'm so sorry you went through that. Did you love him?" he asked.

She met his gaze, hers unwavering. "I thought so."

"Do you still?"

She shook her head. "No. I know now that I never really did. I was infatuated, touched that someone so much older and more sophisticated would love me. I was naïve, I guess. My parents always sheltered me. I'm sure Daddy thought he'd always be around to protect me from the wrong kind of man."

"Temper," he whispered, cupping her face in his hands. "What happened to you was not love. It was selfish and cruel, and it was wrong."

Tears trembled on her lashes. "Show me," she whispered as his arms went around her, and his lips covered hers in a tender caress.

"Oh, no," he denied. "When I take you to my bed, it'll be out of love. Only love. It'll be because we both want it, and because it's right. Not that I don't want you, Darling," he assured, his voice husky. Craig picked her up and carried her to the living room. Settling himself on the couch, he cradled her in his lap.

"Can I ask you something?"

She nodded into his shoulder.

"The other day, when I kissed you like that, did it bring all this back?"

She shrugged. "Sort of. It was never far from my mind. As much as I tried to deal with it, it continued to haunt me."

"The nightmares?"

Again, she nodded.

"Explains the delirium, too. Scott was right, people who are delirious cry out from the deepest part of their souls. I would never hurt you that way. You know that, don't you?"

"Yes, I know. Your stopping when you did showed me that. It wasn't the kiss itself, but the intensity that frightened me. I never knew that desire could be felt with such passion and depth, almost as powerful as anger. I'd never experienced it. Your kiss touched me so deeply, so intimately," she blushed. "I wanted you in a way that I never thought proper. It surprised me. And shamed me."

"There's no shame in what we feel for each other, Sweetheart," he chided, his tone gentle.

"Maybe not," she insisted. "But I don't believe it's proper out of wedlock."

"Scott was right again," Craig muttered, humbled by his own stupidity.

"Why did you leave like you did? Why didn't you talk to someone, me, or Scott, or Gramps, or even Maria? You can't solve anything by running from it."

"I wasn't running away. I knew I would have to face up to it, Craig, and I couldn't do it at the ranch. I had to come back here, where it happened, and rid myself of it for good.

Otherwise it would ruin what's happening between us." Her voice was soft, thick with emotion.

"What's happening, Temper?" he queried, daring to hope that her feelings for him were as strong as his were for her. He felt her smile.

"I'm not sure, but something is definitely happening," she admitted, repeating what he told her not too long ago.

Craig's heart thrilled. "Would you find it hard to believe that it's love?" he asked gently, rubbing her back. "For me, anyway," he whispered, still afraid to say the words.

"No," she admitted with a soft sigh. "But I'd have to ask since when."

Craig chuckled. "Since the first time I laid eyes on you and you threw water in my face. I think I fell in love with you in that moment."

"Now, *that* I'd be hard-pressed to believe," she said with a smile. "Will you forgive me for being such a coward?"

"Oh, Sweetheart, you're no coward. You're the strongest woman I've ever met; and the smartest, and the most beautiful. Add it all up, and you could be quite intimidating."

"For a lesser man, maybe," she confided, snuggling closer to his hard chest.

Craig wrapped his arms around her protectively, wanting nothing more than to take her home where it was safe and secure, where nothing or no one would ever harm her again. "Let's go home, Love," he suggested.

"I am home," she replied.

Her eyes were shining. *Convince me otherwise,* they begged.

Craig's smile was tender, his eyes soft and warm, like liquid metal.

"No, you're not. True, this will always be your house, but the ranch is your home now." He cupped her face in his hands. "Come home with me, Temper," he urged with a tender kiss.

"Is Gramps very angry with me?"

"More worried than angry," he assured. "But he'll be furious if I don't call him soon with the news that I found you, and that we're coming home. I did promise to bring you back," he confessed. "Even if I had to drag you kicking and screaming," he admitted with a grin.

She rolled her eyes, glad he'd come after her, glad to be in his arms. "Arrogant jerk," she muttered, wrapping her arms around his neck and burying her face in his collar.

Craig continued to hold her, stroking her body in a gentle, soothing manner until she relaxed more fully against him. He felt her breathing slow and deepen as the tension drained from her and the effects of endless, sleepless nights washed away. Rolling gently to one side, he laid her down, not stopping his soothing caresses. She opened her eyes with a soft moan.

"Don't leave," she whispered.

His smile was tender, his voice gentle. "I'm not going anywhere without you, Sweetheart. Rest," he ordered. He kissed her forehead and eyes then her nose and finally her mouth. He groaned when her lips parted, giving him a full taste of her sweetness, but Craig kept a tight rein on his desire, showing her the tenderness born of love. He stayed by her side until he was assured she was sound asleep. Taking the afghan off the window seat, he covered her, and then called Gramps.

After their conversation, he went out and checked on Temper. Only after he left the confines of the house did Craig unleash the anger that had been simmering inside since his arrival nearly two hours ago. He beat his fist against the stable wall, wishing to God it were the face of the man who'd hurt her so horribly. His anger spent, he wept for her lost innocence, her broken trust, her shattered dreams, and her torn and tattered faith. Though badly abused, she wasn't broken. Her spirit was intact. Knowing how strong she was made his love even stronger.

Going back in the house, he washed his face and hands then decided to take a shower. Retrieving his bag from the jeep he checked on her once more, then found the bathroom.

Dressed only in jeans and a T-shirt, he walked through the house, smiling at the pictures on every wall of her growing up. He could envision her, feel her presence in every room, hear her soft, tinkling laugh throughout the house; imagine her as she grew from a bright-eyed little girl dressed in ruffles and lace to the beautiful young woman she was now.

He grinned, noting how few and precious were the pictures of her in a dress and feminine surroundings, compared to those of her in jeans surrounded by horses. He wondered if her mother realized what an incredible job she'd done in raising her to be the woman she was now. Somehow, he felt she knew, and he could feel her father's pride as he gazed at a photo of the two of them. Being in the house where she spent so many cherished years gave him a sense of peace. Exhaustion began numbing his mind. Going back into the living room, he picked her up and carried her into what could only be her bedroom. Curling up beside her, he slept with her wrapped securely in his arms.

* * * * *

Tamera awoke with her face nestled in Craig's shoulder, her arm possessively around his waist. She smiled, remembering his voice: *"Just call me Prince Charming."* He was. And he was hers. He'd all but come right out and confessed his love. Dreamily, she dragged her hand up over the firm muscles of his stomach. Her palm tickled; desire warmed her blood in slow degrees as she caressed the dark curls dusting the wide expanse of his broad chest. Just a touch, a caress, and she wanted to feel more, so much more. She shook her head, embarrassed at her own thoughts. Tucking her hand under her cheek, she snuggled closer to his warm body, surprised at the rush of warmth pulsing through her. Closing her eyes, she dozed off once more.

* * * * *

Craig awoke feeling chilly. As usual, he'd tossed his T-shirt sometime during the night. Tamera had turned away from him, taking her warmth and the afghan. The chill was quickly replaced with heat as he remembered her shy, hesitant caress. Drugged with the lazy bliss of dreams, it had taken every ounce of self-control he possessed to keep from responding to that touch.

Propping himself up on one elbow, he watched as she sighed softly and stretched. He smoothed the hair off her cheek and waited for her to wake up. She rolled over, curling into him as she opened her eyes.

"'Morning, Sweetheart," he drawled, kissing her lightly. A groan escaped him when her lips parted invitingly, and she teased his mouth with hers. He accepted the invitation without hesitation, his lips slanting across hers in a heated caress. He held her firmly against him as the kiss deepened.

Lost in passion, Tamera wrapped her arms around his neck, fitting her body to his. Her fingers got lost in the luxurious softness of his thick, black hair. A soft murmur of protest escaped her as he dragged his lips from hers.

"Man," he rasped. "Looks like I need another cold shower," he mumbled. Pushing away from her tempting presence, he headed for the bathroom.

Tamera blushed, snuggling deeper into the soft mattress. With a groan she buried her head as his voice assaulted her ears when he began singing—or rather, attempting to sing—in the shower. She was ready for him when he walked out of the bathroom toweling his hair vigorously.

"What did you do with the money your grandfather gave you all these years?" she asked.

"What money?"

"For singing lessons. It's obvious you didn't take them," she teased.

He grunted. "You saying I can't sing?"

"Nope," she assured with a grin. "Can't carry a tune in a five gallon bucket."

Picking up a brush off the dressing table, Craig regarded her in the mirror with glittering gray eyes. "I thought I sounded pretty good, myself."

"That's what you get for thinking when you're not used to it, you conceited jerk."

He grinned. "Not conceited, Sweetheart, convinced. There are plenty of women to back me up, too," he taunted.

Tamera forced down the angry retort.

Craig chuckled, arching an eyebrow at her.

"That's 'cause you've got them all brainwashed," she hissed, wondering why the thought of him with 'plenty of women' made her want to knock the smirk off his face.

He turned around. "Brainwashed? How?"

"Oh, come on, Craig," she muttered. "With looks like yours, a body like that, and..." she bit off her tirade, blushing furiously.

"Oh, please, do continue," he taunted with a smug grin. "I didn't think you'd noticed, Temper," he teased.

She ground her teeth and shook her head.

Sitting beside her on the bed, he nuzzled her cheek. "Think I could ever brainwash you?"

She sniffed daintily. "Never," she denied, shaking her head for emphasis.

"Liar," he accused his voice soft. "You're already well on your way. Admit it," he urged, nibbling at the corners of her mouth.

Wrapping her arms around his neck, she admitted it without saying a word.

After breakfast, Craig rented a tow bar in order to pull her car and trailer behind the jeep. Tamera spent the morning with her father's attorney making sure he would continue to keep an eye on the house until she decided what to do with her inheritance, which she found was quite large.

Though her father had always lavished her and her mother with outrageous gifts, they'd lived modestly. Her father had instilled in her a healthy virtue of working hard and making her own way, therefore, Tamera had no idea that she was a wealthy young woman. The means by which she inherited the wealth left much to be desired and she had absolutely no idea what to do with so much when she really needed so little to be happy. Her father had trusted his attorney for over thirty years so Tamera felt she could trust him for as long as it took to decide what to do with it all.

* * * * *

Craig took her to the cemetery on their way out and stood by her side as she wept softly over her parents' graves.

He ached for her, wishing there was some way to absorb the pain, to erase it from her beautiful eyes. He swallowed his most violent arguments when she told him she wanted to visit Tony's grave. She gazed up at him, her eyes wide and pleading, and, as usual, his resistance waned.

"Don't look at me like that," he growled. "You know I'm powerless against it," he complained.

"I have to, Craig."

He stroked her cheek and nodded. "Okay," he whispered. "I don't like it, but okay." Leaving her where she stood, he waited for her by the jeep.

Tamera walked over to where Tony was buried, her feelings mixed between anger and pain. She prayed silently for God to take away the pain and to show her what she needed to do in order to let go of the anger and bitterness that still bound her heart. As she knelt beside his headstone she could feel God's love and peace grow in her heart; the peace she once knew and had been searching for since her parents were killed. She knew what she had to do: *forgive.*

She had to forgive Tony despite the pain he'd caused her, despite what he'd taken from her, even though what he'd taken was more than physical. He'd taken a piece of her heart and robbed her of her faith, stripping her of her ability to trust and love.

She no longer felt whole.

Tamera knew the only thing that would enable her to feel whole again was the Grace of God, which would be supplied in abundance through her act of obedience.

Through forgiveness.

Taking a deep breath, she offered the words that would set her free. "I forgive you," she whispered, swiping at the tears that continued to pour from her heart. Though she meant it at that moment, Tamera knew there would be times when she'd resent Tony for what he'd done. Still, she had to let go.

"May God have mercy on your soul," she added and felt the burden lift.

Now I'm free to love and to feel again, she thought as the peace of God filled her heart to overflowing. Tamera knew God would give her the strength and courage to make the journey to complete healing, to total victory and, though it may be a rocky road, the journey had begun.

She rose and turned toward the jeep. The sight of Craig leaning against it, patiently waiting, filled her with peace, joy and love. Her smile was brilliant as she walked toward him. "I think I've been brainwashed," she whispered, slipping her arms around his waist.

Craig buried his hands in her thick blonde hair and his lips on hers, giving her a long, thorough kiss. The tender light of love shone deep in his eyes. Tamera felt the warmth and the strength of it.

"So have I," he murmured against her mouth. "By a beautiful, blue-eyed, seductive little witch." He kissed her again. "Let's go home."

Chapter Fourteen

The ride home, though long, was pleasant; a time of quiet, intimate conversation interspersed with long stretches of companionable silence. They stopped regularly to stretch their legs and let Temper stretch his. Craig laughed when Temper balked at getting back in the trailer on one of their stops.

"Poor thing, he's never going to load easily again."

"He's just showing a little typical male stubbornness," Tamera teased, babying the big horse until he reluctantly got back in the trailer. "You want to let me drive a while?"

"Nah, I'm okay."

She sidled up to him. "Don't be a macho man. You need your rest, too," she chided, sliding behind the wheel.

Craig rolled his eyes, closed her door and got in the passenger seat. He woke up three hours closer to home.

"How ya doin', Sweetheart?"

"I'm fine," she smiled over at him. "Have a good nap?"

He grunted. "As well as can be expected in this cramped area."

"That's what you get for having such long legs," she teased with a grin, fighting the urge to reach over and massage his thigh.

As though reading her thoughts, Craig's body tensed, waiting. A frustrated sigh escaped him when she visibly clenched her fist and kept her hand to herself.

She shot him a tender look and smile. "I can't wait to get home," she confessed with a sigh. "The first thing I'm going to do is take a long, hot bath and sleep for a week."

"The first thing you're going to do is get that cast checked. Then you can sleep for a week. And I just might join you." His voice softened with insinuation. Unable to resist, he leaned over, rubbed her thigh and teased her ear with his lips. "No comments?"

"You're welcome to join me. As long as you sleep in your own bed."

"Then I wouldn't be joining you," he argued.

Desire curled through her in hot flames. She moaned. "That's right. You won't be joining me literally, only in sleep. Now quit," she ordered breathlessly, pushing his hand away.

"Why?" he queried, continuing his torturous teasing.

"Because you're going to make me wreck this jeep and hurt my horse, and then I'll have to kill you," she insisted between clenched teeth. Soft, encouraging sighs belied her words.

"Pull over," he ordered. "Pull over and let me drive or I'll never be able to keep my hands off you," he admitted in an agonized voice.

Tamera pulled in at the next truck stop. They took advantage of the rest rooms and coffee and gave Temper another break. It was their last stop.

Craig took over the driving and pulled into the ranch driveway nearly twenty hours after they left Mississippi. *Home.* The word never meant so much or sounded so good as it did just then.

Leaning over, he woke Tamera with a kiss. "We're home," he whispered, a tender light in his eyes.

Excitement pushed past the sleep in her eyes. He smiled. "Why don't you go on in? I'll tend to Temper. We can unhitch and unload your car later."

Her smile was brilliant, her eyes shone as she scrambled from the jeep. "Tamera," he called as she reached the porch. "Give him a hug for me, too." Her lip trembled as she nodded and went in.

Knocking softly on his door, Tamera entered Gramps' room. "Good morning, sleepyhead," she greeted with a tender smile while opening the blinds.

"You're back," he whispered, holding a hand out to her.

Relief flickered in the familiar gray gaze, and Tamera could have kicked herself for the worry she'd caused. "Yes, I'm back," she said. Placing her hand in his, she leaned down for a much-needed hug. "Craig threatened to drag me back kicking and screaming if I didn't come peacefully," she teased as he walked into the room.

"Thank you, boy," Gramps told Craig, welcoming his hug.

He chuckled. "Anytime, Gramps. I'd go to the ends of the earth to make you happy. If having this ill-tempered brat around works, well," he shrugged, "so be it," he teased, giving Tamera a tender look. "I'm going to call Scott and see if we can get you in to see about that cast."

"It's okay, Craig," she argued. "It's not bothering me at all, and it's due to come off soon anyway."

"It's cracked." He traced the fissure. "I'd feel better if we get it checked out. Even if I have to drag you in kicking and screaming," he warned.

She rolled her eyes. "I know you tried real hard, Gramps, and you did your best, but this is the most stubborn, hard-headed, arrogant jerk cowboy I've ever met."

Though he could see the glint of laughter in her eyes, Gramps sighed. "Okay, you two, I know you're teasing but someone always ends up angry."

Tamera rubbed her cheek against his hand. "Don't worry Gramps; nothing can make me angry today."

"Me neither," Craig admitted, stroking her hair.

Tamera kissed Gramps' cheek and went to help Maria with breakfast.

"She looks good," Gramps remarked after she'd closed the door behind her.

Craig nodded. "I think she'll be okay."

"Did you tell her you love her?"

He grinned. "Yeah, kinda."

Gramps snorted. "Kinda? How can you 'kinda' tell someone you love 'em? You either told her or you didn't."

Craig chuckled. "She knows that I care a great deal, and that something is definitely happening between us."

Gramps rolled his eyes. "Things were a lot simpler in your grandmother's and my day, when people were just plain honest and open with each other."

"I'm sure they were," Craig remarked, helping him to get out of bed and into some clothes. "I just don't want her to feel pressured right now, or afraid. She's been hurt badly by someone she thought she loved. I want her to be sure it won't happen again, and I want her to feel confident in herself and in her feelings about me."

"I guess you're right," Gramps agreed. "She's going to need your patience more than anything right now, Craig. It won't be easy loving her the way you do. You're going to have to draw on your self-control now more than ever. The Lord will help you."

"I know," Craig admitted with a weary sigh. "I think He already has and is. In fact, I know it. I could have killed that man when he hit her." His eyes narrowed at the memory. "It's a miracle I have any self-control left, as much as I've been drawing on it," he muttered.

Gramps chuckled. "Like God's mercy, it's renewed and strengthened every day."

"That's encouraging. We'll be fine Gramps, I'm sure of it," he reassured his grandfather as they went in for breakfast.

Later, Scott met them in the emergency room. "Someone want to tell me what's going on?" he asked, examining the crack in Tamera's cast, noting the signs of fatigue in her face and the slight bruise on her cheek. His brown eyes glared into Craig's tired gray ones.

Seeing the questions, Craig arched an eyebrow at him. "You know me better than that, Scott," he growled.

Scott sighed, raking his fingers through his hair. "You're right. I'm sorry. Been a rough one already today," he said by way of explanation, then turned to a nurse.

"Let's get this cast off and get an x-ray of that arm," he ordered.

"You want to tell me how she got that bruise?" he asked, leading Craig into a private office. What Craig told him made his blood run cold.

Tamera waited quietly while Scott examined the x-ray. She could feel the tension in him and knew Craig had told him what happened.

"I don't see any signs of it being re-broken."

"I told Craig it would be okay. But you know how stubborn he is."

Scott smiled. "Overprotective," he countered.

"Oh, is that what it is?" she queried.

He chuckled, noting the soft light in her eyes. "Knowing Craig, it's hard to tell. He told me what happened," he ventured, "I want you to know, if you ever need or want to talk, I'm here. Or I can refer you to someone else if you prefer."

"You mean counseling?"

He shrugged. "You've been through a very traumatic time, Tamera. There's no shame in talking to someone who can help you deal with it, if you need to, but there is a thing called patient-doctor confidentiality. Anything you tell me will not go further than this room."

"Even with your best friend?"

He nodded his assurance. "Even with my best friend."

"Thanks, I'll remember that," she promised in a soft voice, her cheeks flushed with embarrassment. "Now, what about this arm?"

He looked at the x-ray again and fought the urge to take her in his arms. As a friend, he wanted to comfort, as a doctor he couldn't cross the lines drawn by his profession. He shrugged mentally, leaving the comforting to Craig.

"I think we'll put on another cast just to be sure. Sometimes a hairline fracture doesn't show very well on x-rays."

She groaned. "How long?"

"Two additional weeks."

"Can we do it later? If I promise to just go home and take a long, hot bath and go to bed?"

He laughed. "I'd rather do it now while you're here. You can never tell what might happen between here and home."

Tamera sighed wearily and submitted herself to his tender ministrations.

* * * * *

Maria and Tamera were sitting in the den visiting with Gramps when Craig got in. He paused outside the door, listening. He wasn't interested in what they were saying, just in the laughter coming from the room. The sounds of joy filled him with a warmth and wholeness he'd never experienced. Love, peace, and joy were mild words to express the way he felt, but the best he could come up with.

They'd been back nearly two weeks, and he hadn't ventured far from Tamera's side. The first couple of days he stayed home, watching as she slipped quickly into her normal routine. As the days passed, he too got back into the swing of working his ranch. The tenderness she'd gotten a glimpse of was now a permanent part of his demeanor. Only once did he kiss her in a way that threatened to overwhelm.

He'd been out working cattle and ended up staying all night. When he got home, he swung her up into his arms, his lips covering hers in a hungry kiss. "Boy, I missed you," he admitted huskily, kissed her again then released her lips with a ragged sigh. "Guess I shouldn't be holding you like this."

Her smile was tender, as was the light in her eyes. "Why not?"

He took a deep, inhaling breath. "Whew!" He shook his head, grinned. "Because I need a shower and a shave."

She giggled, rubbing her soft cheek against his hair-roughened one. "Yeah, you do," she teased.

He gazed into her shining eyes. "Then can I hold you like this?" he asked, his voice soft and tender.

She locked her fingers behind his neck and her gaze with his. "Nope. You had your chance, and you took it. No more. Not today, anyway," she conspired in a soft whisper, leaning her forehead against his.

He chuckled, kissed her again, and put her down. "Yes ma'am," he complied. "You probably need a shower now, too."

Since then he'd remained gentle, his kisses tender, his caresses teasing.

Tamera's smile was welcoming when he joined her, Maria and Gramps. She tilted her head up to receive his kiss as his hand caressed the back of her head.

"How was your day?" Gramps asked.

"Good," Craig answered, walking to the window. "Everything's in order around here. I'll be leaving for San Antonio in about an hour."

Maria got up to pack him some food.

Gramps smiled to himself at the look of disappointment on Tamera's face. "Why don't you take Tamera with you? She's never been to San Antonio. Have you, dear?"

She shook her head. "No. What are you going there for?"

"A stock show and auction." Her face brightened with excitement.

"Really? Can I go?" she asked.

Craig shrugged, knowing that he could deny her nothing when she looked at him like that. Just a smile, that particular smile and that look, those eyes, wide, full of hope and pleading, ripped his composure to shreds. She knew it, too, though he doubted she had to force the expression. It seemed to come naturally. Or from years of practicing on her father, he mused silently, thinking he would be made of tougher stock if he had a daughter.

"You really want to go?" he asked, dragging his thoughts back to the situation at hand.

She nodded.

"It'll cost you," he warned, his voice husky, teasing. She blushed, a wary look crossing her face.

"What?" she asked.

"A kiss. Come here," he opened his arms to her.

Tamera's blush deepened as Gramps chuckled. She smiled over at him. "Pretty bad, wouldn't you say, Gramps, having to bribe me for a kiss? I figured he'd say I could go as long as I behaved like a lady or something." An idea came to her. She winked at Gramps. "Make a deal with you," she told Craig.

"You promise that I can go and I'll show you how movie stars kiss."

It sounded innocent enough, but Craig had the feeling he'd get caught in this one.

"Deal?" she asked, walking toward him.

He nodded as she slid her hands over his chest. Her arms caressed his shoulders as they wound around his neck. Slowly, teasingly, she pulled his head down. "Cut," she said in a stage whisper, his lips a breath away from hers. She pushed out of his embrace, laughing.

Gramps roared. "She gotcha there," he choked.

Craig grinned, promised to get her back and told her to go pack. Before she could walk away he pulled her firmly against his chest, his lips covering hers in a thorough kiss. When she began trembling in his arms, he released her. "That's how movie stars kiss," he assured, chuckling at the blush that rushed to fill her cheeks.

He sighed heavily as she bounded up the stairs. "Why did you suggest that I take her with me? How on earth am I going to keep my hands off her fifty miles from this house and alone in a hotel?"

Gramps laughed. "By getting separate rooms."

Craig grunted. "Fifty thousand acres and it's hard. Difficult," he amended quickly, flushing at Gramps' chuckle. "Unbearably difficult. What on earth makes you think separate rooms will make any difference?"

Gramps laughed again, unconcerned at his predicament. "Maybe it's time you actually did something about the situation. Like propose," he added at Craig's raised eyebrows. He retrieved something from the desk and handed it to Craig. His smile was tender when Craig's surprised gaze met his.

"These were Grams'?" he asked, indicating the solitaire diamond engagement ring and matching wedding band in an antique gold setting. Gramps nodded. "Why haven't I seen them before now?"

"None of the women you've been involved with before now were deserving of them. I wanted to give them to your mother, but you know how your father was."

Craig laughed softly. "And Tamera is deserving?" He shook his head in mock disbelief. "She's hard headed, temperamental, sassy-mouthed..." he trailed off at his grandfather's quick shout of laughter. "And sexy as sin," he admitted with a sheepish grin.

Gramps chuckled, "Oh, yes, she's deserving all right. If I were in your shoes, I'd have begun courting her the day we met. If that didn't work, I would've crawled into bed with her then insisted that she marry me. But like I've said, things were much simpler in my day."

Craig shook his head. "Right, like any of that would work with her," he drawled. "And you! I'm shocked you would even suggest such a thing, being a Christian and all; especially since you got angry with me when you thought I'd done just that," he teased, slipping the rings in his pocket.

Gramps chuckled. "I haven't always been a strong Christian, Craig. Just goes to show the power of God's grace," he added, as Tamera came down the stairs carrying a suitcase and an overnight bag.

"You didn't say how long we'd be gone," she remarked.

"About a week," Craig said.

"What about this darned cast?"

He laughed. "We'll get it removed over there."

"What about Temper?"

"Temper will be fine. He'll let Shorty feed him and let him out. Jimmy will be coming after school. Temper's gotten used to Jimmy, so he can groom him *and* take care of the foals," he assured before she could ask. "My word, you'd think they were your babies," he teased, laughing when she made a face at him.

"How are we getting there?"

He frowned. "I was going in the jeep."

"We could take my car," she offered and laughed at his skeptical look. "Don't worry. There's plenty of room for those long legs of yours."

"Works for me," he agreed, taking her bags out and transferring his to the trunk of her car. He came through the door with a frown creasing his brow. "Can I ask you something without sounding like a dumb, hick cowboy?"

She eyed him. "Oh, I would never consider you a hick cowboy," she said, her voice laced with innocence.

He grinned. "I caught that."

She giggled. "See, you're not dumb, either."

"Do you want to go with me, or not?"

"Of course."

"Then answer the question."

"You never asked it." Tamera tried not to smile as she waited expectantly for the question she knew was coming.

"How on earth do you get that low-slung sports car to pull a horse trailer?"

"And I thought I'd found the one person who could figure that out," she teased.

He shook his head and grinned. "I'm a rancher, not a mechanic."

Tamera winked at Gramps. "But I thought cowboys knew everything," she purred, her voice laden with sweet sarcasm.

Craig couldn't help but chuckle. "Brat."

She laughed. "I get asked that question all the time. Believe me; I'm used to the wide eyes and gaping mouths whenever I pull it. The body has been totally reinforced. Spacers lift the back end, and custom-made sway bars take most of the weight off the car. Daddy had the trailer made out of lightweight metal and reinforced enough to carry its load."

"Never heard of it, but I can see it works," Craig admitted.

Less than an hour later they were on their way. Craig accepted the keys, curious to see how the car handled. He'd always wanted a Corvette but never indulged in getting one. A jeep was more practical and he'd drive it until it gave out. This car suited her, he thought, sleek and sexy, yet strong and beautiful.

Reaching over, he turned on the radio, frowning at the static when her C. B. radio came on, too. "I didn't realize you had one of these."

She smiled. "Daddy insisted I get one since I was on the road so much between college and work. He had a base at the house. You don't have one?"

He shook his head. "I didn't think Rocky had enough horse power to keep it running," he teased, chuckling at her snort of laughter.

"I thought everyone had one these days," she remarked as a man's voice broke into their conversation.

"Hey Corvette, got your ears on?"

She eyed Craig. "You gonna answer him?"

He shook his head as she reached for the mike. "You got us, go," she spoke into it.

"Hey, little Sweetheart! What's your handle? Where you headin'?"

"Alamo City," she replied giving the truckers' term for San Antonio. "Who we got?"

"You got Peterbuilt, Darlin'," he cooed. "What's your handle, little doll?"

Craig's eyes narrowed at the intimate tone and fought the urge to jerk the thing out of the dash.

She smiled over at him and keyed the mike. "Well, Peterbuilt, my sidekick here doesn't have a handle. Help me give him one?"

Told ever so subtly that she wasn't alone, Peterbuilt sighed. "What's he like?" he asked in a neutral voice.

Craig chuckled at the change of tone.

Tamera laughed. "A typical, arrogant, jerk cowboy," she answered sweetly.

"Thanks, Temper." Craig scowled. "I appreciate the fact that the whole country will soon know I'm an arrogant jerk."

Peterbuilt roared. "Looks like he's got a built-in handle then. Now, Sweetheart, you gonna tell us who you are?"

She laughed. "You got Temper Tantrum," she replied.

"Well I'll be. How'd a sweet soundin' little thing like you ever get a handle like that? How about it, Jerk Cowboy, she got a temper?"

Craig saw the opportunity to get back at her and eagerly took advantage of it. Taking the mike from her, he keyed it. "Sayin' she's a hot one is puttin' it mildly," he remarked, sending Peterbuilt into guffaws of laughter.

Tamera jerked the mike from him, a hot flush on her cheeks. "Jerk," she spat, not missing the double meaning to his words and knowing Peterbuilt hadn't missed it either.

Nor had anyone else who was listening.

Keying the mike, she signed off the radio. "Gonna listen to the good time radio now. Have a safe trip. Temper Tantrum said it; we're gone. Bye, bye."

Peterbuilt passed them with a blow of his horn and a wave.

Craig laughed at her, enjoying the flashing blue gaze, which quickly gave way to excitement. Pulling her toward him for a quick kiss, he answered her endless questions about where they were going, why they were going, and what they'd do while they were there.

Chapter Fifteen

"Why do men have to be so crude?" Tamera turned angry, accusing eyes to glare at Craig.

They'd been to the stock show early that morning and to get her cast removed afterward. Missing lunch, they stopped around two o'clock for a hamburger. That's when all hell broke loose. A man who'd obviously been drinking made lewd eyes and crude comments about her anatomy, particularly the part of her encased in "painted on jeans," infuriating Tamera.

Craig agreed to take her somewhere else, but excused himself to go to the restroom first. On the way there, he very politely asked the man to watch his mouth. His request went unheeded. The confrontation was inevitable when the man approached Tamera. Craig managed to drag her out of the restaurant before she lost complete control of her temper and came completely unglued on the guy. Now they were back in her room, and she was still fuming.

He bit back a smile, attempting to calm her. "Not all men are like that, Temper. I've never treated you like that."

Her look of complete incredulity had him backing up. "Okay, okay. But not since we first met," he defended himself and his species. "No one that I know has, either. Not that I'm aware of, anyway. Calm down, no harm was done."

She snorted. "Huh! And as for you! Where I come from a gentleman would have defended a lady! But I guess, as a man, you saw the humor in the situation," she snarled.

Unable to resist, he chuckled. "Not really. Aw, c'mon, Temper," he coaxed when she turned away in an angry whirl. "Normally I would have defended you, Sweetheart, but you were doing a pretty good job of that yourself. Besides, the guy was drunk. It wouldn't have made for a very fair fight."

Tamera burned. "Guess I'll just have to get all fat and ugly, then I won't have to put up with all this bull!" Craig's soft laugh grated on her nerves. "What?" she asked, nearly stomping her foot in agitation.

"Look at you," he whispered, turning her to face the mirror. "You could never be ugly."

His soft, husky voice made her tremble. She blew out her cheeks, made a face, and laughed. "Maybe not" she conceded. "But the next time someone comes at me like that, I'm going to slap his face," she threatened.

He chuckled throatily. "Yeah, and get yourself and probably me thrown in jail or killed," he muttered. "It's not fair for you to be so beautiful," he groaned, desire streaking through him like lightning. "Temper," he moaned turning her to face him. His lips covered hers in a hungry caress.

Craig wrestled with temptation, knowing he should walk away from her while he still could. He struggled with his new convictions, wavering between what was proper and what was basic. He knew it wasn't fair. It was wrong. He was taking advantage of her agitated state, but he couldn't help it. The past three days in San Antonio had put an unbearable strain on his self-control.

Gramps was wrong. Separate rooms made absolutely no difference whatsoever.

Today had been the worst. Her knowledge of horseflesh had astounded him. Her excitement set fire to his blood. The passionate display of anger only inflamed the desire that had been simmering in him since the day they met. He struggled. He lost. He'd wanted her forever and denied himself too long. His hands caressed her back in a soothing manner as she relaxed in his arms, caught up in the kiss. A soft, encouraging moan escaped as she pressed her soft body into his passion-hardened one.

"I want you, Temper," he groaned. "I need you."

"Craig," she whimpered.

"What, Love?"

"Please," she begged. "I can't think straight."

"Don't think. Just feel. I want you, Temper. What do you want?"

"I...." she moaned again, clinging weakly to his frame as he placed feathery kisses over her cheeks and throat.

"Do you want me?" he asked in a husky whisper. "Do you want me to make love to you?"

"No," Tamera mumbled, trying desperately to regain some measure of control over her weakening will. He didn't give an inch, but continued to batter away at it with soft words, tender kisses, gentle caresses.

"You say 'no', but your body says 'yes'. Every ounce of you is screaming for me to take you over there and make love to you. Say it, Temper. Say, 'yes'. That's all I need to hear. Do you want me?"

"Yes," she surrendered, wrapping her arms around him.

"Yes," he agreed with an answering groan. Picking her up, he carried her to the bed. "I'll make you mine this time, my beautiful Temper Tantrum," he assured, his voice ringing with triumph.

Tamera gave up all hope of reasonable thinking when he laid her on the bed, his lips clinging to hers in a fiery kiss. There was no fear, no apprehension. Nothing existed but this burning need to love and be loved by him.

Craig's head swam with the intensity of desire roaring through him. Taking a deep breath, he commanded control over his raging senses and ignored the voice within that was trying desperately to get his attention. His kisses were tender as his mouth traveled from her lips to her ear and down her throat to caress the skin showing through her open collar, leaving trails of hot, scorching kisses over her silky flesh. Mumbling incoherently, soft words of love and desire, Craig fumbled in his haste, determined to be gentle despite the strength of his need. He felt her stiffen, heard her soft whimper as fear snaked in, robbing him of her full surrender.

"No," she struggled in his arms. "Please, stop."

He moved quickly, covering her lips with his. His desire waned as he pulled her firmly in his arms, stopped her struggles with a gentle hand and held her tightly against his chest. "Please," he begged in an agonized voice. "Please don't be afraid of me. I won't hurt you."

Tamera knew he was too much the gentleman to use force. "I know," she choked as a huge tear rolled down her cheek. "I can't help it. I don't want to be afraid of you," she cried, wrapping her arms around his neck. Her lips clung to his in a desperate kiss.

A frustrated groan escaped him, but Craig checked his desire. He held her a long time, talking softly, his hands moving over her in a soothing caress.

"I'm sorry," she cried. "I'm afraid I'll never be able to enjoy a normal life with a man. And I want to. I want to with you," she wailed.

"It's okay," he soothed. "Shh, Temper, it's okay. Give yourself a break, it's only been a few months and you've been through so much. I'll wait. I love you." She gazed up at him, surprise evident in her electric blue eyes.

"Really?"

He smiled. "You have to ask?"

"You never said it before," she argued. "I mean, you insinuated it, but you never really said it."

"I didn't want to scare you away and I wanted you to be confident that it wasn't just desire. And, to be honest, I wanted to be sure of that myself. Although," he smiled tenderly, "I can promise you it's plenty of that." Wariness clouded her shining blue gaze.

"How can you be positive it's really love?"

"Because I've never felt about anybody the way I feel about you."

"But you were engaged before," she hedged.

Craig knew she wanted to believe, to trust.

He grinned, understanding her reluctance. Not liking it, but understanding. "Yes, I was engaged before. But I didn't feel this way about her."

"Then why were you engaged?"

He chuckled remembering his naive hopes about his and Stephanie's marriage. "Gramps wants to hold his great-grandchildren, and Maria's always fussing about the house needing babies in it. We'd dated off and on for a long time. I thought marriage would appeal to her. I was wrong. We were engaged, but she didn't like the idea of an old-fashioned marriage." He shrugged, knowing in his heart that would be the only kind of marriage for Tamera.

"What other kind is there?" she asked innocently, confirming what his heart had told him.

"An open one. You know, the kind where you don't have to forsake all others," he explained at her confused look. "Stephanie doesn't consider herself a one-man woman."

"Oh," she blushed, grasping his meaning. "When did you realize what you feel for me is love and not just desire? And don't give me the bull about the moment I threw water in your face. You didn't like me at all, then."

Craig laughed. "Oh, but I did, Sweetheart. I loved your spirit, though I never would have admitted it." He considered her question thoughtfully. He'd wanted her from the beginning, but it went deeper than that.

Soul deep.

He stroked her cheek and looked into the brilliant sapphire gaze he'd grown to love so much. "When I thought I'd lost you," he confessed in a husky whisper, his lips covering hers in a tender caress. "Both times."

"I love you, too," she admitted when he released her lips after another breathtaking kiss.

Craig chuckled. "You sure? I think you just lust after my body."

She blushed again, but refrained from comment. Wrapping her arms around his neck, she covered his lips in a thorough kiss.

"That, too," she admitted, kissing him again. "I'm hungry," she informed him with a pout.

"Me, too," he groaned capturing her lips again.

"For food," she corrected when he released her lips.

"Food? How can you think of food at a time like this?" he asked, rolling his eyes.

Her stomach growled as if answering his question. She giggled at the look of surprise on his face. "We never did eat," she countered. "And it's been a long time since breakfast."

"Okay," he relented. "I get the message." Rolling over, he pulled her gently atop his long frame. Wrapping his arms around her, he cuddled her to his chest. "I love you," he whispered, reluctant to release her. Her smile was brilliant, her eyes tender.

"I love you, too," she replied, just as reluctant to move. "We could call room service," she offered.

He shook his head. "If I don't get you out of here, I may not be able to stop myself again."

"Oh, please," she muttered rolling her eyes expressively. "You just said you would wait," she teased. Her voice softened. "Thank you for being so gentle and understanding."

Craig held her close, loving the feel of her body against his, yet aching with desire from holding her so intimately. His kiss was gentle, his smile tender, his voice soft.

"You're welcome." He rolled onto his side, keeping her firmly in his arms. "I could hold you like this forever."

"We'd never get any work done and I'd never get to eat," she teased her eyes bright and shining. "Other than that, I could let you."

Craig consulted his watch. "How hungry are you?"

"Famished."

"To the point of being weak?"

"Yes," she admitted. Her voice lowered to a husky purr. "But I don't think it's only from lack of food."

He grinned arching an eyebrow. "Keep talking like that and we won't leave this bed," he warned.

"Why?" she asked.

"Why do I want to know, or why won't we leave the bed?"

She shook her head. "Why do you want to know how hungry I am?" she inquired in a voice reserved for the very young, or very dense.

He laughed at her tone. "Well, it's almost five now. Why don't we get showered and dressed and go out for the evening. That is, if you think you can wait to eat," he teased. "Don't want you passing out on me."

She grinned. "I can wait. Let me up."

"Do I have to?"

"Craig, if you don't let me up so we can get ready and go eat, I'm going to start gnawing on the nearest thing to my mouth. That happens to be you," she threatened.

"That could be interesting," he observed wryly.

"Let me go, you jerk," she muttered, struggling in his grasp. "You twist everything I say into some kind of sexual innuendo."

He emitted a sound, something between a groan and a chuckle. "That's because you're so beautiful when you're flustered. And so easily riled," he taunted, and with one slight shift of his body stopped her attempt to escape and kissed her before releasing her.

Fifteen minutes later, he knocked on the door adjoining her room to his and entered at her command. She was sitting at the dressing table brushing her hair. "Wear it down tonight," he requested, running his hand down the length of it.

She smiled at the tender light in his eyes. "Okay. I was going to put on a little makeup before we go. It'll just take a minute."

"You don't need makeup. You have a natural kind of beauty that women work for hours trying to create."

She flushed at the compliment. "How do you know so much about what women do?"

"Because I used to watch my mother. It took her hours to get ready to go anywhere. She tried everything she could think of to look good and get a little attention from my father."

"Tell me about your parents," she encouraged. "I never hear stories about them. Every time we talk, all you ever talk about is Gramps." Tamera saw his frown and the quick flash of pain in his eyes before he shrugged. "Only if you want to," she amended.

He smiled, ran his hand down her hair again. "No secrets, remember? There's not much to tell. My father was plain no-good, a throwback from our ancestors, I guess."

"What were they, pirates?" she inquired sweetly, imagining him in black leather britches, white billowing shirt, a red sash around his waist, wielding a sword and wearing a patch.

He chuckled as though reading her thoughts. "Probably more like bandits and thieves. Anyway, despite Gramps' best efforts, my father was wild, a maverick. The only reason he married my mother was because she was pregnant, and he never let her forget it. He drank, gambled, and womanized relentlessly. There was no end to his selfishness."

She watched his eyes darken as he continued.

"My mother was a weak, clinging woman. That's why I love your strength. Among other things," he mused. "You would never put up with the things she did."

"No way; I'd geld the guy who cheated on me."

He chuckled. "Any man would be a fool to cheat on you, but I'll remember that should I ever be tempted. Anyway," he continued. "She was only sixteen when they got married. She was so tiny, so fragile. I'd watch her vying for his attention, then hold her while she cried over the way he treated her. I swear, there were times when I could have killed him for hurting her so much."

His face hardened. Tamera's eyes filled with tears, aching for the childhood he had missed and grateful for the one she'd had.

"Don't say anymore, she whispered, reaching up to stroke his cheek.

His eyes bored into hers. "I want to," he whispered, squatting down beside her. He'd never felt the desire to share his dark past with anyone else, to rid himself of the bitterness and pain. He'd dealt with the rumors and gossip, but had never felt inclined to share the truth, as he knew it, with anyone. Only Scott, Gramps, and Maria knew how terribly hurt he'd been by it all. It was the ultimate sacrifice of trust in her and in God.

At her nod, he continued.

"I was fifteen when they died. It was hard at first, then relief overwhelmed the grief. Gramps was always there for me and for her. I think her death hurt him more than my father's. Oh, he loved him, but he never understood him. The harder he tried, the wilder my father got."

"You never had any brothers or sisters?"

"Not that I'm aware of. Not legitimate anyway. I'm sure there are plenty out there, though. My mother had a miscarriage a few months before they died. I think it's what pushed her over the edge."

"Scott?"

He shrugged. "His mother said no and his father stood by her. Guess we'll never really know. I asked Gramps once, when I was eight or nine, how it was possible that we looked so much alike.

"What did he say?"

"He said it was one of God's great mysteries. Then, after my parents died, I asked him again. He never really answered, just asked me if it would make a difference in the way I felt about Scott. When I said it wouldn't, he said that sometimes the truth is not always what looks obvious." He shrugged again. "It didn't matter to us either way, Scott and I have been best friends since the first grade."

"How did your parents die?"

"It's recorded as a hunting tragedy. My mother loved to hunt. It's the one thing that she was really good at, and about the only thing he considered good about her. They'd gone out for a weeklong trip. When they didn't return, Gramps sent a search party. They were both dead. The police thought it was a murder-suicide, but at Gramps' request didn't pursue it. There was enough scandal surrounding my father anyway so why add to it? It was written up as an accident. Guess that's another thing we'll never really know the truth about."

"You have no other family? On your mother's side?"

He shook his head. "A couple of uncles. They started a big bunch of trouble after she died, trying to get me and her share of the ranch. At first Gramps put it off as grief. Then he realized they were just after the money. What they didn't know was that there wasn't much of that, either. It took a lot of years and hard work to pull the ranch back up out of the ruin my father left it in. Anyway, Gramps ran them off with a shotgun. We've never heard anything more from them.

"It's really strange how many relatives you find out about when you start accumulating wealth. They never wanted anything to do with my mother. She was thrown out and disowned when she got pregnant, but when we started pulling things together, getting ahead, showing a profit, they came out of the woodwork."

"My, God!" she exclaimed. "I'm sorry you had to go through that," she whispered wrapping her arms around his neck and leaning her forehead against his.

He pulled her in his arms feeling like a huge weight had lifted off his shoulders. "I'm all right. I used to think about my mother a lot. I always wished I could have protected her somehow." He shrugged. "Gramps spent a lot of years talking to me, teaching me about life, helping me through the tough times. It made an old man out of him before his time."

"It's made you as strong as you are too."

"Maybe. It's strange how God uses tragedy. I learned a lot from the situation. Good and bad. Through His grace and Gramps' love, I've retained the good, and I know how to avoid the bad. I had to grow up fast. And hard. I guess that's why I have this attitude," he grinned. "What everyone calls arrogance. I swore early on that no one would do to me what he did to her. And what her family tried to do. I also swore I'd never treat another human being the way my father treated my mother. I know I'm a hard case most of the time, but sometimes you have to be in order not to get taken advantage of. I always try to be fair, though. Tough, but fair."

She smiled. "Well, I love you, you arrogant-jerk cowboy. All of you," she admitted, her lips tracing his in a gentle caress.

"How do you know?" he queried.

A teasing light glistened in his eyes, like dewdrops dancing on sheet metal. Tamera smiled tenderly. "Because I've never felt this way about anyone," she assured him, using the same words he'd used to assure her.

"Never?"

There was no doubting what he really wanted to know. Tamera wrapped her arms tighter around his neck and locked her gaze with his. Electricity shivered between them.

"Never," she said her voice tremulous. "The way I felt about Tony was child's play compared to how I feel about you."

No other words could have meant more.

Chapter Sixteen

After a quiet dinner, Craig took Tamera to Cowboy's for some country music and two stepping. They laughed and danced until well after midnight. The band took a break and someone played a Johnnie Rivers song on the jukebox, a song about slow dancing with your girl. Craig pulled her firmly in his arms, molding her soft body to his, unnerved at how well she fit and how good she felt against him. He pulled her closer still as the song played until she was dancing on her toes, her arms wrapped securely around his neck. He could feel her heart thudding against his. He kissed her tenderly, caressing her lips with his until their senses hummed like high-tension wires.

"Let's get out of here," he suggested his voice no more than a husky whisper. At her nod, he turned to lead her off the dance floor only to be interrupted by a very drunk woman.

"You dance so well, Craig, Darling," she slurred. "Dance with me."

"No thanks," he said, stepping away. Something about her seemed familiar, but for the life of him, he couldn't place her; not with his senses so full of the woman by his side.

Her eyes narrowed, "Oh, the little veterinarian," she hissed, getting a glimpse of Tamera behind him. "When you get through baby-sitting, come back and we'll make a night of it."

It took less than a minute to register the voice, to recognize the face beneath the bleached blonde hair. Tamera must have recognized her immediately. He felt her stiffen, heard her sharp intake of breath.

"I don't think so, Stephanie," he said, pulling Tamera firmly against him. Without so much as a backward look, he walked away.

Stephanie's screech of anger could be heard well above the noise of the crowd. "Bet you can't please him the way I do," she taunted at their departing backs.

Tamera jerked from Craig's grasp, turning with an angry growl.

He grabbed her, pulling her firmly against him. "Let's go, Temper. Now," he insisted softly. "Before there's trouble."

"You mean before I tear every poorly-bleached hair out of her head?" she muttered, clenching her fists in fury.

"Yeah, before that," he agreed.

His steely gaze danced with amusement she didn't understand or appreciate. Tamera glared at him for a moment. Jerking away, she turned, head held high, and walked out, leaving him to follow in her wake. The ride back to the hotel was in total, strained silence. When they got there, she walked straight to her room and slammed the door. Craig followed without the slightest hesitation. She turned on him in an angry huff. "Well, you're through baby-sitting. Why don't you go back?" she bit out, an icy edge to her voice.

He pulled her in his arms. "Your anger is justified, Temper, but jealousy doesn't become you," he chided gently.

"Who says I'm jealous?"Her voice was calm, cold.

Too much wine and too much excitement had need jolting his system, shocking in its intensity. Desire poured through him like hot, molten lava. Craig pulled her firmly against his body, wrapping his arms around her. His lips covered hers in a hungry gesture until she trembled, clinging weakly to his strong frame. "No one has to say you're jealous, it's written all over your pretty face," he assured with a husky chuckle, tightening his arms when she struggled in his embrace.

"You jerk. Curse your fool head, Craig Harris, for what you do to me."

"I love you," he whispered. "Only you. Forget it, Temper. She's not worth it," he insisted his voice soft, his lips capturing hers once more, his hands roaming over her in a gentle caress.

Anger and passion, pleasure and pain, desire; emotions raced through her so quickly, so fiercely that it was impossible to tell one from the other. Tamera felt the changes occur swiftly, forcefully, leaving her breathless, weak and hungry.

Power unleashed.

Wrapping her arms around his neck, she took as much as he gave, giving the same measure in return.

Lost in desire, a primitive moan escaped from somewhere deep within her, but she tensed when Craig picked her up and carried her to the bed. Principle warred with passion as his hands caressed her slowly, teasingly, until she relaxed in his arms once again. Burying his face in her hair, he struggled, praying for control. "God," he rasped, "I need help here."

He stroked her cheek; gazed hungrily into her soft sapphire eyes. He saw the need there, and the fear. "I know you're still afraid, Tamera, but I want you. I want to revel in your beauty. To touch you, taste you, to hear your sounds of pleasure, and feel you against me. I want to see the hunger and satisfaction in your eyes while I make love to you. Temper," he groaned. "I don't want you to be afraid of me, and I don't want you to regret what we'll share. Stop me now," he begged, "before there's no stopping."

Even through their clothes, Tamera could feel the power and strength of his need, the heat of his desire. Panic seized her but she fought it. She loved him. He loved her.

He was giving her a choice.

She eased her arms from around his neck, running her hands over the strong muscles of his back, then up the firm wall of his chest. "I love you, Craig," she whispered. "And I do trust you. Although I am still afraid."

She kissed him tenderly, stroked the tense muscle in his jaw, and considered her words carefully. "I don't believe in premarital sex. I've always been taught that purity is an honorable thing. The Bible confirms it. However you, my arrogant jerk cowboy, could be the exception to the rule."

Craig saw confusion warring with the other emotions in her eyes as she continued.

"I've always wanted to wait until I was married. I know that sounds crazy, especially after..." she hesitated, fighting what she felt for him, fighting fear, and fighting the need to feel normal, to feel healed and whole.

"I do love you, Craig, and I want you, but I still feel that way."

Her eyes begged his for understanding. He felt her trembling response as need battled, control strained. Craig nodded and eased himself away from her, waiting for the tension to pass and sanity to return. "It's not crazy. We'll wait," he promised, and held her a long time, leaving sometime deep in the night to sleep in his own bed.

* * * * *

Craig awoke in a state of agony from dreams more erotic than he'd ever imagined. *If this prolonged state of self-imposed misery doesn't end soon, I'll lose my mind,* he thought, dragging himself into the bathroom. *Or drown from too many cold showers. It's a wonder my blood hasn't turned to ice water.*

Getting a firm grip on his thoughts, he finished his shower, dressed, and called room service. Glancing at his watch he decided to let Tamera sleep until breakfast arrived. Picking up the phone again, he called home. While waiting for the call to go through, his mind wandered back over the events of the past evening.

Last night had been wild, to say the least. This morning he'd let Tamera sleep as late as he could. This would be their last day in San Antonio. The auction started around eleven and lasted sometimes until eleven at night. Tomorrow he'd promised to take her shopping as long as her little heart desired before they returned home.

A knock sounded at the door, signaling the arrival of room service. Taking the cart, he tipped the waiter and poured himself a cup of coffee. The food would stay warm for a while in its containers. Finding no newspaper, he picked up the Bible off the bedside table. Opening it to a page that had been earmarked, he read Galatians chapter five.

Verse sixteen leapt off the page and straight into his heart. *I say then, live by the Spirit and you will certainly not gratify the desires of the flesh... Now the works of the flesh are obvious: immorality, impurity, licentiousness...But the fruit of the Spirit is love, joy, peace, patience, generosity, faithfulness, gentleness and self-control.*

The implication couldn't have been clearer than the Voice he'd heard deep in his soul the night of Tamera's accident. He had been so wrong! Though she'd been violated, Tamera was a virgin at heart. She'd remained pure for reasons far deeper than any he ever imagined understanding before. Now he knew why.   Finally, he understood. Her decision to wait until she was married was more than just moral upbringing; it was a command of God.

A command of God that he'd ignored most of his life.

Being experienced in the ways of the flesh, it was up to him to maintain control when they were together and not tempt her into immorality. Remorse filled his soul.

"God," he prayed. "Forgive me. And help me to be a better man than I've been in the past. I love her, and I thank You for giving her to me. Help me to show her and You the respect you both deserve."

Once again, Craig felt the very real presence of the Lord surround and fill him to the deepest recesses of his soul. "Thank You," he whispered.

Not many minutes later, he heard water running in the adjoining bathroom. He smiled to himself, anticipating Tamera's surprise when she finished her bath.

* * * * *

Tamera tied her robe securely around her waist and shook her hair loose from its towel. She ran her brush through it until it cascaded down her back in a silken mass. A startled gasp escaped her lips and color rushed to her cheeks when she stepped out of the bathroom to find a breakfast cart in the room and Craig leaning casually against the door.

"Morning, Sweetheart," he drawled. "Hungry?" he asked, holding his hand out to her.

She nodded, placing hers in it.

"Me, too," he answered, kissing her fingertips. Unable to stop there, he kissed her mouth, his lips covering hers in a gentle caress. "Sit," he urged, pushing her gently on the bed. In a single, sweeping motion, he handed her a rose nestled in green paper.

"It's beautiful," she breathed, fingering its soft petals and inhaling the sweet scent.

"I'll get some water," he offered, picking up the empty vase off the tray. He watched through lowered lids as she reached for the ribbon around it. Seeing the ring tied securely to the knot, her eyes widened in surprise then lifted to meet his.

"Craig?"

"Will you marry me?" he asked, kneeling in front of her. Tears filled those beautiful blue eyes and streamed down her cheeks.

She nodded.

"Is that a 'yes'?"

His voice was soft, husky, teasing.

"Yes," Tamera said, throwing her arms around his neck.

"Thank God," he breathed. "I hope you don't like long engagements."

She shook her head, too choked up to speak.

"When? Today? Tomorrow? Next week?"

His insistence made her laugh. "As long as it takes to plan a wedding."

"What do you mean a wedding? I say we go to the nearest Justice of the Peace and do it now."

She shook her head. "Oh, no, Cowboy. You're not getting off that easy. I want a wedding. You know, the dress, the cake, the witnesses," she teased.

He chuckled. "I'll give you a week," he said, thinking it was a generous offer indeed after the agony he'd suffered to date.

"A week! How about a couple of months?"

"No way," he argued. "I'll die if I have to wait that much longer to make you mine."

"You're a big boy," she assured him.

"One month and not a day more," he insisted.

"Oh, all right!" she agreed, her eyes dancing merrily into his. "One month. I guess Maria and I can throw something together in that amount of time."

A hint of sadness clouded her face. "What?" he queried.

"I always wanted a beautiful, white gown with lots of satin and lace and pearls," she whispered, at that moment hating Tony for the fact that she was not pure.

Cupping her face in his hands, Craig stroked her cheeks with his thumbs. "Wear white, Love," he whispered. "You only get married once, and you'll always be my virgin bride," he assured her, his voice husky, his kiss tender.

"I love you," she replied, her voice tremulous. She fingered the ring. "When did you get this?"

He smiled, untying the knot and placing the ring on her finger. "It was my grandmother's. Gramps gave me the set before we left. If you don't like it, we can pick out something else."

Tamera shook her head. "Oh, no, it's beautiful! I'd be honored to wear them."

* * * * *

Tamera tossed her book aside with a bored sigh. They'd been home from San Antonio less than two weeks. The first few days had been filled with excitement and plans. Their engagement announcement had appeared immediately in the newspaper, causing a flurry of activity. Overwhelmed at the deluge of gifts, she spent several hours a day writing thank-you notes. Even that dwindled down, though, and she found herself with less and less to do. The invitations would be ready in a few days, tand until then she had nothing to do but wait.

Since the rodeo, her veterinarian skills were not needed much. Which was why they'd offered the job for the summer only. She still worked with Silver's foals, but that took a mere two hours out of her day. A couple of days she rode with Craig, but being an inexperienced wrangler, she wasn't much help. To top it all off, for the past three days it had done nothing but rain relentlessly, and she hated being cooped up.

The weather caused Gramps' arthritis to flare up, so he wasn't much company. Maria accepted her help in the house, but there usually wasn't enough work to occupy a whole day, much less three and it was so wet outside, she didn't dare try and go to town for fear of burying her car axle-deep in mud.

Going to her room, she managed to wile away an hour by gazing at the picture of her dress and sample invitations, and daydreaming of the wonderful life she and Craig would have. With a frustrated groan, she decided to workout and take a hot bath. That took another two hours. Still bored, but less frustrated, she picked up her book and continued reading until Craig came in, and then it was time for supper. They'd barely finished eating when Shorty came in to inform Craig that Temper had broken out of his stall and was with Silver, who was in heat.

With a frustrated sigh and a muttered curse, Craig left the table. This was all he needed. It had been an awful day out there, cows and calves stuck in the mud, fences down, rain and more rain, and now this! Tamera entered the barn as he took a whip off its hook. He heard her startled gasp.

"What are you going to do?" she asked, putting a restraining hand on his arm.

"Get that blasted horse away from my mare."

"Not with that whip, you're not!" The thought of Temper's beautiful, spotless, white coat streaked with blood made her tremble.

He shook her off. "Get out of the way, Tamera," he warned. "The last thing I want is my mare bred with that ill-tempered brute of yours!"

A low growl escaped her clenched teeth. "I'll have you know that ill- tempered brute is a hundred times more horse than any you have on this ranch. Maybe it's high time you upgrade your stock!" she hissed. "If you touch him with that whip, I'll use it on you!"

Craig snorted and stalked off, only to be told it was too late, the mating was accomplished. Stomping back into the barn, he threw the whip down with a curse. "Can't you control him?" he barked, his fists clenched in frustrated fury.

Tamera's blood boiled at his unwarranted and unfair attack on her. "What could I do?" she queried in a furious voice. "He just responded the way any normal male animal does."

Craig heard the emphasis she put on the words male and animal and grabbed her by the arms. "Is that so?" he queried in a soft, deadly voice. "I guess you're an expert at normal *animal* responses?" he hissed through clenched teeth, seconds before his lips covered hers in a bruising kiss.

She remained cool and passive in his arms until he released her lips. Tears smarted her eyes, but Tamera didn't dare lower her gaze from his. They glared at each other for a moment.

Craig let her go before he lost complete control. "Do something with that horse, before I wise up and shoot him," he ordered, thrusting her away.

He saw the rage in her eyes and easily caught her wrist before her palm connected with his cheek. "Oh, no, you don't. You've gotten away with more than any man would dare attempt. But no more, Tamera, never again. If you *ever* slap me again, I'll beat you," he warned. "You hear me?"

Jerking her arm from his grasp, Tamera turned in an angry whirl and stomped off, not bothering to dignify the question with an answer and went to get Temper, who was prancing and snorting, proudly showing off for his conquest. She led him back to his stall, tethered him up short, and began brushing him. The more she thought about what had happened, the madder she got. The madder she got, the rougher she was with the brush. When she neared his tender flanks, Temper stomped and snorted in undeniable threat. Undaunted, Tamera slapped him on the rump.

"Don't you dare threaten me, you big brute or I'm liable to shoot you myself."

She looked up as Shorty leaned against the stall door. "He didn't mean it, you know."

"Didn't he, Shorty?" she asked, arching an eyebrow at him.

"You know he didn't. He's had a rough few days with all this weather. He just temporarily lost control."

She snorted. "Well, I've had a rough few days with all this weather, too, but you don't see me treating him like that."

Shorty shook his head. "I don't understand you two. Why don't you just sleep with that boy, and get it over with," he suggested. "You're going to be married shortly, anyway." Her eyes shot sparks at him.

"What in heaven's name will that solve?"

He grinned with a wink. "It sure will ease most of his frustration. Yours too, I bet."

Tossing the brush aside she glared at him, hands on her hips. Tamera could tell he was teasing, but she wasn't laughing.

"See this, Shorty?" she asked, indicating the engagement ring on her finger. At his nod, she continued.

"Well, it's one ring. One ring does not make a marriage. He's not getting in these britches until the vows have been said and the rest of the rings are in their proper place," she assured, slapping her thigh for emphasis.

Shorty threw back his head with a laugh. "Good for you, Missy. It's high time young Mr. Harris realizes he can't control everything. Don't let him intimidate you and don't let him get by with treating you this way," he urged with a grin.

"I don't intend to," she assured.

* * * * *

Craig walked out of his bedroom as Tamera entered hers. He spoke her name softly, wondering if she didn't hear or was ignoring him when she closed the door without so much as a glance in his direction. He heard the shower start and decided to wait to apologize.

167

He had regretted his behavior the moment she'd walked away from him. He was wrong, and he knew it. This hadn't been her fault at all. The last few days, combined with the excitement of the wedding and the frustration from needing her so much while having to wait, had strained his patience to the limit. A poor excuse for treating her the way he did, but the truth. Giving her enough time to finish showering and dressing, he knocked on her door and entered without waiting for a reply.

She glared at him. "What are you doing in here?"

"I wanted to apologize."

"Oh, really?"

He sighed, raking his fingers through his hair. "Yes, really," he said, reaching for her. "I'm sorry, Temper. I shouldn't have lost it like that."

Though quick to anger, he was also quick to admit when he was wrong. Tamera stroked the cheek she'd wanted to slap earlier. She hated that tense, frustrated look and the pulsing muscle that throbbed in his jaw when he was angry or upset.

"Me, too, Craig," she whispered. "I guess we're like two sticks rubbing together. There's going to be sparks."

He chuckled. "Guess so, but I can think of a lot more pleasant ways to expel those sparks than fighting."

She rolled her eyes and muttered "jerk" with a tender smile, then went willingly into his arms.

"Have I told you today how much I love you?" he queried, knowing very well he had.

She shook her head. "No."

He chuckled. "How remiss of me. I love you."

"I love you, too. You sure you want to be hitched for life to an ill- tempered brat with an ill-tempered brute of a horse?" she teased.

He laughed. "You sure you want to be hitched with an arrogant jerk cowboy?"

She nodded. "Yes. I love you, Craig. We'll probably have many more fights, but it'll take much more than that to make me stop loving you," she assured him. "Like you shooting my horse," she added, chiding him with a firm look followed by an impish grin.

He laughed, pulling her gently in his arms for another kiss. "I am sorry," he whispered.

"You should be."

"Like to see me grovel, don't you?" he teased, knowing she wouldn't anymore than he would do it.

"A little humility never hurt anyone," she assured with a sweet smile "How is it Shorty put it? 'It's high time young Mr. Harris realized he can't control everything.'" she taunted, laughing at his frown.

"Looks like I need to have a talk with Shorty," he remarked, knowing darn well it wouldn't do him any good. "Just cause he's been around longer than I have gives him no right to undermine me."

Tamera laughed. "Sure it does. You said your father wasn't a good one. Seems to me that God made sure there were plenty of strong, good-hearted men around to raise you right."

"And Maria, to boot," Craig admitted with a grin, knowing, without a doubt, how truly blessed he was.

Chapter Seventeen

Craig finished his paper and poured another cup of coffee. Though the rain had stopped yesterday, it was still too muddy to rush out the door. Besides, all the fences had been checked and cattle rescued two days ago. Nothing else could go wrong. Or so he thought. He and Gramps were discussing what to do about Silver when Tamera came down for breakfast.

Wrapping her arms around his shoulders, she whispered her love, surprised that he wasn't gone yet. Three days had passed since their fight, and both made sure the other knew it was over. No grudges would be held in this relationship. Glancing out the window, she sighed with relief to find the sun already rising and hot. Maybe today she would go into town and do some bridal shopping. She'd finished her juice and poured a cup of coffee when Craig spoke.

"Give Silver something to abort the foal if she's pregnant."

She blanched. "What?"

His eyes widened at the look of horror on her face. "Tamera, you know good and well that ranchers and breeders do this all the time. Why are you acting so shocked? You, yourself, said she needed a break. She's my best brood mare. People around here don't need Arabians, they need well bred, well trained Quarter horses. I have no use or market for half-breed horses," he insisted in as gentle a tone as he could summon.

"I can't believe you would be so cruel as to take her baby away from her. Is that what you're going to do if I get pregnant before you're ready? Make me have an abortion?"

Craig groaned. The reaction was typical of a woman, but Tamera was a veterinarian! "There's a big difference between a child and an animal," he chided, again doing his level best to speak in a gentle tone.

Tears filled her eyes. "It's still a baby," she choked, leaving the table.

Craig shook his head in dismay and massaged his throbbing temples. "Is this what the rest of our lives will be like?" he asked Gramps. "Disagreeing on everything?"

Gramps chuckled. "No, but now she's got an equal say in the way things are done around here. You may not like it, and you may not always agree, but that's the way it is. And should be," he added when Craig started to argue.

"She's a smart woman and a brilliant veterinarian, but she is a woman. Women love babies. All babies. Women were put on earth to nurture. Forcing an abortion is not nurturing. I'd suggest you think of an alternative."

Craig left the table with a muttered curse. "Quit looking so pleased, Gramps. I get the picture," he mumbled as Gramps burst into a fit of laughter.

As the morning wore on Craig found himself concerned about her reaction. It wasn't like her to get so choked up. Anger he could handle. Insolence he could tolerate. Down right refusal, he wasn't so sure about. But tears? Tears were his downfall, especially tears from those beautiful blue eyes. Unable to concentrate, he turned Rocky around and headed home.

"Tamera!" he called the minute he walked in the door.

She came bounding down the stairs. "You're home early. Something wrong?"

The difference in her demeanor in just a few short hours puzzled him. "I was worried about you. You weren't your usual self this morning. What was that all about?"

She blushed. "Oh, that," she remarked with a wave of her hand. "That was a little depression, a touch of nerves, and a whole lot of hormones."

Depression. The word struck a chord in him; a warning signal went off in his mind. He hated that word. "Depressed about what?" Sadness clouded her shining blue eyes.

"I miss my parents," she admitted, tears rushing to her eyes, her lips trembling. "Mama's not here to help with the wedding arrangements and Daddy won't be here to walk me."

He sighed with relief as he pulled her in his arms. "I'm sorry, Love. I know it's difficult. Is that all?"

"That and normal, raging hormones," she explained, her cheeks a delicate shade of crimson.

He grinned, getting the drift of her meaning. "Oh. You get like that very often?"

"Only a few days a month."

He chuckled. "Can you warn me next time so I can go camp out on the range or something?" he teased.

"No. Jerk," she muttered, punching him on the arm as he pulled her firmly against him.

"Do you know what the thought of how very much of a woman you are does to me?" he asked, his voice husky and teasing. She shook her head her eyes bright and shining.

"Make you want to tuck tail and run?"

"Not a bit," he assured with a husky chuckle, pulling her firmly in his arms for another kiss.

They turned at the knock on the door. Craig opened it.

"Miss Tamera Collins?" a boy holding a very big box asked.

She walked to the door.

"I have a delivery for you from Martha's Bridal Shop."

"Just a minute," she begged off, closing the door in his face. "Go in the den," she urged Craig and then called for Maria.

"Why?"

"My dress is here. You can't see it."

He shook his head. "I can't imagine you believing in all that superstitious hogwash."

"I'm not taking any chances, Cowboy. Now get, please," she pleaded when he hesitated, teasing her. She followed until he was safely in the den with Gramps. "Don't let him peek," she urged.

Craig sighed, rolling his eyes as Gramps promised. "This is the longest month of my life," he muttered with a grin, his eyes a bright, glinting shade of silver. "Actually, it's been the longest four months of my life."

Gramps laughed. "Life will never be dull. I promise you that."

* * * * *

The next few days continued in a flurry of activity. The invitations were delivered and mailed, causing another deluge of gifts. Neighbors called, dropped by, and invited them over for endless rounds of parties. Excitement overwhelmed and tension ruled until Craig and Tamera were at each other's throats, bickering over the pettiest thing. It came to a tumultuous head one evening. An extremely trying day was made even worse when Stephanie showed up unannounced and uninvited right at suppertime.

Tamera heard her high-pitched, feminine purr and threw down the dishtowel. "All I need is that..." she bit back the word that came to mind ... "Cow here, fawning all over him."

"Hush now," Maria chided, giving her a hug. "He loves you. I've never seen him show so much feeling and emotion toward anyone else in all his born days. Not since his mother. And especially not Stephanie."

Pasting a smile on her face, Tamera walked into the den where Craig was holding a weeping Stephanie. He looked at her helplessly and shrugged.

"Is there a problem?" she tried to sound concerned. She really did.

The flashing sapphire eyes belied the polite tone. Craig tried to explain. "Stephanie is having trouble with her father again."

"Craig!" Stephanie protested. "You don't have to tell the world!"

"I'm not, Stephanie," he consoled, patting her shoulder. "Just explaining to my bride-to-be."

"He's such a jerk," she wailed. "And all I need right now is you throwing her, and the fact that you're getting married, in my face," she sobbed pitifully into his shoulder.

Well-versed in her theatrics, Craig rolled his eyes with a sigh and patted her again.

Maria walked in clucking her tongue. "There, there, now. Come with me, and I'll fix you a nice, hot, cup of tea.

It'll make you feel better and help you sort things out," she soothed, whisking her from the room.

Craig waited, knowing a gale of hurricane proportions was about to hit. He wasn't wrong. Tamera walked up to him, and in one smooth motion unsnapped his shirt and jerked it off him. Tossing it in the trashcan, she turned toward the door.

Stunned to say the least, he grabbed her, whirling her around to face him. "Let's have it, Temper," he insisted. "But understand this, I will not put up with another hysterically-theatrical female."

"I don't want her here, Craig," she informed him, jerking free from his grasp. "At all, if possible, and especially not at my wedding."

Her eyes were like jeweled daggers of ice, slashing his composure in cadence with the chilliness in her tone. "What do you expect me to do? Her family and mine go back generations."

"I don't care. I'll be your wife, and I don't have to put up with her presence. Especially if she insists on finding a way into your arms every time she's around," she ground out. "How would you feel if the situation was reversed, and it was me in another man's arms? Suppose things hadn't happened like they did, and Tony wasn't dead? And suppose you found us like this?"

"If Tony wasn't dead, and he showed up here, I'd kill him," he informed her. "It's as simple as that. Same goes for any man who thinks he can put his hands on you."

"My point exactly. But I'm supposed to put up with her just because your family and hers go back generations?" she queried, hating the fact that her lip trembled and tears clung to her lashes. She blinked furiously to keep them from falling.

Craig sighed and rubbed at the tension in the back of his neck, at a loss for what to do. She had a point, a very valid point. So he did the only thing he could think of and pulled her into his arms.

"I love you, Tamera," he whispered, his lips covering hers in a tender caress. "Please don't put me in this situation.

The invitations have already gone out. But," he cupped her face in his hands. "I promise I will keep her at an arms' length from now on. I won't even dance with her at the reception."

He pulled her firmly against his chest, hating every shuddering sob she tried valiantly to suppress. "Please, don't cry. I can't bear it when you cry."

"It doesn't seem to bother you when she soaks your shirt with her tears," she bit out between clenched teeth.

"Right. She doesn't bother me at all," he assured. "Now, can I have my favorite shirt back if I promise to have it washed before I wear it again?" he asked, unable to mask the amusement in his voice.

She glared at him. "Burn it, for all I care." Her eyes narrowed. "She didn't give it to you, did she?"

He laughed and shook his head. "No, she didn't give it to me."

"Good. If you have any that she has given you, I want them out of this house. Anything she's given you for that matter. I may not be able to keep her away, but I don't have to have any other reminders of your relationship around."

"Yes ma'am," he agreed as meekly as possible, pulling her into his arms for another luxurious kiss.

"At least she no longer thinks she's a blonde," Tamera muttered, her voice thick with sarcasm. Craig chuckled and agreed.

Supper was a quiet, strained affair since the only proper thing to do was invite her to stay, and Stephanie didn't have the decency to decline.

Later, Craig paused by Tamera's door at the sound of her weeping. Suppressing a groan, he entered without knocking. "Temper, what's wrong?"

"Nothing," she sobbed. "Everything. Go away."

He grimaced at the sound of her continued crying. "Let's go for a walk," he urged.

"I don't want to go for a walk. I want to be left alone."

He pulled her firmly off the bed. "And I'm not going to leave you alone until we get this settled. Whatever it is," he muttered with a frustrated sigh, thinking everything had been settled between them earlier.

Tamera could tell by the look on his face that there was no use arguing the point. If he wanted her to go for a walk, she would go. Her only choice was to go peacefully or go kicking and screaming. Sliding her feet into her sandals, she followed him.

Craig avoided contact with her until they reached the porch. Sliding his arm around her waist, he pulled her gently against his side, rubbing her body in a soothing caress as they walked toward the barn. "You want to talk to me?" he urged in a soft voice.

"My parents never fought like this," she muttered, unable to choke back a sob or stop the tears.

Craig pulled her in his arms, burying her face in his chest until her sobs subsided. "I'll bet that's because your mother was a docile little thing that never lost her cool, which you, my little Temper Tantrum, are not," he remarked with a tender smile. "You are passionate, high-strung and fretful, like a high-spirited, untrained filly. All you need is someone with a gentle touch and a slow hand to soothe you through the rough spots."

Tamera didn't know words could melt bones. His low, husky voice, thick with emotion, did just that as his hands eased the tension from her body. Desire ignited in them so swiftly, so forcefully, all she could do was cling to him as his lips swooped over hers in a scorching kiss.

Craig pulled her firmly against his chest. One arm held her in place while the other caressed her back. Burying his hand in the thick, silken mass of her hair, he tempered his response. "I love you, Tamera," he rasped. "I don't like this tension."

She sighed. "I just want everything to be perfect."

His smile was as tender as his words.

"It will be perfect," he assured her, "whether it's a fancy, fairy tale wedding or blue jeans, boots, and a Justice of the Peace. Do you know why it'll be perfect?" At the slight shake of her head, he continued. "Because we will be celebrating our love. That's the only important thing, Temper, the rest are just trappings. Relax. Enjoy yourself. Everything will be all right," he promised.

"I guess I do get carried away sometimes," she admitted. "And her *'visit'* just topped it all off."

His reply was a gentle chuckle. "Like I said, a soft touch and gentle hand to guide you, and a baby at your breast real soon. That's all you need to settle you down."

She rolled her eyes in an exaggerated manner. "That's a male chauvinist remark if I've ever heard one. Typical coming from a male chauvinist pig," she muttered.

He laughed. "That's me," he teased. "I guess I haven't been much help, have I?"

She shook her head. "You're always so tense. I don't know if you like the plans we've made or not."

"I just want you to be happy, Temper. It's your day."

"Yours, too," she whispered.

He nodded, "I like everything you've planned," he assured her with a kiss. "Let me explain something to you," he whispered, releasing her from his embrace. Cupping her face in his hands, he stroked her cheeks with his thumbs. "Do you know what happens to a man when he chooses to remain celibate for an undetermined length of time?"

He felt the heat rush to her cheeks as she shook her head. "Nothing," he assured her. "Unless God decides to play a trick on him, presenting him with an angel in the flesh, one that's smart and beautiful, who's talented, strong, and beautiful, with eyes that could seduce a saint and lips that would tempt the strongest of men. Then do you know what happens when he's forced to walk around in a state of arousal for as long as I have?"

Again, she shook her head, another surge of heat rushing to her cheeks.

"It makes him crazy, Temper. To the point of total loss of control."

"But, you're always in control," she argued. "Thank God. I, on the other hand, feel like I'm losing my mind."

He chuckled. "Oh, no, I'm not the one in control. The only reason I've held off as long as I have, and remained even slightly sane, is because I begged God to make me the man you need me to be, and because I not only love you, but I respect you. You needed time after what you went through.

Added to all of that is the fact that you don't believe making love is proper out of wedlock."

He grinned. "Not to mention Gramps would have killed me for dishonoring you in any way. I'm no saint, Tamera, but I'm trying to do what's right. I know God created sex to be within the bounds of marriage. Though I haven't always abided by that, I'm trying to respect it now. Believe me; it's taken a lot of prayer and many cold showers for me to even get to this point."

"I love you, Craig," she assured him. Rising up on her toes, she slid her arms around his neck, her lips covering his in a gentle caress. "It won't be long now, Cowboy," she whispered when he trembled in her arms.

"Thank God," he groaned. "'Cause this has been the longest month of my life," he complained.

She merely giggled.

Friday morning he entered her room just as she finished her workout.

"Ride with me today," he urged, his eyes sweeping over her in a hungry gesture.

"I can't. I've got too much to do."

"What?" he demanded.

She looked at him wide-eyed then grinned. "Nothing, I guess. It's all done."

He nodded in approval. "Good. If anything comes up, Maria can handle it. Unless I miss my guess, you're playing this traditional all the way. That means I won't be able to see you tomorrow until the ceremony."

"That's right," she admitted.

"Not even for breakfast?"

She shook her head.

"Then today you're all mine, pretty lady. From now until midnight, I don't intend to let you out of my sight. I'll tolerate no arguments from you, Tamera," he insisted when she started to protest. "You can come willingly or..."

"I know," she interrupted. "Kicking and screaming."

He grinned. "Or I'll chain you to my side," he finished. "Be downstairs in five minutes, or I'll come after you."

She laughed, caught up in the excitement in his eyes. "Yes sir," she complied as meekly as possible.

"I kinda like the sound of that," he remarked, leaving so she could change.

"You would," she muttered. Hearing his arrogant chuckle, she smiled to herself as he closed her bedroom door.

He took her out to the same spot by the river where they'd gone before and they spent the whole day together. He did let her out of his sight, but only when and as long as absolutely necessary.

That evening when the night had settled down around them, he held her close, lying with her until her eyes rolled tiredly, and she begged him to let her sleep. Then he held her while she slept. As the clock struck eleven, he went to his own room to find Shorty waiting for him. He and a bunch of the guys urged Craig out for his last night as a bachelor. Though a bit reluctant, he went with them.

It was the usual bachelor party with lots of beer, women and music, all the way to the scantily clad girl jumping out of the cake and dancing exotically. She sidled up to Craig, her body moving in tantalizing ways. Though his eyes swept over her with amused appreciation, his heart compared her to the passion evident in his young bride waiting at home. He just smiled when she ran her hands up his chest.

"Last night as a bachelor, Cowboy?" she asked in a suggestive purr.

He laughed, gently removing her hands. "Lovely though you are, darling, you don't hold a candle to my bride-to-be," he assured her, leaving in the midst of their teasing, jostling, jeering and name-calling.

Sneaking back into Tamera's room, he kissed her awake.

"Craig," she exclaimed, "it's after midnight!"

He laughed. "We'll pretend it's Friday until the sun comes up."

She held him a while, allowing his kisses and caresses until she thought she'd die from the hunger he elicited in her. Then she wrapped up securely in the covers where he couldn't touch her, and insisted that he leave, which he did with a reluctant, frustrated sigh and definite pout to his sensuous lips.

Chapter Eighteen

Saturday dawned bright and clear, a perfect day for a wedding. It was after eight o'clock when Craig joined Gramps for breakfast. He'd already tended to Temper, Silver and the foals, and requested that Tamera be left to sleep as long as she wanted, confessing that he had kept her awake pretty late last night.

"How was the party?" Gramps asked.

Craig grinned, "I don't know. I left, but there's a lot of moaning and groaning coming from the bunk house."

"What do you mean, you left? It's tradition for the groom to have a bachelor party."

Craig grunted. "Tradition. If I hear that word one more time I'll puke. It's because of tradition I can't see Tamera until two o'clock this afternoon. Why did we schedule the ceremony for that time, anyway? Why isn't it scheduled for ten o'clock?"

Gramps laughed. "For the simple reason that, because of the bachelor party, you shouldn't be out of bed before ten."

"Oh," his grin was sheepish. "Well, I figured I was wasting my time when there was a woman dancing half-naked in front of me, and all I could think about was the one sleeping upstairs," he admitted.

His eyes glistened. Gramps chuckled. "That's the way it should be for a new groom. And that's the way it should stay forever," he added in subtle warning. "I don't think I've ever seen you looking so happy, Craig. I pray that it lasts a lifetime. It won't always be so full of excitement."

Craig laughed. "What makes you think I have any illusions about the happy-ever-after syndrome? You forget I know Tamera pretty well. No, it won't always be easy, but, like you said, it will never be dull. And it'll be worth it."

His expression turned serious. "I've been waiting all of my life for someone like her, Gramps. I'll never take her for granted, that I can assure you."

"Just love her, Craig, and give her room to grow. That's all you have to do. In the heat of battle, remember your love and your vows. Remember that it is God who blesses our lives with love, and nothing will destroy it. The Bible says, *nothing shall prosper against you.* Believe in God's word. Trust in it. Build your life and your marriage on it, and you will not fail."

"I will," Craig promised, walking over to his side. "I love you, Gramps. Thank you for putting up with me all these years. Thank you for all that you've taught me. Thank you for your love."

Adam Craig Harris Sr. pulled his grandson against him, his gray eyes filled with tears. "I love you, too, Craig. You've been more of a son to me than your father ever was, God rest his soul. You're getting a prize today, Craig. There aren't many like her in the world these days. Hang on to her, son."

Craig grinned, "Oh, I plan on it. Even if I have to beat her into submission and chain her to my side," he teased, a hint of arrogance in his voice.

Gramps chuckled. "As if that'll work."

* * * * *

Tamera awoke to a soft knock on the door and watched as a card slid beneath it. She smiled to herself and went to pick it up. She could feel his presence through the door. She opened the card and read....

Until later, my love. I'll be waiting anxiously. I'll be the guy in the white tux, the one with gray eyes and no mustache.

As his best man, Scott would be dressed similarly.

She smiled at his teasing. As if she wouldn't know which guy in the white tux she was marrying, even if they could pass for twins. Raising the envelope, she could smell his after-shave lotion on it. Her heart skipped a beat. She placed a hand on the door. "Craig?"

"I'm here," he whispered. "This is the stupidest tradition of them all," he muttered.

She giggled. "Are you sure 'stupidest' is a word?"

He grunted. "Well, it is now. One kiss, Temper," he urged.

Tamera felt herself weaken at the soft, seductive tone of his voice. She hesitated, only a moment, but long enough to stop herself from opening the door. "No, Cowboy. I'll see you at two o'clock. Then you can kiss me all you want. I'll be the girl in the wedding gown. I love you," she whispered. She waited for his disgruntled reply and the sound of footsteps as he walked away from her door.

As arranged, Craig left for the better part of the day so Tamera wouldn't have to be cooped up in her room the whole time. Caterers and decorators turned the ranch house into a fairy tale wedding chapel. As the clock neared two, Tamera found herself nervous to the point of tears.

Downstairs, Craig was in no better, if not worse, shape than she was. He was, as Scott diagnosed, past the point of nervous groom and well on his way to certifiable basket case.

He paced the floor, tugging relentlessly at the stiff collar and bow tie at his throat. Raking his fingers through his hair in an agitated gesture, he glared at the clock then cursed because it had moved less than five minutes from the last time he'd looked at it. A frustrated sigh escaped him as Gramps and Scott chuckled.

"If you glare at it any harder, Craig, you're liable to break it. Then it won't move at all," his grandfather warned.

He grimaced. "This is the longest day in the longest month of my life," he complained, tugging again at his collar.

"Stop that." Maria bustled in, dressed in the new pale pink dress that he and Tamera had bought for her. "Don't make me have to press that shirt this late in the day," she insisted, slapping at his hands. Straightening his tie, she smoothed the front of his shirt.

Her hands ran over his shoulders in a soothing caress. "The best-looking groom this county has ever had to boast of," she assured him, her eyes shining with the love she reserved just for him.

Her soothing, motherly fussing eased his tension some. Craig grinned. "Yes ma'am," he obliged, justly chastised. He placed his hands on her ample waist and kissed her cheek. "And thank you, but I believe your opinion is a bit biased."

"What's this?" Maria demanded. "Where's that cocky, self-assured cowboy I raised?"

He grinned. "Lost somewhere in this ridiculous monkey suit. Have you seen Tamera?"

She nodded, smiling.

"How is she?"

"About as nervous as you and very beautiful."

He groaned. "I knew we should have eloped," he complained good-naturedly.

Scott laughed. "What, and miss all this fun?" he asked, walking through the door.

"Where are you going?" Craig demanded.

"I'm going to check on the bride," he informed him with a smug, cocky grin.

"Dog!" Craig muttered, clearly jealous, glaring at him until he stood at Tamera's door. He watched barely a moment before Maria dragged him back into the den.

Scott knocked, "It's Scott," he announced, opening at her command. "How ya' doin', Sweetheart? I sure hope you're in better shape than the groom."

Tamera lifted huge, pleading eyes to his amused brown ones. "Scared to death. I should have listened to Craig when he suggested a Justice of the Peace."

He laughed. "Scared of what?"

"Everything."

He walked over to her, cupping her face in his hands. "Tonight?"

Tears rushed to her eyes and she nodded.

"Craig will not hurt you," he assured her, his voice soft and tender.

"It's not Craig I'm afraid of, it's sex," she said, her lips trembling, too nervous to be anything but blunt.

"Listen to me," he urged. "You just relax. Remember how very much he loves you and, I promise you, after tonight you'll never be afraid again. Sex is a beautiful gift given to us by God to celebrate life, and it's a vital part of marriage. And Craig is a very tender lover."

"How do you know what kind of lover Craig is?" she queried, making a feeble attempt at teasing.

He chuckled. "Because his reputation precedes me into every relationship I enter. Although the women I date haven't been with him, they know *of* him, which means I'm constantly up against his reputation."

"And how do you hold up?" she asked, her eyebrow arched with interest. He grinned, that same arrogant grin she loved so much on Craig, and she was again astounded at how alike they were.

"I don't compete," he admitted with a wink. His eyes twinkled as surprised understanding registered on her face.

"Anytime you're ready, Sweetheart," he remarked, glancing at his watch. Kissing her on the cheek, he left her alone once more.

She took several deep breaths, waiting for him to reach the bottom of the stairs where, after she descended, he would escort her to Craig's side. Picking up her bouquet, she gazed in the mirror, pleased at what she saw.

The Victorian-style wedding dress was covered with tiny eyelet lace and glittering pearls. The waist was tight, accentuating her tiny form, and the train flowed down to the floor two feet behind her. She chose a small, white velvet hat in lieu of a veil. She wanted nothing to block her view as she gazed into her groom's eyes to say and hear their vows.

Saying a short prayer to still her racing heart, she walked to the door, opened it and waited for Scott's signal. A hush fell over the house as the bridal march began. Taking a deep, steadying breath she walked from her room to the landing and paused for a full minute as rehearsed then began her descent in small, slow steps. Rounding the curve in the staircase, she got her first glimpse of Craig and stopped.

Craig's eyes widened when he saw her. She was a vision from heaven, an angel wrapped in white satin, silk and lace. Her eyes sparkled like rare, precious sapphires and a soft flush covered her cheeks. Radiant didn't come close to describe how beautiful she looked, and he was infinitely grateful for the flashbulbs going off all around him. He took a step forward, only to be detained by the gentle touch of Gramps' hand on his arm.

Their eyes met. Electricity sizzled between them. Tamera stood a full moment, immobilized by the emotions glowing in his eyes: love, desire, pride, triumph. His eyes swept over her in a look so blatantly male, so incredibly masculine, that it made her knees weak. She smiled. A smile so brilliant, it would later be said, that it melted the tension in the air, like the first warm days of spring melt snow.

Placing one hand on the banister for support, she continued as Scott took a step toward her. She placed her hand in his and looked up into his warm brown eyes.

He grinned. "It's not too late to change your mind and marry me," he whispered.

She glanced over at Craig, so handsome in his black-trimmed, white tuxedo. His eyes were warm and tender, like liquid metal. She locked her gaze with his. "Thanks," she whispered under her breath. "But I don't think so."

"Figures," Scott muttered. "Some guys have all the luck. Maybe I should just thank you for taking him off the market," he teased. Tucking her hand firmly in his arm, he escorted her to her groom's side.

Craig took his eyes off his bride long enough to shake his friend's hand. Gray eyes meshed with brown in mutual love, admiration and respect. A lifetime of friendship passed between them in a split-second look that said it all.

Taking Tamera's hand in his, Craig pulled her firmly against his side, and the ceremony began. The vows were traditional and blessedly short. Craig turned, cupping her face in his hands even before the minister told him to.

"I love you," he whispered, his voice so husky, so full of emotion that it brought tears to her eyes. "I love you," he repeated, seconds before his lips covered hers in a tender caress.

The kiss deepened for a brief moment, sending sparks of desire shooting through her already trembling body. She grabbed his wrists as her knees threatened to buckle beneath her and tears slid down her cheeks. He brushed them away with his thumbs. With a tender smile he pulled her against him, and they turned so the minister could pronounce them 'husband and wife'.

They proceeded through the line of guests to the reception area.

As the reception wore on, Craig grew restless. He was tired of being dressed, tired of the crowd, tired of dancing with women other than his wife, and extremely tired of watching her dance with other men.

He heard Stephanie's high-pitched laugh and watched as she walked toward him, arms outstretched, a hundred dollar bill in one hand, a straight pin in the other.

"My turn to dance with the groom."

He caught her hand before she could pin the bill to his lapel. "I think I'll just sit this one out." So far, he'd kept his promise to Tamera and kept Stephanie at arms' length.

She pouted prettily. "You've been avoiding me all evening. What's the matter, afraid the little wife will get upset?"

"Don't flatter yourself," he muttered, surprised at her sharp, hissing intake of breath.

"I remember a time when you enjoyed being in my arms. What happened?"

He shrugged. "I grew up and realized what I wanted out of life. Maybe you should think about doing the same."

She practically snarled at him, tossing her hair off her shoulders with a haughty shake of her head. "Maybe I should give the little veterinarian—a virgin no doubt—a few pointers on how to take care of you," she insinuated.

Craig grabbed her firmly by the wrist. "Listen carefully, and hear me well, Stephanie. If you do anything, anything at all, to ruin this night for her or to hurt her, ever, I'll pay you back in spades," he warned.

His voice was calm and deadly; his eyes were narrow slits of glinting steel. Stephanie felt a tiny tug of fear. She squashed it. "Just how do you propose to do that?" she asked sarcastically, determined not to be intimidated by the man who had jilted her because of her modern, feminist attitude.

He shrugged nonchalantly. "Oh, a nice little chat with your father might work."

Jerking free from his grasp, she stalked out of the room.

Hopefully that put an end to that, Craig thought with a sigh. He walked over to Gramps as the song ended, and the band took a break. "We're outta here," he whispered.

Gramps nodded, smiling in understanding. Clearing his throat, he announced their departure, raising his glass in salute.

"A toast," Scott insisted, chuckling at Craig's glare. "To you, my friend," he raised his glass in salute to Craig.

"May God bless you and your new bride, and may He bless your life with a house full of children: girls as lovely as your beautiful wife. And boys just like you."

"Huh," Harry snorted. Since they'd met in his restaurant, he was one of the honored guests. "A blessing for him; a curse on the rest of us," he teased, laughing with the rest of the crowd.

Craig grinned, shook Harry's hand, and hugged Scott who, in turn, kissed the bride, whispering encouragement in her ear. The guests cheered as Craig swung her up in his arms.

"What are you doing?" she demanded, a hot blush rushing to her cheeks.

"Why, Darling, it's tradition for the groom to carry the bride."

"It's tradition to carry her over the threshold," she countered.

He grinned. "Yes, but our threshold is up there. And we can't disappoint our guests by ignoring tradition now can we?"

She rolled her eyes. "You just want to show off, you arrogant jerk," she muttered, burying her hot face in his collar.

"That's right," he agreed with a throaty chuckle. "I want to show every one, especially the male members of our honored guests..."

"And one certain female," she interjected.

He grinned with a nod and continued. "And one certain female, just who has wed and who shall bed you," he teased, laughing at her muttered insult.

Despite her hot cheeks, Tamera lifted her head and smiled lovingly into his eyes. Brushing the hair off his forehead, she ran her fingers tenderly through the thick locks, and nuzzled his cheek, determined that no one would doubt her feelings for him.

He carried her into the master bedroom suite that had been scrubbed, redecorated and refurbished in the last month. Putting her down, his hands slid over her in a subtle caress.

"You are so beautiful," he whispered, his voice so thick he could barely get the words past his raw throat.

She smiled. "You don't look half bad, yourself, all dressed out in a tux."

He grinned, tugging at the bow tie that had been doing its level best to choke him for hours. "Let's get changed and get out of here," he suggested.

"Wait," she urged. "I have something for you." Walking to her suitcase, she withdrew a tiny package and handed it to him with a shy smile.

Craig opened it, gasping with pleasure at the sturdy gold cross on a solid gold chain. Turning it over, he read the inscription: *Always, Tamera.*

"It was for my father," she informed him, a soft catch in her voice. "I bought it for him for Father's Day but he never got a chance to wear it." Her voice trembled. She swallowed a sob.

"I was wrong, Craig, there is another man like him in the world. You. I know he'd want you to have this. So do I."

Pulling her against his chest, he kissed her, stroking the hair off her face. "I'll treasure it always," he assured her, his voice thick with emotion. "And I'll treasure you always," he promised, hoping her father could hear him and would entrust him with his daughter's love.

She went into the bathroom to change while he used the bedroom. They escaped through the mob of rice-throwing guests to the waiting car. Tamera had no idea where they were going, since she had left the details of the honeymoon up to him. She looked at him in surprise when they abandoned the car for the jeep.

He avoided answering her questions, simply saying that their destination was a surprise. After a thirty-minute drive, they arrived at what looked like a deserted cabin. Once again, he carried her over the threshold and into the darkened building. Putting her down, he lit a candle, took her hands in his, and kissed her.

"In the old days the bride and groom were closeted in their room for a week. The only person they saw was the maid who brought their meals. We have the rest of our lives for trips and crowds. I thought it would be neat to be here alone, just the two of us, for our honeymoon. Do you mind?"

Excitement curled in the pit of her stomach. She tried not to smile and turned wide, innocent, eyes to his. "What about food? Don't tell me you have to catch or kill everything we intend to eat?"

He chuckled and opened the refrigerator, which was stocked to the hilt with wine and food.

"Looks more like you've planned for a week-long drunk," she teased.

He chortled. "Yep. A whole week of drinking wine and making love."

"What exactly are we going to do all day for a whole week?" she queried in a soft voice. "There's no television or anything."

In answer, he swung her up in his arms and carried her to the bed, his lips capturing hers in a fiery kiss. He felt her tense slightly and warning signals went off in his brain.

Rolling over he pulled her atop his long frame. His hands traveled over her body in a soothing caress. Ironically, he didn't feel the raging desire he'd felt for her since the day they met, but more like a slow, burning need, and what he needed most was to feel her relax. He desperately wanted the feel of her lips on his, the taste of her kiss, and her hands on him in mutual desire. Talking softly, he urged her to relax.

Slowly, shyly, she kissed him. Her lips traveled from his mouth over the smooth skin of his cheek and down his throat. Her hands moved timidly across his chest until she caressed every inch of the wide expanse of well-muscled flesh. She felt him tremble as a groan escaped him.

His arms tightened around her automatically, but Craig kept his desire in check, letting her explore and become familiar with his body.

Guided by instinct alone, she kept on, caressing him with her hands and lips until her own desire pulsed through her in heated waves. A soft moan escaped her as he rolled her over onto her back to return her caresses with some of his own.

"I didn't know love could hurt so much," she whimpered.

"What hurts, Love?"

"Everything," she admitted. "I love you so much it feels like my heart will burst wide open any minute, and I ache in places I never knew existed."

"Tell me where it hurts, Love, and I'll kiss it away," he promised in a low, seductive whisper. His lips followed his hands as he caressed her, leaving whispers of fire across her skin.

Soft, encouraging moans escaped her as he continued to kiss and caress, mumbling incoherent soft, sweet words of love and desire. "I love you, Tamera," he whispered. "I won't hurt you," he promised.

Somewhere deep in her heart, Tamera heard the still, small voice of God assuring her that all was well and right. Wrapping her arms around his shoulders, she offered herself to her husband, her lips covering his in a melting kiss.

Afterward, Craig lay in her arms as long as his love-spent body would allow, whispering sweet words of love and praise for what they shared. He relieved her of his weight and pulled her firmly in his arms, wrapping her in his love for the first night of their life as husband and wife.

* * * * *

Craig awoke the next morning to find Tamera already awake and out of bed. He held a hand out to her as she came from the bathroom, a puzzled look on her pretty face. "What's the matter, Temper?"

She put her hand in his, not sure what to say. Pulling back the covers, she slid beneath them and curled up in his arms. "Craig, why would I bleed? I mean," she hesitated, a hot blush rushing to her cheeks. "I know the usual reasons, but why again?"

Craig's mind whirled in confused excitement. "Temper, you said that you fainted when Tony attacked you. When exactly did you faint?"

Her blush deepened. "When he tore my dress and put his hand...." she broke off, too embarrassed to finish her sentence.

He swallowed hard praying desperately to grasp what God was trying to tell them. "Temper, maybe he didn't finish what he started. If a woman passed out on me, I certainly couldn't." Hope glowed in her eyes.

"You think so?"

Craig knew she wanted it to be so. She'd wanted to be a virgin when she married, more than anything else. He shrugged, knowing he was probably grasping at straws for her, but he'd do his best to rope the moon and lasso a couple of stars if she asked him to. "That's something you'd have to ask Scott, or another doctor, Love. But if it is so, then you know what?

She laughed, feeling happier and more carefree than she had in months. "Yes, my darling husband, it means that you'd better be glad you didn't seduce me before we were wed, otherwise you'd have stolen my virginity, you arrogant jerk cowboy," she teased.

Craig roared while rolling her over, desire already pulsing through him. "Steal? No way," he teased, his voice soft and husky. "Had I decided to seduce you before we were wed, you, my sweet little Temper Tantrum, would have been begging this arrogant jerk cowboy to take your virginity," he assured her, hushing her arguments with his lips.

Chapter Nineteen

After a week of sheer wedded bliss, things returned to normal for Craig and Tamera. Actually, things were becoming better than normal. It amazed them how well they got along since their marriage. They very seldom disagreed, so there were very few arguments. They slipped into a solid routine, laughing and loving, learning to operate as a team, as husband and wife, instead of rancher and veterinarian. Things seemed to be going smoothly until Craig came home late one blustery fall evening barely three months later, to find Tamera beyond agitated.

"Where have you been?" she demanded.

He looked at her with a puzzled frown. "What?"

"I've been worried sick," she insisted, stomping her foot in an agitated gesture. "It got dark hours ago!"

"Whoa, there, I've been riding this range all of my life. It's not that late, Tamera, it just gets dark a lot earlier than usual. What's the matter with you?"

She sighed raking her fingers through her hair. "I don't know," she whispered tears filling her eyes. "I was just worried, that's all."

He grinned shaking his head. *Women!* "If you're through fussing at me, can I have a kiss?" he queried, pulling her firmly in his arms.

Tamera's worries melted as his lips covered hers in a gentle caress. The kiss deepened until she was wrapped firmly against his hard body. A soft moan escaped her as her breasts pushed painfully into his chest.

Assured she was trembling from desire and no longer upset, or mad, or whatever the case, Craig gently released her from his heated embrace. "Wow! What you do to me," he rasped, his voice hoarse, his heart pounding in his chest as desire washed over him in angry waves.

They gazed at each other, pleasantly surprised at the depth of need they felt for each other.

"Who said heaven ended when the honeymoon was over?" he asked.

She shook her head, her body reeling from the impact of that one kiss. "I don't know."

"Well, whoever it was is wrong. Dead wrong," he assured her, his lips covering hers in a gentle caress.

Tamera went into the kitchen to warm his supper while Craig went to see Gramps.

"You have any idea what's wrong with Tamera?" he asked his grandfather.

Gramps smiled. He had an idea, but wouldn't be the one to bring it up. His thoughts wandered back over the last few days, recalling how strange she'd been acting. She was tired and moody, and, just this morning, she'd paled at the sight of her food instead of devouring it as usual. In answer to Craig's question, he simply shrugged. "She's probably just experiencing the holiday blues."

Craig shook his head. "Women," he muttered, grinning when Gramps laughed. He visited with his grandfather until he was called in to eat.

Afterward, he led his wife upstairs. Pulling her firmly in his arms, he reveled in the pleasure of her love. Ever grateful, he shared that pleasure with her until, sated, they fell asleep in each other's arms.

* * * * *

Tamera groaned, turning away from the stinging water of the shower. She felt tender and ached all over, especially her breasts. Closing her eyes she let the warm water run down her back, thinking maybe it was time for her period. Her eyes flew open at the thought. Excitement curled in the pit of her stomach as she realized she hadn't had a period since before she and Craig were married.

Turning off the shower, she dried off and double-checked her calendar. Her heart fluttered with anticipation, as her mind comprehended what her body was telling her. Jumping to her feet in enthusiasm, she swayed as a wave of nausea and dizziness assailed her. She slumped into the chair as the symptoms she'd been experiencing spoke loud and clear.

She was going to have a baby!

Craig walked in, and she ducked her head to hide her emotions. She wouldn't tell him until she was sure.

"You want to ride with me today?"

She shook her head, thinking quickly. "No, I think I'll run into town and do a little Christmas shopping."

He peered at her. "You look incredibly beautiful this morning, My Love," he whispered, tugging at the towel scantily covering her body. "On second thought, maybe I'll just stay home with you today," he suggested, caressing her mouth with his.

Clasping the towel with one hand, she placed the other against his chest. "Go to work, Craig, so I can go spend some money," she teased.

He chuckled. "And I thought you married me for my body."

She grinned, an impish light in her eyes. "That, too," she admitted, nipping at his hand which insisted on caressing the tender skin exposed above the towel.

Craig watched as desire turned her eyes from brilliant sapphire to smoky, midnight blue. Unable to resist the invitation in them, he picked her up and carried her back to bed. It was some time later before he left for work, and she left to go to town.

Later that evening they were in the den. After last night's scene, Craig decided to come home earlier, though it was still dark. The house was warm and cozy, a feeling he'd come to appreciate to a much greater degree.

Tamera and Gramps sat looking at a catalog, laughing and talking softly. Craig began to go over the latest financial reports from his accountant, relieved to see that the ranch had shown a nice profit again this year. Wise investments ensured their continued success.

Putting aside his reports, Craig watched as Tamera leaned forward, whispered in his ear, and Gramps chuckled. Excitement rent the air. His curiosity aroused, he walked over to them.

"Okay, you two, what's going on?"

"What makes you think something is going on?" she asked, raising innocent eyes to his.

"Don't give me those innocent eyes, Tamera. You two are plotting something. What gives?" The smile she shared with Gramps took his breath away.

"We're just looking at new furniture," she replied sweetly.

"New furniture for what?"

"Well, I was thinking about getting some pieces for the area your mother used as a sewing room. You want to help me pick them out?"

Not taking his eyes from hers, he reached for the catalog she held out to him. The excitement in her eyes set fire to his blood. Dragging his gaze from hers, he looked at the book in his hand. A puzzled frown crossed his face. "This is baby furniture..." his voice broke, breath stuck in his throat, hands trembled. "Baby furniture?"

At her nod, he grinned, tossed the book aside and pulled her out of the chair and into his arms with a laugh. "A baby? We're going to have a baby? When? How?"

She squealed with delight at his reaction. "When? In about seven months. How? Surely you know where babies come from," she teased.

He laughed; Gramps chuckled; she giggled. "It's okay to shout or dance with joy," she assured him. "We're going to have a baby," she sang out, twirling around.

"You're doing enough of that for both of us," he countered. "Don't you think you ought to sit down? Take it easy?"

She made a face at him. "No. Scott said I'm as healthy as a horse. He said I could keep on doing what I do everyday unless I have any cramps or bleeding. Don't worry," she assured him, "I asked him about everything," she whispered loudly, conspiratorially.

He fell for it. "About what?"

She smiled. "You know, exercise, riding and," her voice lowered to a stage whisper, "sex."

"And just what did he say?" Craig asked with a grin.

"He said okay to all of the above. Just don't turn flips, jump fences, or get kinky. What did he mean by that?" she asked, all innocence again.

Craig roared. Picking her up he whispered in her ear, laughing at the blush that stained her cheeks.

She closed her eyes in mortification and buried her hot face in his collar. "Definitely not," she mumbled, embarrassed to the core.

He laughed, stroking her back. "A son," he said with a dreamy expression on his face.

She glared at him. "Oh, no, it's going to be a girl."

"I want a son," Craig insisted.

His gray eyes glittered. "And what if it's not?" Tamera wanted to know.

He grinned. "That's what divorce courts are for."

She struggled from his grasp. "Well, go see your lawyer, Cowboy, 'cause it's going to be a girl. She's gonna have black hair and blue eyes, and I'm naming her Amber Nichole," she assured. "Amber Nichole Harris. Has a nice ring to it. Doesn't it?"

"Don't I have a say in the matter?"

Her grin was smug. "No. You did your part. Now just leave the rest up to me."

The phrase holiday joy took on a whole new meaning. The house came alive in hopeful anticipation of new life. Maria was in her element, constantly fussing over Tamera.

Gramps seemed happier and more content. Craig was more protective than ever, especially when it came to her riding.

After hearing of one incident when Temper was unusually difficult for her to handle, he insisted that Tamera stop riding, threatening to kill, or at the very least geld, Temper if she got hurt.

Tamera, herself, was calmer and more serene. Though she disagreed with Craig about riding, she relented when he enlisted everyone's support on the issue. She still worked with the colts and yearlings, and her veterinarian skills were occasionally called upon, but mostly she just took it easy, enjoying the extra special attention she received.

As winter deepened and the days grew shorter, Craig stayed home more, riding the range only a couple of days each week. It was one evening while they were getting ready for bed that the full impact of her pregnancy hit him.

She was standing at the window brushing her hair. The full moon illuminated her silhouette, and he got a glimpse of her slightly rounded abdomen. Emotions rushed through him so fierce, so primitive it took his breath away and scared the living daylights out of him.

He was going to be a father!

He walked to her on trembling legs and pulled her firmly against him. His hands traveled slowly over her body, feeling the tender fullness of her breasts and smooth roundness of her stomach. "You are more beautiful than ever," he whispered, turning her in his arms, his mouth covering hers in a tender caress. Picking her up, he carried her to the bed and loved her with exquisite tenderness.

While they lay in each other's arms, amazed at the depth of passion they shared, Tamera felt the tiny flutters of life within her womb. Tears of joy and wonder filled her eyes. "Did you feel that?"

Craig shook his head. "Feel what?"

"She moved." Taking his hand, Tamera placed it on her abdomen as the tiny flutters occurred again.

His eyes reflected the same wonder and joy as Craig felt his child move sweetly against his palm. His lips moved down her body until his cheek rested against her abdomen, and he felt the baby move again. He whispered soft words of love and thanksgiving for the blessing God was creating just for them.

The next morning he was sharing a cup of coffee with Gramps while Tamera slept in. "Well, Gramps, how does it feel to know you'll be holding your great-grandchild soon?"

His smile was pensive. "I hope so, Craig."

"What do you mean, you hope so? It won't be long now. We felt her move last night." He chuckled. "She's even got me calling the baby *her* already." Gramps' eyes clouded, as did his face.

He gazed into Craig's glowing gray eyes. His smile was tender, his words gentle. "I'm tired, Craig. Very tired."

Fear knotted Craig's stomach. He put down his coffee. "What are you saying?" he asked, noting the pain deep in his grandfather's eyes.

"I'm saying that I'm tired of fighting to do the simplest chores. I prayed that the Lord would let me live to see you happily wed. He has, bless Him, but I'm not sure how much longer I can go on. I don't even think I could hold a newborn, and my heart is weak," he admitted, his voice tender.

Craig's heart thudded against his chest like a trapped bird. His hands trembled. "Since when?"

"I've been having small heart attacks for quite some time now."

"Why didn't you tell me? Why didn't Scott tell me?" Craig insisted, suddenly angry and afraid, angry with them, angry with God and afraid of his ability, or lack thereof, to go on without Gramps.

Gramps saw the pain, the anger and fear in Craig's eyes. "Now, don't be angry with Scott. He's bound by law not to disclose anything I ask him to keep confidential."

"But he's my friend," he protested. "And you're my grandfather."

"I should have told you sooner, but I didn't want to spoil the excitement of the first few months of your marriage, and then the baby."

Craig knelt in front of his wheelchair. "You've got to hang on, Gramps," he pleaded. "I'm not sure I can do all this without you."

Gramps smiled. "You're the strongest man I know, Craig. God has given you the strength to grow into a fine man despite the odds. With His help, you can handle anything," he assured.

Feeling as though he would suffocate with fear and grief, Craig decided to ride the range. He stayed a long time, pondering all that his grandfather had said. His heart ached; his mind repeated the conversation until he had accepted the inevitable and realized it would be soon.

Stopping his horse in the middle of a hundred acre pasture he wept, howling with grief and anger. Emotionally spent, he headed back to the house, determined to stay by his grandfather's side until the end.

* * * * *

Craig awoke with a feeling of dread. Less than a month had passed since his talk with Gramps. He'd stayed home more, spending as much time with him as he could, and watched as Gramps' health deteriorated steadily. Quickly deducing that Tamera was not in the room, he slipped into a pair of jeans and went looking for her. Fear clutched his heart when he searched the rooms upstairs and couldn't find her. Gut instinct led him into Gramps' room where she was kneeling by the bed, weeping. He put his arms around her, whispering her name. She looked at him with tear-drenched eyes that tore his heart out.

"He won't wake up," she choked.

He shook his head, "I know. C'mon, Love, it's cold in here." He picked her up. His heart ached as she buried her head into his shoulder and wept anew.

"I thought he was getting better," she wailed.

"No, Temper. You're the only one who refused to see he was getting worse," he scolded though not too harshly.

"He won't get to hold the baby," she sobbed.

"I know." Craig choked back his grief, more concerned now with the health of his wife and unborn child.

Looking down into the peaceful expression on his grandfather's face, he said a prayer for his soul and walked away. Pulling the door closed behind them, he called for Maria as Tamera's sobs increased.

"Call Scott," he told her. He heard her gasp and read her thoughts. "It's Gramps. He's gone, and I'm afraid Tamera's going into shock. Hurry, Maria," he urged, a worried frown on his face.

Scott came out immediately, his heart aching with grief for the man who'd been like a grandfather to him while growing up. As a physician, he did what was required.

As a friend, he did what he could, staying as constant companion to Craig and Tamera while the funeral arrangements were made.

Less than a month passed after Gramps' death before Craig had to get back to work. Difficult though it was, life went on, and he had a ranch to run. What was most difficult was dealing with Tamera's grief. It grew deeper as the weeks passed, and the anniversary of her parents' death neared. She was depressed more often than not, and Craig was worried. His only consolation was that she took exceptional care of herself and the baby. He rode back to the house with Shorty one afternoon to find her gone.

"Where's Tamera?" he asked Maria.

"Gone to town."

"How long has she been gone?"

"Most of the day. She left early this morning."

"You haven't heard from her?"

"No. Should I have?"

He shrugged, unable to still the uneasiness he'd felt from the moment he noticed her car wasn't there. Something wasn't right. He could feel it. The later it got, the stronger the feeling got. He called Scott, the hospital, and the police department. There was no trace of her. She hadn't been in an accident, and she hadn't been admitted to the hospital.

Where was she?

A sense of foreboding filled him. Suddenly, he knew. She was gone. No note. No explanation. Just gone. He knew where she'd gone too. One call to the airport confirmed his suspicions. She'd left that morning on a flight to Mississippi.

Anger quickly replaced the worry and fear. Craig spent most of the night alternately praying that she was safe, cursing her for leaving and cursing his own stupidity for not guessing that she would. He knew she was depressed. Now she was gone, and he didn't know what to do. Should he go after her? Did she expect him to? She hadn't even called. It didn't matter that she was carrying his child, their child, she'd just cut him out of her heart, out of her life, *and gone home.*

It was that thought that catapulted him into action. The ranch was her home now. It was where she belonged, where his child belonged. He picked up the phone and booked a seat on the next flight out.

Neither the flight to Mississippi nor the drive to her parents' home were long, just long enough to have him primed and ready for a showdown. Until he saw her. Except for dark circles beneath her eyes, she was pale and visibly shaking. Anger turned once again into fear and worry. "What's wrong?"

She brushed a trembling hand through her hair. "Craig, I was going to call."

"When?" he asked, unable to mask the frustration he felt.

"When I got up enough courage."

"Since when do you need courage to talk to me? Since when do you need courage to call and let me know what's going on with you, and that you're alright?"

"Since I realized how selfish I've been. God's been dealing with me since I set foot on that airplane."

The anger was back in full force, evident in the darkening of his eyes to gunmetal gray and in the throbbing muscle in his jaw.

"Selfish? That's putting it mildly if you ask me. How about immature and thoughtless? You say you have faith. You claim to believe in God's word, yet you run away every time something goes wrong. Hear this, Tamera. I don't have time to follow you to Mississippi every time you get a wild hair."

She began to cry. "You're right. I've been all those things and more in not letting go and in not letting God heal me of my grief. I'm just so afraid," she sobbed.

Anger dissolved with the first tear. "Afraid of what?"

"Everyone I've loved, I've lost. I'm so afraid I'll lose you. Or this baby."

Craig pulled her close, praying for the right words to comfort and reassure her. "Oh, Sweetheart, you're not going to lose either one of us. I'm not going to let you go that easily," he added.

The touch of arrogance in his voice made her smile. "As if you have any say in the matter," she chided.

He chuckled. "At least you're smiling," he whispered against her lips. "Don't worry Temper; I have it on good authority that we're going to be fine. All of us," he added, stroking her well-rounded abdomen.

Remorse overwhelmed Tamera as she realized yet another side effect of her selfishness. *It was his grandfather!* She'd been so consumed by her own grief that she hadn't even considered her husband's feelings.

"Oh, Craig," she whispered gazing into his pain-filled gray eyes. "I'm so sorry. I haven't been here for you. I've been so wrapped up in myself that I've neglected you and I've given you something else to worry about," she apologized, reaching for him.

Craig went willingly into her arms. His grandfather's death had had a profound effect on his life. He was more than an heir now, one tolerated by most. Now he was the boss, the only boss, and the sole owner. He had to be stronger now, more tolerant, and wiser.

Gramps had always been there to clean up the mess when he'd made a mistake. He'd always tempered his decisions with wisdom and taught Craig to do the same. Now he had to rely on all he'd learned in order to continue running the ranch as effectively as it had been run during the past fourteen years. Only in his wife's arms, could he let down his guard and be himself. Only wrapped in the security of her love, and God's grace, could he be the man beneath the rancher.

"He was all I've ever had, Temper," he whispered, his voice thick with grief. "He was a father when mine wouldn't be, and mother when mine couldn't be. And he was always there for me. I thank God every day that I have you now. And this baby."

Tamera held him while he wept unashamedly, huge, heaving sobs that shook his whole frame. When it was over, they both felt better; closer and stronger, cleansed, renewed, alive.

Healing had begun.

Chapter Twenty

Tamera awoke to sunlight streaming through the windows and the smell of coffee brewing. She stretched, rubbing her abdomen as the baby stretched within, then massaged a spot where a tiny foot or elbow poked out. "Getting tired of being cooped up, are you?" she whispered. "I can hardly wait to hold you in my arms."

Tears gathered in her eyes and her heart overflowed as she thought about the blessing of this child. "I promise to love her and nurture her, Lord. Just let me hold her," she whispered. "Please, God. Craig was right. It's time I stand on my faith instead of running in fear, and I'm sorry. I love You. I love my husband. And I love this child. I'll thank You every day that you let me keep her."

She smiled at her husband as he peeked in the door. "Come on in, we're awake."

Craig grinned. She was a beautiful sight, all round and plump, that beautiful body forever branded by his love. "How are you feeling, Sweetheart?" he queried, bending down to kiss her.

"Fine."

"And how's daddy's girl?" he asked, rubbing Tamera's well rounded abdomen.

"Ready to be born," Tamera said. "Mama's ready for her to be born, too."

"It won't be long now. Only a couple more months."

Tamera rolled her eyes. "Spoken like a true man. I feel like a big cow, and you say only a couple more months."

He chuckled. "How about some coffee?"

She laughed. "Think coffee earns forgiveness for anything, don't you?"

Craig laughed, nuzzling her neck. "How about if I bring you coffee in bed?"

Tamera smiled. "I'd love some. Craig," she stopped him with a hand on his arm. "Thank you."

He frowned. "For what?"

"For being the man that you are. For coming after me. For understanding. I love you."

"I love you, too, Temper. Don't worry. We'll get through this. You'll see."

"I know," she replied softly, as he went to get them a cup of coffee. "Would you mind if we stayed a day or two?" she asked when he returned carrying a tray.

"I'm one step ahead of you, Darling. I've already called the ranch. Shorty and Maria send their love. Both of them insisted that we stay and that you get some rest."

Tamera smiled. "We are truly blessed, aren't we, Craig?"

His lips covered hers in a tender caress. "We sure are," he agreed.

The next morning Tamera went to the cemetery. She was surprised to see a man standing beside her parents' graves.

"May I help you?" she asked the stranger, surprised at the tug of recognition she felt, despite the fact that she'd never laid eyes on him.

His smile was gentle. "Hello, Tamera. May I call you Tamera?"

"Depends on who you are and what you're doing here."

"I'm Frank Coleman, your caretaker. I figured since I was taking care of their home, I might as well take care of their resting places too."

Tamera looked down at the fresh flowers and scrupulously clean headstones marking her parents' graves. "Thank you," she whispered, tears of gratitude filling her eyes. "I hope Mr. Barker has rewarded you well for your time and labor."

He smiled again. "Very well. I realize we've never met, but I feel like I know you. I have something I'd like to show you. Do you think you could trust me enough to come to my apartment?"

She laughed softly. "If Mr. Barker trusts you enough to let you have free rein to my home for the past year, I think I can trust you enough to follow you home. I'd really like for you to meet my husband, though. Can you bring whatever it is to the house? Have lunch with us?"

"I'd love to."

Frank arrived at promptly twelve o'clock with a large, wrapped package. "I was going to send these to you, but when I saw you this morning, I decided to give them to you in person," he remarked, handing her the package.

Tamera gasped when she un-wrapped the paintings of her home, her parents, and one of herself with her father. "These are beautiful," she remarked, showing them to Craig who murmured his agreement.

Frank beamed. "It's such a lovely home, and the photographs all around are so precious. It's easy to see and feel the love in them. I simply transferred them onto canvas."

"May I take them with me? Back to the ranch?"

"Of course. They're yours. A thank you gift," he remarked softly. "This job has been a real life-saver for me, in more ways than one. Working here has given me a sense of purpose and meaning, made me believe in God in a deeper way. Love lingers in these walls, and where there is love, God is forever present."

They sat down to eat lunch. At Tamera's encouragement, Frank told his story; a story of love and loss, of pain and heartache. A story of how drug addiction had destroyed his faith in himself and in God, ruined his art and health and eventually cost him the lives of his wife and child. A story with a bittersweet but happy ending since he found peace and healing—*since he found God*—in the house where she'd grown up.

Later, after Frank left, they were sitting quietly watching television when there was a knock at the door. Craig got up to answer it while Tamera went to the restroom. Fury swept through him at the visitor. "What do you want?" he demanded.

Anthony Gerard sighed wearily, looking up at him with haunted eyes. "I need to speak to Tamera."

"I thought I told you to never come around here," he growled.

Tamera walked in from the other room. "Craig, Darling, let the man speak," she chided. "Mr. Gerard, please come in."

Anthony hesitated a moment before entering. He knew in his heart what he had to do, have known it for some time. He only hoped she would listen and try to understand. "Tamera, I want to apologize to you, for myself and for my son. There is no excuse for our behavior," he said in a humiliated whisper.

Tamera smiled, her eyes filled with tears. "Thank you, Mr. Gerard. I want to tell you something; maybe it'll help. I hope so, anyway." She led him into the living room.

"Please, sit down. Craig, will you get us some coffee? Please," she added, her eyes begging him for understanding.

Craig's furious gaze swept over her. He knew in his heart what she was going to say. Unable, however, to resist those pleading blue eyes, he nodded curtly and went to do as she asked.

Tamera sighed, praying that Craig would understand. If there was any way to ease this man's pain, she had to do it. They regarded each other in tense silence, waiting for Craig to return.

Anthony gazed with longing at Tamera. She glowed. Even in the advanced stage of pregnancy, she was beautiful. It was obvious that she was happy, and well loved. Her husband's protective demeanor was evidence of that.

"Thank you," Tamera whispered as Craig put the tray in front of them.

"I'll let you two talk," he offered, placing a quick, hard kiss on her lips.

Tamera poured the coffee and offered Anthony a cup.

He took it with trembling hands. "Your husband loves you very much. He's very protective of you," he remarked, unable to mask the pain in his voice.

Her smile was tender. She nodded in agreement. Taking a deep breath Tamera put her coffee down and reached for his hands. Holding them, she chose her words carefully. "Mr. Gerard, I'm sorry for all you've suffered. I know how difficult it is. Maybe what I'm going to say will help." Locking her gaze with his, she continued.

"Tony did not rape me. I know it was his intention, but he did not complete the act. I'm sorry. I didn't know he was unsuccessful until my wedding night. You see, when he tore my clothes, he," she hesitated, a hot flush rushing to her cheeks.

"Uh, when he put his hand on me, I fainted. When I woke up there was some blood so, not knowing any better, I assumed he'd accomplished what he set out to do. I'm sorry for the pain my accusation caused you. I forgave Tony, and you, a long time ago. I hope you can forgive me."

Anthony's eyes filled with tears and he nodded. "Thank you. You've no need of forgiveness. I know how innocent and naïve you were, knew it all along, and I apologize again for saying otherwise. I'm sorry he even considered such a hideous act." Getting to his feet, relief overwhelmed him. He stood on trembling legs and opened his arms to the girl who should have been his daughter-in-law. "Be happy, Tamera," he whispered, as she accepted his embrace.

"I am," she assured him.

Craig stomped into the room. He'd tolerated the man's presence long enough. He stopped, stunned to find them hugging and watched with wary eyes as Anthony Gerard walked toward him.

"You have an angel, there," Anthony remarked.

Craig nodded in agreement.

"Take good care of her," Anthony insisted. "And your baby."

"I intend to."

Anthony hesitated, and then offered his hand to Craig. "I wish you both all the happiness in the world. I've apologized to Tamera. I hope you can forgive me, too."

Craig nodded, not sure he could say the words. He knew by looking at her that Tamera had generously and graciously offered words of comfort and forgiveness to Anthony Gerard. Could he do less? His gaze sought that of his wife.

"I love you," she mouthed.

The peace in her gaze penetrated his anger. Craig shook Anthony's hand. "All's well that ends well."

Tamera watched Anthony talk with Craig and knew by his demeanor that he'd forgiven his son and made peace with God. The knowledge filled her with a renewed sense of peace and a deeper faith. Her mind wandered back over all that had transpired in just one year; the pain, the sorrow, the joy, the blessings. She considered all she'd lost and all she'd gained; her parents and Tony, Gramps and Maria, Craig and their expected child, the ranch, and everyone on it. She contemplated how different her life would be, and how she may never have fully known the blessing of their love, had that fateful day when her parent's airplane blew up, never happened.

Even Frank Coleman, a man whom they'd never known, was inadvertently helped by her parents' deaths.

"Will you be here long?" Anthony asked, forcing her thoughts back to the conversation at hand.

Tamera shook her head. "No. We're going home tomorrow. But we'll come back after the baby's born. You will come and visit, won't you?"

"I'd be honored to," Anthony answered.

* * * * *

In the weeks following, the pain and sorrow of death was lessened by the excitement and anticipation of new life. The rodeo had been canceled due to Gramps' death and the impending birth of Craig's child.

Craig had assured all of the regular contestants that it would resume next year, although he was making some changes in the schedule. He'd come up with a plan to host it later in the summer, hoping to increase participation and improve results. He was also considering entertainment and prizes that would encourage a broader scope of competition and hopefully increase charitable donations. He left Tamera only once, as the baby's due date got nearer, for a short trip to San Antonio. When he returned, she was sleeping on the couch.

"Temper?" he woke her gently. "Are you all right?"

"Craig. Missed you, can't sleep without you," she mumbled, as he carried her up to their bed.

After one of Tamera's visits to her obstetrician, she and Craig were having lunch with Scott. Craig had requested his presence in the delivery room at the time of the birth. Though honored, Scott hesitated. "Childbirth is a very intimate time for a couple, Craig. Dr. Sarver is a very competent doctor. You have nothing to worry about."

"But what if something's wrong with the baby?"

"There will be a pediatrician on standby for that."

"Can't you be there for that?" Craig insisted.

Scott grinned. "I think you just want me there in case you pass out, you big chicken," he accused with a chuckle.

Tamera excused herself to find a rest room.

"I'm not sure if I can hack it, Scott, seeing her in pain," Craig confided.

"You'll be fine. She'll be fine," Scott assured him. "I'll be at the hospital from the minute you call me, but if you really want, I can be in the delivery room. Just be sure Tamera doesn't mind. I mean, I am a doctor and all, but she may not feel comfortable with another man in the room. We've been friends all our lives, but she's only known me a short while."

Craig nodded in understanding, promising to consult her and let him know. He came in early one afternoon to find her pacing the floor, practicing her breathing and timing her contractions.

"You'd better get cleaned up, Cowboy," she told him with a smile. "I think we'll be making a trip to the hospital soon."

"Isn't it a little early?" he asked, a worried frown on his face.

Tamera shook her head and breathed her way through another contraction. "Babies can be early or late. Now hurry," she urged. "My contractions are down to seven minutes apart and getting stronger."

Scott met them in the emergency room. "Check her in," he ordered Craig. "How are we doing Sweetheart?"

She smiled and nodded okay, gritting her teeth to keep from crying out with the contraction that ripped through her midsection. "That was a tough one," she confessed when it was over.

Wasting no time, the nurses prepped her for delivery while Craig, Scott, the doctors and delivery nurses scrubbed up. In the delivery room, Scott stayed by her side while Craig paced.

"How much longer?" he asked, glaring at the doctor after one extremely long, hard, contraction.

Tamera seemed to be handling the natural childbirth relatively well, but Craig wasn't.

The doctor smiled and shook his head. "He's the worst case of expectant father I've ever witnessed. Get him out of here before he goes ballistic on us," he urged Scott.

"You want to leave?" Scott asked Craig.

"Wild horses couldn't drag me out of here," he assured, turning his glaring gaze on Scott.

"Then you'd better calm down," Scott warned.

Tamera's tired eyes sought Scott's amused ones with a smile. "Come here, Cowboy," she gritted between contractions. "Get over here and hold my hand while I have your child."

That's all it took. He settled down, holding her hand and brushing the hair off her face. "I love you," he breathed, as she strained with another contraction.

When it was over, she reached up and stroked the tense muscle that throbbed in his cheek. "I love you, too," she groaned. Another contraction grabbed her, stopping all thought except getting through this and praying it was over soon. The doctor urged her to push one last time. She lay back with a relieved sigh as the baby slipped from her body into the doctor's waiting hands.

"It's a girl," he announced.

Pain and fatigue seemed to vanish. "I told you so," Tamera teased. Craig's eyes warmed to the color of liquid metal when they placed the tiny, squirming bundle in his hands.

"She's beautiful," he breathed. Jerking the mask down he lowered his lips to Tamera's, then handed the baby to her. "I think I'll keep her," he informed her, his voice husky.

"No black market money then Scott, he's decided to keep her. Guess that means you'll keep me, too," Tamera remarked, reminding her husband of his playful threat of a divorce had the baby not been a boy. With a shake of his head and a chuckle, Craig hushed her teasing with his mouth.

Scott grinned and slapped Craig on the back. "Congratulations, Buddy, you made it," he teased. "Now, let's get out of here," he urged Craig, giving Tamera a quick kiss on the forehead as everyone in the room laughed.

Holding her newborn daughter, Tamera truly understood that *all things do work together for the good of those who love God and are called according to His purpose.*

Dear Readers,

I hope you've enjoyed Craig and Tamera's journey as much as I have. It is my prayer that the Truth in these words settles in your heart and warms your spirit. If you don't already, I pray that you'll seek to know Jesus Christ as your Lord and Savior and if you do, it is my hope that you'll be encouraged to develop a closer walk with Him. Regardless, please remember one thing: ***Only when hearts are tempered, minds are open and wills are softened can man discern the will of God for his life.***

Until later...May God bless and keep you –and yours- in the palm of His loving hand!

Sincerely,
Pamela S. Thibodeaux
"Inspirational with an Edge!" ™
http://pamelathibodeaux.com

Get a Sneak Peek at Book 2 in the *"Tempered"* Series!

Tempered Dreams

Dr. Scott Hensley (introduced in Tempered Hearts) has built a wall around his heart since the death of his wife and parents. Katrina Simmons is recovering from scars inflicted on her as a battered wife. Can dreams be renewed and faith strengthened? Can they find joy and peace in God's love and in love for one another? Find out in: *Tempered Dreams.*

Chapter One

Katrina Simmons awoke with a jolt when the car she rode in slammed into the bridge, spun twice and came to a sliding halt against the concrete wall. She sat a moment, stunned, her heart banging against her ribs, her breath escaping in ragged pants. Thank God there was no one around. Reaching over, she shook her husband. "Jack?"

He mumbled, eyes rolling languidly, and passed out.

Rage unlike anything she'd ever known roared through her. Fumbling with the door handle, she managed to get it open and climbed shakily out of the vehicle. A groan, more anguish than pain, escaped her clenched teeth as she considered the damage to her car.

"Great, Jack! Just great," she raged at her husband, who reclined in a drunken stupor. "You've finally done it! You've ruined my car!" she accused, kicking the door.

* * * * *

Dr. Scott Hensley settled in for the drive to New Orleans. It wasn't a long drive from Lafayette, but a trip he wasn't looking forward to. Mardi Gras in New Orleans was not the place to be. Putting the top down on his car, he reveled in the brisk evening air. A nearly full moon gleamed its glory against a backdrop of black velvet in the star-studded sky. A cacophony of night birds and insects sang in harmony, rivaling the sound of tires slapping on pavement. Much to his surprise, Interstate traffic was light. At the sight of an automobile accident, he slowed his vehicle and pulled over. Using his mobile phone, he called the police and climbed out of his car to check on the victims.

"Are you all right?" he asked, hurrying toward the young woman pacing alongside the car.

She whirled around with a screech, lunged through the window, and shook the driver.

"You drunken idiot!" she raged, punching him soundly on the jaw. She shook him again, winced, and shoved away to continue her tirade.

Being a wise man, Scott stepped back from the raging female as the sound of sirens pierced the air. Showing his Identification, he talked with one of the police officers arriving on the scene while the other officer spoke with the young woman.

"Did you see what happened?"

Scott shook his head. "No, I pulled up afterward. Looks like they hit the wall." He glanced toward the stretch of concrete median dividing one of the longest bridges in Louisiana and the United States. Most of its four lanes divided by water, the stretch of highway passed over the Atchafalaya Basin between Lafayette and Baton Rouge, making it a tedious section to travel with few exits. Endless swamps and cypress trees were the only scenery. They watched the young woman pace, answering in monosyllables. She turned in an angry whirl, gestured wildly, then cradled her arm against her.

"She seems to be favoring her wrist," the officer observed.

Scott chuckled. "I'm sure it needs tending. She hit him."

The cop's eyes widened. "What? Who?"

Scott laughed softly and shook his head. "Her husband or boyfriend, whoever is driving. When I arrived, she was ranting and raving about him ruining her car. She lunged through the window, and punched him. I haven't had a chance to check on him. I doubt he's injured too badly. From what I can gather he's probably drunk."

"What did he do?"

Again, Scott chuckled, feeling a tug in the region of his heart. The fiery little lady reminded him of someone he knew. Two people actually, someone he loved and someone he'd lost. "He just groaned and passed out," Scott answered, walking toward them. He presented his I. D. to the other officer, requesting permission to check her wrist.

Katrina balked at the offer. "I'm fine," she hissed, not caring about her wrist. All she wanted was for someone to drag her husband out of the car and let her loose on him!

Scott reached for her, turning her to face him. "Easy, Sweetheart," he said, his voice a soft drawl. "I won't hurt you."

She looked up at him, her eyes wide and angry, her cheeks flushed, and fainted. Scott caught her as she slumped in his arms. Picking up her small frame, he held her as the summoned ambulance arrived with sirens blaring. Carrying her to it, he waited as the EMT's opened the back and retrieved a stretcher before gently laying her there to examine her. Her wrist, swollen and purple, showed signs of a break. The golden band on her ring finger implied that the driver was her husband. Other than restless stirrings, she seemed fine.

Covering her with a blanket from the ambulance, Scott watched the officers pull the driver out of the car. Gut-wrenching fury clawed through him when they hauled the huge bulk of a man from behind the wheel. A tad over his own six-foot height, the man was a giant compared to his tiny wife.

Where Scott's broad shoulders tapered down and narrowed to a slim waist and long, muscular legs, this guy was rock-hard. His chest was easily as broad and thick as his shoulders. He had a solid middle and bulky, muscular legs and hips, the build of a football player, wrestler or body builder. From his belligerent attitude, he obviously took advantage of it.

"You leave me in jail, and you'll pay for it, Katrina," he hissed, slurring the words, obviously unconcerned that his wife lay passed out on a stretcher. When the young woman began to moan and writhe, Scott turned toward her.

"My baby," she whimpered. Clutching her stomach, she curled into a tiny ball and wept.

Scott noticed a widening stain of blood on her jeans as it seeped from her body. Pulling her against his chest, he did his best to soothe the trembling female in his arms. In all of his years as a physician, nothing prepared him for the array of emotions slashing through him. After she had quieted, never fully conscious, he lay her back down.

Walking over to the police car, he hailed the officer. "Add murder to his charges. She just miscarried," he growled, glaring at the man in cuffs.

It took a moment for the words to register on Jack Simmons's booze fuddled brain. He grunted. "Don't need no brats anyway," he slurred. His head rolled languidly, and he slipped into a drunken stupor once more.

Scott's hands clenched into fists and for one fleeting moment, he thanked God that he'd taken an oath to preserve life. He could easily kill the man, so obviously unconcerned with his wife and unborn child that he'd driven, drunk, with her in the car. Domestic violence and child abuse were the two most hated diagnoses in the Physicians Desk Reference and he'd seen enough to leave no doubt in his mind that she had little, if any, say about the situation she was in.

The police drove off with the husband cuffed securely into the back seat, and the ambulance took her away. He watched their departure and then decided to follow the ambulance to see how she was. Turning on his c. b.

radio, he communicated with the drivers and found out what emergency room they were taking her to.

"Well, she's from Lafayette, but we're closer to Baton Rouge, so we're taking her there," the paramedic replied.

Using his mobile phone, Scott put in a call to the hospital he was traveling to and bought some time. Instead of the seven in the morning to seven in the evening shift he'd originally been scheduled, Scott had it switched to the opposite. He pulled in behind the ambulance and talked with the doctors and nurses on staff in the emergency room at Baton Rouge General. Then he waited.

* * * * *

Katrina swam up from the pain-induced fog to awareness. Tossing in discomfort, she opened her eyes. Surprise and shock widened them as she gazed into the soft brown eyes of a stranger.

Scott moved closer when she stirred. He'd been watching her for hours. The sunlight streaming in the room bounced off the red highlights in her thick, golden hair, turning it into a fiery mass. Her skin, silky smooth and the color of a sun-ripened peach, made him wonder about the color of her eyes. Probably the blue or green that usually accompanied her coloring, he thought. Hazel perhaps.

Wrong.

They were brown; deep, dark brown, like two huge chocolate drops in a bowl of peaches and cream. He smiled tenderly and she glanced away with a blush.

"Do I know you?" she queried in a timid voice.

"I'm Dr. Scott Hensley. I was at the accident last night. I thought you might appreciate seeing a familiar face when you woke up. Can I get you anything or call someone for you?"

Her lip trembled as she shook her head. "My husband?"

Biting back a growl, he softened his reply. "In jail, Sweetheart. That's all I know."

"Good," she muttered, blushing at the relief she felt but still trembling with the fear. Jack always threatened to hurt her if she ever had him put in jail or left him if he landed there on his own. This morning she didn't care. He'd caused her pain for the last time and cost her the one thing she wanted most in life—her baby. The minute she returned home, she planned to call a lawyer.

Scott watched the emotions cross her lovely, fragile features and fought back the urge to take her in his arms. Professional ethics insisted that he remain objective, but it was difficult to adhere to ethics when a lone tear escaped from one of her tightly closed eyes to leave a trail down her silky cheek. He waited and watched, his heart cringing, as she fought valiantly against the tears, and lost. Her breath started to hitch and she succumbed to the sobs wracking her small frame.

Forget ethics.

Sitting on the bed, Scott pulled her into his arms and held her against his chest. The icy reserve he'd built around his heart over the last several years began to melt under the onslaught of her tears. His fingers sank into the luxurious softness of her hair while the other hand caressed her back in a soothing manner. Her sobs subsided into soft, hiccupping sounds; silence ensued.

Katrina stiffened fearfully when she realized the strength in the arms of the man holding her, arms of a stranger, of a man other than her husband. Grinding her teeth in mortification, she pushed herself away, a hot blush warming her cheeks. "I'm sorry," she mumbled, not daring to look him in the eye.

"It's okay, Sweetheart. I'm a doctor. I won't hurt you. Are you sure there's no one I can call for you? Your mother or some other family member?"

She shook her head. "No. No one," she admitted, knowing that her mother wouldn't be able to come even if she wanted to. Her stepfather would see to that. Coming from a long line of abused women, Katrina was determined to break the pattern. Never again would a man take advantage of her.

Scott's voice broke into her thoughts.

"Is there anything I can do?"

"Leave me alone." She turned away knowing her words were rude and not at all grateful for the comfort he so easily and gallantly offered.

Totally unprepared for that answer, Scott frowned. He'd dealt enough with grief and pain to know when a patient was talking out of emotion, lashing out. He respected that. But coming from someone so tiny, so fragile, so vulnerable, it seemed out of place. He remembered her fury the night before and bit back a grin. Maybe not.

"Okay," he said, brushing the thick mane of red-gold hair off her face then stood. "I need to be going, anyway." Still, he hesitated. Something about her pulled at him. Maybe her fragile beauty, or the subtle waves of fear. Perhaps the gentle elegance of her fine, porcelain-like features giving the impression of a china doll, or the fiery passion he had witnessed last night.

He shook himself mentally. Maybe he was just tired.

With a slight shrug, he walked around the bed and toward the door. Turning, he got a glimpse of the tremble that shook her slender frame. He walked back to the bed, reaching for his wallet and pulled out a business card.

"Look, here's my card. If there's anything, anything at all I can do for you, please don't hesitate to call." He wrote the phone number to the hospital in New Orleans where he would be for the next couple of weeks. She remained silent as he set the card on the bedside table.

With another subtle caress, he brushed the hair off her cheek and felt her stiffen. Of their own accord, his knuckles swept gently across her cheek again, soothing. He bit back words of comfort. It was evident though needed she didn't want them. Turning quietly, he left.

Trina's fingers trembled when she reached for the card and noticed that he resided in the same town as she. Questions rolled around in her head and all she could do was speculate about the answers. Dr. Scott Hensley. Who was he? What did he want? Was he like this with all of his patients or just the helpless females?

* * * * *

The two-hour drive to New Orleans passed without further incident; giving Scott plenty of time to think about the woman he left behind. Something about her stirred memories long since buried, some better off forgotten. Unable to resist, he picked up the phone and dialed the hospital. Requesting her room, he waited for her to answer.

"Hello?"

"Mrs. Simmons..." he hesitated. What was he supposed to say? He didn't even know why he called! Clearing his throat, he tried again.

"Katrina, I'm serious about what I said. If there's anything you need, please feel free to contact me."

"Dr. Hensley," she huffed out a sigh. "I know you're aware that I'm a married woman. I don't know what you want from me, but you won't get it. I'd appreciate it if you just leave me alone," she insisted, slamming the receiver into its cradle. *Men!* Her mind screamed, drowning out the voice in her heart chiding her for the unfairness of her attitude.

Put ever so completely in his place, Scott hung up. A smile crossed his face as he thought about the defiant tone that belied the soft, sensual voice. Maybe it was time for a challenge in his life. He sighed, wished once again he was going anywhere but New Orleans, and slipped a cassette in the deck. Soft, soothing Jazz notes oozed out of the speakers as his mind roamed lazily along the path of his career.

In all of his years as a physician, his one desire—the desire to help those in need—was finally being fulfilled in this job. He was one of the leading physicians for the Louisiana Charity Health Care System, a system that served the needy. One of the joys of being on contract with the State was traveling to different facilities and working with various people. One of the disadvantages was not being able to refuse. But at least he no longer had to journey with missionaries to do the good he so desperately wanted to do. He'd given up on that after the death of his wife and parents.

Leaving his home in Texas more than six years ago hadn't been an easy decision, but a necessary one. Necessary for his sanity. Home was too full of memories. Memories he hadn't dragged out in a long time. Memories that surfaced now. His jaw hardened and fists clenched in automatic defense against the swift tug of anger followed by sorrow and grief that always accompanied the recollections of his wife and parents, and how they died.

He'd been on a three-month mission in South America. His family had flown down to visit him his second month there, his mother and father always so proud, and Melissa, his wife. He'd been swept away by her passion, not seeing until it was too late that there was very little substance beneath. Though not a happy marriage from the beginning Scott did his best to adhere to his vows. Still, he was on the verge of divorce when he received the offer to travel with the missionary. He'd known then, even as he knew now, that the trip had only been an escape hatch and that when he returned home he'd have to make some serious decisions about his marriage.

As fate would have it, he went home sooner than expected when the plane they occupied was blown out of the air by terrorists. To date, their deaths were recorded as a senseless, unsolved tragedy.

He'd returned to Bandera, Texas to bury his family. Unable to deal with the grief, the heartache and the guilt, he sold the ranch to his friend Craig Harris, who then turned most of it into an arena and campground. The house was turned into a Bed & Breakfast, and the charity rodeo that the Rockin' H had hosted for over thirty years was now held there. The rest of the year, it was merely an extension of the Rockin' H. Guests came and went at the B & B, giving a substantial monthly income, which, at Craig's insistence, Scott retained. That decision made, Scott had moved on. Craig and his family remained his closest friends. Now, when he returned to Bandera for a visit, it was with joy—joy tempered by memories and heartache.

His mobile phone rang once, jerking Scott out of his revere, which was a good thing since he nearly missed his exit. When it didn't ring a second time, he shrugged it off, knowing that if it were important, whoever it was would call back. Arriving in New Orleans, he ordered flowers to be sent to Mrs. Katrina Simmons then took a much-needed nap.

The next ten days flew by with little time to dwell on the fiery little lady in Baton Rouge General, but she was always in the back of his mind, making him smile.

From the weekend before to the weekend following Fat Tuesday, New Orleans ran wild, parties ending in fights, fights ending in brawls, brawls ending in injury or death. It was rough to say the least. New Orleans was notorious for its parties and passions.

Beautiful and old, the city graced the banks of the Mississippi river, as it had for more than a hundred years. In the old days, the French filled this port city with style and elegance. To date, it still held all the magic and beauty, with its river walk, shops and boutiques, French Market and, of course, the notorious Bourbon Street. Restaurants offered the best of French Cuisine and nightclubs offered the best in Jazz music. New Orleans was a beautiful place to visit, but Scott wouldn't want to live there, especially during Mardi Gras.

Scott knew the city and its people would settle down after Fat Tuesday. Rich in tradition, they would shelter in for the Lenten season, repenting of their wicked ways and drawing closer to God. This spiritual side increased the charm of New Orleans. Full of life, the people exuded laughter, love and faith, but like all of God's children, they had their rebellion and tantrums. During Mardi Gras, these aspects came out in the worst ways.

* * * * *

Katrina stared at the single, rebellious rose still alive amongst the bouquet of dead flowers. The arrangement had graced her kitchen table for almost a week now. A smile curved her lip. That one rose reminded her of him, the strange doctor with his tall good looks and Texas drawl. Stubborn too, she thought, but a gentle stubbornness. Trina knew she'd never met a man like him before.

Taking the flower from the center of the bouquet, she placed it in a slender vase. Burying her nose in its soft fragrance, she inhaled deeply, then exhaled on a sigh. This one rose spoke so boldly of life, life and hope, especially considering the rest had long since been dead.

A tear rolled down her cheek and emotions swarmed through her as she faced the sad facts. No life existed in her marriage, and no hope. Nothing left to cling to after nearly ten years of abuse. There was only now, her life and her future, if she wanted one, if she wanted to live long enough to have one.

Trina knew the facts, the statistics. Most battered women lived frightened, lonely lives, if they lived at all.

For some unknown reason, she had survived through the years of abuse, first as a child then as a wife. Trina found it hard to believe that it was God who looked after her, not after all she'd been through and tolerated in the name of love.

Despite everything, she still believed in the sanctity of marriage. But she could no longer consider her's a true marriage. Until suffering the loss of her child, she'd never faced the fact that what she lived in for the past nine and a half years was not a marriage, not in the real sense of the word. In truth, it didn't even come close. Trina knew what she had to do. Picking up the phone, she called Legal Aide.

Books 3 and 4 in the *"Tempered"* Series

Tempered Fire
Amber Harris is a good girl on the brink of womanhood. Stanley Morrison is a young man at the start of his life. For each other, they have always felt the fireworks that two people in love should feel. However, the questions about his past, his pride, and Amber's father might be the end of what could be a strong relationship. As the two try to protect their budding romance, some unlikely but powerful forces conspire to keep them apart. Will they survive the wishes of everyone around them with their relationship intact?

Tempered Joy
All around rodeo cowboy and heir to the Rockin' H Ranch, Ace Harris is determined not to fall in love. He's only loved one woman in his life, his mother, and no one can even come close to filling her boots. Lexie Morgan thinks rodeo cowboys have rocks for brains and a death wish for a soul. A broken childhood and the death of her father and best friend leave her doubting and questioning God (despite her years of religious upbringing) and afraid of love. Can two young people who clash from the onset learn to trust in the healing power of God and find love and happiness amidst tragedy and grief?

About the Author

Pamela S. Thibodeaux grew up in the town of Iowa, Louisiana. She is a mother, grandmother and deeply committed Christian who firmly believes in God and His promises.

"God is very real to me and I feel that people today need and want to hear more of His truths wherever they can glean them. People are hungry for practical (and real) Christian values, not some 'holier-than-thou' beliefs that are impossible to believe and impossible to live up to," Pamela says.

"I do my best to encourage readers to develop a personal relationship with God. The deepest desire of my heart is to glorify God and to get His message of faith, trust and forgiveness to a hurting world."

Email Pamela at: pthib07@gmail.com
Visit her website: http://www.pamelathibodeaux.com
Or blog: http://pamswildroseblog.blogspot.com

Other Titles by Pamela S Thibodeaux

Love is a Rose

Music is the magical entry into the spirit world; the golden gate into the Kingdom of God. But we mustn't be of the mindset that God only uses Christian music to reach out and touch our mind, heart and spirit. God uses any and **every** means available to speak to His children.

Our job is to be open and receptive.

In this devotional, Pamela S Thibodeaux shares how God opened her spirit to a deeper understanding of the abundance of His grace and mercy through the words of the song, The Rose sung by Country & Western artist Conway Twitty.

Pamela offers Seeds to Ponder and a prayer as she parallels the love of God and the Christian life to each verse of the song.

Lori Strickland (introduced in *Tempered Fire*) has always been known as her father's "wild child" with no desire to change until she meets ex-bull-rider-turned-preacher Rafe Judson. Her attempts to change her wanton ways come to naught until she realizes redemption only comes with true repentance. Can she find redemption and win the heart of the cowboy preacher? Find out in **Lori's Redemption**

A visionary is someone who sees into the future Taylor Forrestier sees into the past but only as it pertains to her work. Hailed by her peers as *"a visionary with an instinct for beauty and an eye for the unique"* Taylor is undoubtedly a brilliant architect and gifted designer. But she and twin brother Trevor, share more than a successful business. The two share a childhood wrought with lies and deceit and the kind of abuse that's disgustingly prevalent in today's society.

Can the love of God and the awesome healing power of His grace and mercy free the twins from their past and open their hearts to the good plan and the future He has for their lives? Find out in ***The Visionary*** ~ Where the awesome power of God's love heals the most wounded of souls.

The Inheritance *is about the chance we all long for...the chance to start over.* Widowed at age thirty-nine and suffering from empty nest syndrome, Rebecca Sinclair is overshadowed by grief and loneliness. Her husband has been deceased for a year, her oldest child has moved to New York in pursuit of an acting career and her youngest child is attending college in France. Having spent over half of her life as a wife and mother, she has no idea what God has in store for her now. Will an unexpected inheritance in the wine country of New York bring meaning and purpose to her life and give her the courage to love again?

US Postal worker Raymond Jacobey has been in love with the little widow since he first set eyes on her. A wanderer searching for the ever-illusive soul mate, Ray has never stayed in one place too long. Raised by self-centered, high-power executives, he's longed for the idyllic life of residing in a cozy house in a small town with the love of his life. Will he gain the heart of the lovely widow or will he lose her to the wine country of New York?   Find out in ***The Inheritance***

Single mom Cathy Johnson is tired of running her life alone...what she needs is a well-trained angel to help out. Jared Savoy gave up the dream of having a family when he discovered he is sterile. Can a confirmed bachelor and the mother of four find love amid normal daily chaos? Find out in ***Cathy's Angel***

Best-selling novelist and songwriter, Camie Rogers has penned numerous accounts of the secret love she holds in her heart. Country-Music Superstar Kip Allen has changed from the shy, humble boy, to the epitome of "star." Can the two rediscover each other after one night of his Home is Where the Heart is Tour? Find out in **_Choices_**

Anthony Paul Seville is known as the 'most eligible bachelor' in New Orleans, possibly even the entire state of Louisiana, but finds himself alone—completely and explicitly alone. Jessica Aucoin is a writer on her way to fame and fortune, but is haunted by a man from her past. Will the "champion" lawyer and the author of romantic suspense find love written in their future? Find out in **_A Hero for Jessica_**

Sienna has survived what most succumb to - the death of a spouse and child and has maintained her faith despite her troubles. William has never met anyone who actually lived out what they say they believe. Is it true love between the faithful optimist and broody pessimist or simply **_Winter Madness_**?

Grade school teacher Carson Alexander has a gift—a gift that has driven a wedge between him and his family. Worse, it's put him at odds with God. Feeling alone and misunderstood, Carson views God's gift of prophecy as the worst kind of curse...that is until he meets Lorelei Conner, landscape artist extraordinaire, and perhaps the one person who may need Carson and his gift more than anyone ever has. Lorelei Connor is a mother on the run. Her abusive ex-husband has followed her all over the country trying to steal their daughter. Distrusting of men and needing to keep on the move, she's surprised by her desire to remain close to Carson Alexander. Through her fear and hesitation, she must learn to rely on God to guide her—not an easy task when He's prompting her to trust a man. Can their relationship withstand the tragedy lurking on the horizon? Find out in **_In His Sight_**

Jason Stockwell has been commissioned to interview Kylie Erickson and to review her books. Only problem is, she won't give the time of day much less an interview to someone whose type of writing she deems not worthy of respect. Can they suspend their judgmental attitudes and find true love? Find out in ***Review of Love*** (A FREE read from White Rose Publishing!)

**Temperance
Publishing**